Richie

Best Wishes

THE GUARDIANS OF IMAGINARI

The Book Of Imaginari - Part Three

Richard Hayden

Richard Hayden

Copyright © 2023 Richard Hayden

This is a work of fiction. Names, characters, places, and incidents either are the product of the author's imagination or are used fictitiously. Any resemblance to actual persons, living or dead, events, or locales, is entirely coincidental.

All rights reserved. No part of this book may be reproduced or used in any manner (physical, digital, or broadcast) without written permission of the copyright owner except for the use of quotations in a book review. For more information, contact the copyright owner: richard.c.hayden@outlook.com

First paperback edition May 2023
First Kindle ebook edition May 2023

Paperback ISBN: 9798387631542

Book and cover design by Richard Hayden & Naomi Hayden
Images by Richard Hayden

Twitter: @r_c_hayden
Instagram: @r_c_hayden
Facebook Page: Richard Hayden Author (@rchaydenauthor)

Dedication.

This is an Amazon Kindle Direct Publishing first edition of The Guardians Of Imaginari, which is the final part in The Book Of Imaginari.

The series would not exist without the love and support of my friends and family. To get to this point has been a rollercoaster of edits, changes, late nights, long days, updates, and more.

To those that have read draft after draft, I thank you. I would like to thank by name; Amy, Imelda, Jane, Janet, Jo, Josie, Lesley, Martyn, and Steve, though there are many more that have known about this project in some way, these people have contributed in no small way to this adventure.

Most of all though I would like to thank Naomi, without her inspiration, love, and support, I would not have got any further than chapter one. In many ways, Imaginari belongs to us both, and now I am sharing it with the world.

To everyone that has helped or has been aware of this project, however small, thank you.

I hope everyone enjoys reading it, as much as I have enjoyed writing it.

Richard.

CONTENTS

Title Page
Copyright
Dedication
Chapter 1	1
Chapter 2	8
Chapter 3	25
Chapter 4	34
Chapter 5	37
Chapter 6	55
Chapter 7	68
Chapter 8	80
Chapter 9	93
Chapter 10	99
Chapter 11	109
Chapter 12	115
Chapter 13	130
Chapter 14	150

Chapter 15	158
Chapter 16	168
Chapter 17	187
Chapter 18	196
Chapter 19	209
Chapter 20	217
About The Author	225

CHAPTER 1

Not so long ago.

Driving in the dark is not a problem. Darkness combined with a downpour from the sky the likes of which have only been written about in books is a different position altogether. This however was the position that Christian found himself in. He was driving home from work after a long week of meetings, travelling, and general headache inducing long days. Despite the terrible weather, Christian was in a an upbeat mood. He was driving home, to see his fiancé, Gemma. Gemma was his world and there was nothing he would not do for her, or their son. They were new parents; Christian had only just returned to work after a couple of weeks whilst Gemma was still off taking care of their beautiful boy. It had been a tough time, indeed there had been more arguments lately mostly related to tiredness and exhaustion rather than anything real. Christian did not blame Gemma for any of it, he knew he could do better and had set himself the goal of doing just that starting right now. On his way home he had picked up a bunch of lilies, Gemma's favourite flower, and the ingredients to make her favourite meal; homemade pizza. This was a small thing and a tiny gesture, but he needed to start somewhere and was confident that this would be good for their new future. He drove down the road, past a line of shops watching people running from takeaways to their cars trying to get out of the deluge. He continued down the hill and stopped at the traffic lights by the Brown Dog pub, outside was a sign exclaiming, '*Book now for Christmas!*'. He made a mental note, Gemma liked it there and going out for a meal in the coming weeks would be a lovely thing to do. The lights turned green and he pulled forwards, the rain still bouncing off the road and car bonnet. It was the sort of downpour where wipers made no difference due to the volume of water falling. He turned right onto the country lane that led to the village where he and his family lived. It was a small village, sitting atop of a lone hill. At the top of the hill stood a folly visible for miles, or at least visible for miles when the sky was not filled with rain and clouds. The road narrowed as Christian crossed the canal and then the railway line, the car headlights lighting up nothing but rain and hedges as he went. He turned a bend to a stretch of road that was straight and a little wider. Following his normal instinct, he accelerated a little but kept the speed under control given the visibility and potentially slippery road. As Christian rounded a corner, he was forced to bring the car to a screeching halt. He squinted and tried to peer through the seemingly increasing downpour. Standing in the middle of the road was a man. At least, it looked like a man. He was glowing with his own white light and the car headlights seemed to pass directly through him, he appeared to cast no shadow on the hedge behind. Christian sat there for a few seconds almost paralysed by confusion. The figure did not move nor did he make any effort to communicate with him. Christian blasted his horn, nothing, he wound down his window allowing torrents of water to come splashing in.

"Oi, move," he shouted above the rain, still the man did and said nothing. Christian used his horn again, still nothing. "Unbelievable," he muttered to himself and undid his seatbelt. With one final sigh of frustration, he got out of the car pulling his coat over his head as he did so.

"What's your problem?" he shouted as he walked over to the figure in the road.

As he approached, he noticed that the ghost white figure was not solid. He could see the trees and bushes behind him and indeed could now see for sure that the car headlights were passing straight through him, leaving no shadow. He reached out a hand, to try and touch the figure.

CHAPTER 1

"What are you?" he asked quietly.

The figure did not reply but shot sideways at such a speed he was a blur to Christians eyes. He turned to look, but the figure moved again and was now standing between him and his car.

"Listen, I don't want any trouble, I just -"

"I know what you want," a soft, chilling voice cut across him. Christian fell silent.

"And I can give it to you, Christian Lloyd."

"How do you know my name?" nerves were setting in now, and Christian was beginning to wish he had not got out of the car.

"I know more than that, I know everything. Would you like me to show you?"

Christian said nothing for a moment. "No, I just want to go home," he said as bravely as he dared and started to march towards the figure and his car.

"I'm afraid," the figure added, "I must insist." As he finished this, he brought his hands together in front of him with a blinding flash and deafening bang.

Christian was knocked to the floor and immediately protected his eyes and ears. After a few moments, he relaxed a little and realised that everything had stopped. Even the rain. Christian was lying in a ball on the floor, where the road used to be. He looked around, his car was a short distance away with the floating figure still between them. They were no longer on the road, instead they were surrounded by purple vapour. It was moving constantly in swirls and making Christian feel quite sick.

"Where am I? Who are you?" he asked, real fear in his voice now.

"I am, the Man Of Mow, and I am here to help you, Christian." Christian lifted himself to his feet and stood facing the floating figure. "Man Of Mow?" he asked, confusion in his tone.

"Yes, I am he."

"Never heard of you," Christian replied, trying to pass it off as if someone had suggested he listened to a new band or try a new type of food.

"I know you have not, but I know you. I know your village. I know your world and it is doomed."

"Sorry, what has that got to do with me?" Christian folded his arms. "This is some kind of joke or prank and I'm not buying it."

"No joke. I am here to help you."

"Why would you want to help me?"

"Because I believe we can help each other."

"So, in exchange for your help you want, what?" Christian asked, gaining in confidence a little now.

"Exactly, I propose an agreement. I can give you what you want, and in exchange you will give me what I want."

Christian narrowed his eyes, "And what do you want?" he asked.

The figure said nothing for a moment, just floating in front of Christian a short distance away. "I want your son."

This sent a shot of ice through Christian's body, he felt his heart skip a beat and his entire body tighten. "You will not touch him," he snarled.

"All I want is to try something, I want to see if your son holds the key to your world's salvation. Are you really telling me, Christian, that you will not allow me to try and save your world for the sake of your son?"

Christian took a few steps forward, and said again more defiantly, "You will not touch him."

He started to move closer still.

As he got to within what felt like arm's length of the figure, the Man raised his hand showing his palm to Christian. Christian stopped, not because he chose to but because he could not move any closer.

"Let me past," he demanded.

"No, you will listen to me and see that my way is the only way." With a flick of his wrist, golden strands of light shot up from the floor and wrapped around Christian's wrists, pulling him to his knees on the purple ground.

"Let me go!" he screamed.

"Shhhhhh," the Man hissed, and with another flick of his wrist, Christian found that he could no longer speak. "That is better, now listen as I explain what I need and why."

The Man glided down to Christian's eye level, moving his face within inches of Christian's nose.

"I come from a world that observes yours, a world that needs yours to survive. My world needs the energy that flows through all your living things. Plants, animals, people, everything that is living provides energy to my world. The world of Imaginari."

Christian listened to this, pulling against his restraints and trying to call for help. All to no avail.

"My world cannot live without yours, and if our world perishes, yours will be next."

He moved away, lifting himself back to his full height.

"There is a prophecy that states that my world can be saved if a sacrifice is made by someone in your world. Someone that makes a sacrifice so bold that it will ensure the flow of energy between our worlds continues as it always has. This was done once before, centuries ago and now it is needed again."

He pointed at Christian who looked up to meet his eyeline.

"I have chosen you, Christian Lloyd, to make this sacrifice so that both worlds may prosper and grow. Will you allow me to try and save my world and keep yours from harm?"

He waved his palm as he lowered his hand, and Christian immediately felt his throat release.

He took a few deep breaths, "Why me?"

"Because the person I choose must be willing."

"Why do you need my son?" he choked on the last word, it got stuck in his throat as he tried to say it. Tears started to form in his eyes at the idea of something happening to his boy.

"I need a willing person to sacrifice and take the pain of loss. Then I need a pure soul, a child's soul, to give its energy to the barrier between worlds. The lock, the folly on the hill."

"The folly? In Mow Cop?" Christian asked, confused but also aware this was the first thing that had been said that he properly recognised and understood.

"Yes. That building has stood as a secure lock and control between our worlds, the child's energy will reinforce it."

"No," Christian said boldly.

"No?" the Man hissed.

"No, you will not use my son for anything."

The Man flew down and put his face right in front of

Christian's.

"I can offer you what you want. I can give you peace with your beloved, Gemma," he made a sweeping gesture to his side, within seconds Gemma appeared.

Christian looked and called out to her, but she did not respond.

"She cannot hear you; this is just an image of her, she is home safe with your son."

Christian looked back at the Man, "What do you mean, peace with Gemma?"

He was trembling now, shaking with a potent mix of fear and anger.

"I can make all the anger and frustration between you disappear. I can make it all as it was. That is what you want, is it not, Christian? You want your life back with Gemma?"

Christian looked at the moving image of Gemma, "Not at the cost of our boy. Never."

"You dare to defy me?" the Man rose now, the image of Gemma faded. "You dare to resist and deny me what I want?"

"Yes," Christian said, sounding much braver than he felt. "You will not touch my family, not now, not ever. Whatever it takes you will not touch them."

"Very well," the Man's voice was soft but strong now, this instilled more fear in Christian than when he appeared to be shouting. "I shall not touch them."

Christian exhaled, relaxing slightly.

"But," the Man continued, "Neither shall you." In a moment he dropped down to Christian's level once more and this time came straight for him.

Christian screamed as the Man's ghost like body slammed into him, through him. For a moment everything went dark. Christian opened his eyes, looking around he could see the ghost like figure floating not too far away. He turned to face him.

"What did you do?" Christian called out, but his voice sounded different. He looked at his hands they were different. They were white, ghost like, and glowing against the moving purple landscape. He looked around, and to his horror saw his own body, still tied by the wrists a short distance away. It was his body, lifeless and still, but his all the same. He walked, no, he was gliding now, over to the still version of himself.

"I tried to make you understand," the Man commented. "I tried to make you see, to get you to help. You refused. So now, you are one of us."

"What?" Christian replied in a soft hiss of a voice.

"I have removed your spirit from your body, but unlike other times I have done this, it cannot be returned. Your body will perish, your spirit will live on in my world, or should I say, our world."

Without thinking, Christian charged at the man with a roar of anger.

As he got close, the man simply moved aside revealing a large black hole. Christian, unable to stop himself fell through into a black space of nothing.

"You will never see, or touch, your family again," he heard the Man call down as he fell.

All Christian could do was call back, call back the only thing that came to mind as he tumbled through the darkness.

"I will protect my son."

CHAPTER 2

Today

"Simon are you even listening to me?" Ellie asked of her friend, in a sympathetic but strong tone.

They had been on the bus for a matter of minutes and Ellie had been trying to talk to him. In this time, he had done nothing but look out of the window, showing no interest or acknowledgement of her the whole time she had been speaking.

"What?" he asked, in an apparent daydream, turning to look at her, his eyes glazed over.

Ellie squinted. "What's up? You've not been yourself all day, distracted or something. Everything ok?" She tilted her head to one side in the way she did when trying to work something out and smiled, "Talk to me."

He sighed, "Sorry Ellie, I'm just preoccupied I guess, always difficult about this time of year."

He turned away and looked out of the window again.

It was early September; the sky was still blue but there was an autumn chill in the air, and they were heading to meet their friends. They all had a good summer, apart from the short timeframe which only Ellie can now recall in full. The events surrounding the Statue of Mow were remembered differently by her friends, they could not recall Emilia. The version of Ellie had been created by the Man. This was difficult for Ellie as she could remember all of it, and most of all she could not forget the pain she felt when Emilia faded in front of her eyes allowing her to return home. They were meeting their friends at a park in the town to go for a walk and then for some food in the shopping area, and Ellie was keen to try and help Simon clear his mind to allow him to enjoy it. She was not exactly sure what was bothering him but could have a good guess.

"It's about your dad, isn't it?" she asked softly.

Simon grunted a sound of agreement but said nothing.

She decided to probe a little, "Is your mum ok?"

Simon sighed and turned to look at her, his eyes red, not tearful but clearly hiding deep emotions and feelings.

"She always is, she pretends that it's not a big deal. She acts like it doesn't bother her, but it kills me every year, Ellie. Every year I see her try to hide it, it breaks my heart that I can't help her, that I can't take the pain away."

Ellie took his hand in hers, "You help her every day by being the man she needs you to be. Usually it's mothers protecting sons, but you protect her and help her. I've seen it, we all have. You are a true gent Mr Lesley, and your mum is very proud of you," she smiled.

"She said that to you?" he asked, a quizzical look on his face.

"She doesn't need to, I know it. We see the way you talk about her, and the way she talks about you. You are her world, and you are wonderful. Give yourself a break."

He smiled back.

"It's not your fault, or indeed hers, that he ran out on you both all those years ago. Think of it like this, if that hadn't happened you wouldn't be the man you are today."

"You think so?"

"I know so. Even negative things shape us and make us who we are, sometimes for the better and sometimes for the worse, but it all adds up to who we are."

"When did you get so wise?" Simon asked, a cheeky grin on his face.

"Ever since I got dragged into a spiritual battle to save the world," she beamed. "Twice," she added with gusto, holding up her first and middle fingers to him as if to prove the quantity.

"Show off," he smirked.

"All I'm saying is, I get it, I really do understand but you shouldn't let this one time of year ruin the rest of your year, which is generally pretty good."

They smiled at each other.

"Can I ask you something though?" Ellie queried.

Simon nodded.

"You've never really told me about what happened, at least what you know and what your mum told you. Do you think it would help if you shared it?"

Simon's face faded a little, he swallowed, and Ellie knew he was swallowing tears in the form of a lump in his throat.

"Do you really want to know?" he asked shakily.

"It's not that I want to, I mean I do, but it's more if it will help you. If it will help and make you feel better, then tell me. If it won't, then don't," she squeezed his hand. "I'm on your side."

Simon smiled and squeezed back, "I'll think about it. Now can we change the subject?"

They did and had a wonderful day. The six friends chatted, gossiped, and generally watched the world go by. Tyler had been on holiday for the events surrounding the statue, so he needed to catch up and the others took great pleasure in sharing the stories, adding bits here and there. Ellie sat smiling as her friends told the story as they saw it, with elements of what she had seen and told them thrown in. It was quite a tale.

"So, you're telling me," Tyler asked. "That whilst I was off looking at pyramids, you were all here saving the world, again?"

"Pretty much," Simon replied with a grin. "I mean, I did most of the work of course, Ellie just did the actual moving around based on my plans," he winked. Before being punched in the arm by Annabelle and falling off his seat.

"Now, now," Ellie stepped in. "It was a team effort; I couldn't have done it without you."

"Clearly can without Tyler though," Leo mocked.

The laughter was natural, the group had settled, and all felt that everything was back to normal once again. Ellie was very aware that they had never really had the chance to enjoy 'normal'. After arriving in the village, the events with the Man had taken over her life and indeed that of her friends. But without those events, her life would not be what it is now. She looked at Annabelle, who in Ellie's opinion was the most beautiful girl in the world, with her dark hair perfectly highlighting her round face and her beaming smile that could light up a room. She looked at the others, Tyler, Leo, Dan, and finally Simon. Her friends were special to her and there was not anything she would not have done for them. She was pretty sure that they would do anything for her as well. Ellie's mind had wandered along this path many times since the summer, the path that seemed to always lead to the Man. She knew he would be back and was certain that this time one way or another it would be the last. She needed to be ready, ready to fight. To that end, she needed help from her friends again, but now was not the time. Now was the time to enjoy herself and be who she wanted to be.

Later that night, Ellie was home with her parents. They were all relaxing in the living room when she was asked a question she had been anticipating for a while.

"Do you want to go to university, Ellie?" her mother asked.

Ellie had been considering this, her options that is, trying to work out what the best thing to do was. She had looked at universities near and far, and courses in a wide array of subjects but in truth everything that had been happening in the real world had taken priority for her.

"Not sure mum," she replied, and immediately braced herself for the questions that would be coming her way. To her surprise though, there were none.

"I didn't think you would," Nicholas joined in.

Both her parents looked at her.

"Whatever you choose to do, as long as you are choosing it for the right reasons, we will support you, Ellie," Katherine replied, smiling.

This immediately relaxed Ellie, though she had not worked out what to say or do if this was the way the conversation went. She was a little taken by surprise.

"What do you mean right reasons?" Ellie asked, a little confused.

"Well, there is a lot going on in your world right now, university, work, Annabelle, and your friends. All are very important for different reasons and as long as you pick the right ones for the right reasons then you will have our full support," Katherine smiled.

Ellie smiled too, she loved her parents and even though they only knew some of what had gone on, she knew they loved her and would help in any way they could. It was now or never.

"I think I want to take a year out, work full time to get some money behind me and then see what happens. What do you think?"

These were the plans she had decided to share, but in fact there was another reason. She wanted this time to prepare for his, the Man's, inevitable return.

"I think that is a wonderful idea, have you spoken to work about it?" Katherine commented.

"Sort of, they seemed keen to keep me. Must have forgiven me for breaking that jar of pasta sauce last month, but I think they're in need of the help."

"Perfect. That means you can pay your way for our family get away next month then, can't you?" her father asked with a cheeky knowing wink.

"Dad!" Ellie exclaimed and threw a pillow at him. "Ok I will, if Annabelle can come." Ellie had been meaning to ask this, but not right now. Now it was out there it could not be unsaid, however.

"No issues from me," was Katherine's reply, who then looked at her husband.

"Nor me, we like her a lot Ellie and we see how happy she makes you. Invite her."

Ellie beamed, "Thank you."

This was of course the reaction she had been hoping for, but it still took her by surprise a little. Later, after Ellie had gone to bed she decided to text Simon and Annabelle, the first message was to Annabelle.

'Got some great news gorgeous, will tell you all about it tomorrow morning when you come over. Sleep well x'

The second was for Simon.

'I know I said it earlier, but please know that I will help you if I

can, you know where I am so talk to me if you need to. Always here. Ellie x'

Satisfied that this would intrigue Annabelle to the point of annoyance, and comfort Simon, she put her phone on silent and settled down to sleep, thinking nothing but happy thoughts as she drifted off.

Ellie had got used to dreaming. Sometimes they were not even dreams but visions being imposed on her by the Man or ones that she was creating herself. On this occasion though, it was a dream of rolling hills, clear blue skies and rippling streams. Ellie did not recognise this place, but it felt as familiar to her as if it were her own back garden. She looked around, but there was nobody there. Certainly nothing that made it feel like a vision or recreation like she had experienced before with the Man or Guardians. It was beautiful, peaceful, and tranquil. Ellie looked down and found a rock that was shaped like a seat and decided to sit on it. It looked as if it had been placed there deliberately. The view was stunning so maybe it was a seat. Even though dreaming, Ellie felt in full control of the situation and could not work out why this stone was puzzling her so much. She could not think about anything else other than this stone seat. There she sat, as dreams go it was quite a dull one. Sitting on a rock, or seat, looking out over hills, valleys, streams, rivers, and lakes. Ellie was about to stand and leave when she heard a faint voice call her name.

"Eleanor."

It was soft, as if being carried by the wind. Unlike previous experiences though she did not feel unnerved or scared by this sound, but neither could she place as to where it was coming from. She turned around, nothing and no one. Then without thinking she looked down and to her horror the floor had vanished. She was still sitting on the stone seat, but the path and hillside had vanished into a huge black nothing. There was nothing but her and the seat. She tried to stand up but found that she could not; her legs would not straighten as if they had been locked in the sitting position. The voice was getting louder now, chanting her name over and over. The calmness that had filled Ellie earlier had vanished now and was replaced with fear. She could feel her heart rate rising and her breathing increasing.

"Eleanor," the voice continued.

She turned, and was greeted by the site of a cloud, a thick, heavy looking cloud moving towards her. It was only when she focused on it that she realised this was the source of the chanting of her name. She could not move, could not run, and even if she could Ellie was not sure if she could cross over the blackness surrounding her. The cloud was close now, and Ellie could feel the air moving around her as it started to take over. She closed her eyes and braced herself for whatever was about to happen.

"Eleanor."

"Eleanor."

"Eleanor."

The voice chanted, almost sounding like there was more than one. Then she opened her eyes, and to her surprise, she was greeted by Annabelle's concerned face. Sitting up quickly, she realised she was in bed and Annabelle was sat on the end of it looking down at her.

"Ellie, are you ok? I've been trying to wake you. You wouldn't wake up."

"What time is it?" Ellie asked, trying to process everything and wake up as quickly as possible.

"Nearly ten, I expected you to be up by now. Your mum let me in." Annabelle answered, her eyebrows furrowed. "Were you dreaming again? Dreaming of him?"

"I don't know, I was dreaming but it was different." Ellie looked at Annabelle, "There was a hill, and a rock, and a cloud that was shouting my name."

"A cloud?"

"I know how it sounds."

"It sounds like you've lost it," Annabelle responded with a grin.

"Maybe, but I think there is more to it. I think, I think I need to be ready."

"Ready? Ready for what?" all signs of humour had vanished

from Annabelle's face now.

"Him."

"Ok, come on Ellie, fill me in. I'll go make a cup of tea, you wake yourself up and let's talk. Feel like you're five chapters ahead of me here."

Ellie nodded, a sense of comfort spreading through her body. She needed to tell Annabelle, she needed to ask for her help to allow them to work out what to do next.

Ellie showered quickly whilst Annabelle was making tea. Soon enough they were back in the bedroom together drinking tea and dunking biscuits. Biscuits always helped, Ellie found.

"Start from the beginning, tell me everything that I don't already know," Annabelle stated, concern on her face but a reassuring look to her eyes.

"Ok. I think he will be back. The Guardians said as much before, they also said they didn't know if he was gone for good." Ellie paused for a sip of tea, "Anyway, they basically said that I should be ready. That the only way to beat him for good was to be prepared."

"And attack him or something?" Annabelle asked, "Seems a bit extreme to me."

"This whole thing is extreme. Think about it, it has always been about him. He wants to do something so he does it. He tried to make me sacrifice myself, then created Emilia to be used as a sacrifice. Always on his terms. What if next time, assuming there is a next time, I make it on my terms?" She paused and looked out of the bedroom window that had once seemed so innocent and normal but now with a hidden meaning that only a few knew. "I just want to feel in control again, that's all."

"Ok, I get that. Where does that link into this dream though? Fill me in on that and then we can work out what is best to do next," Annabelle smiled.

The reassurance was comforting beyond measure to Ellie.

"The dream was new. It started off as a beautiful hillside, grass, blue sky with a soft breeze. It was gorgeous. Then it changed, I sat on a rock."

"A rock? What kind of rock?"

"I don't know, a rocky rock. I sat on it and then everything vanished, everything apart from me and the rock. Everything gone and replaced with black. Then this faint voice was calling my name over and over. As I looked around I felt it was coming from this cloud that was moving towards me."

"What happened when it reached you?"

Ellie turned away from the window to face Annabelle, "It didn't. That's when I woke up as your voice became the soft cloud voice. I don't know what happened next."

"What do you think it was? Do you think it was him?"

"No," Ellie said certainly, "Not his style, this felt more-" she paused, trying to think of the right word. "Pure."

"Pure?" Annabelle had a look of confusion on her face again. "What do you mean pure?"

"It felt clean, new, I have no idea what was going to happen, but it felt like it wouldn't have been all bad."

Ellie smiled a small smile at Annabelle.

"So, could it have been the Guardians?"

Ellie raised an eyebrow, "Maybe. There was no purple smoke or anything, but it was more their style I suppose."

"Maybe they are reaching out again? Maybe they want your help?"

Ellie put her cup down and fell backwards onto the bed. "Everyone wants my help, who do I go to for help?"

"Well, that's a little hurtful." Annabelle commented as she moved round the bed to lie next to Ellie. "You come to me, to us. We may not be able to see what you see, hear what you hear, or experience what you experience. We only know what you tell us, but we will always listen and do what we can to help. All of us."

Ellie sat bolt upright, "That's it. Annabelle you're a genius."

"Well yes, I know, but why exactly on this occasion?" Annabelle asked, a cheeky grin on her face.

Ellie turned to face her, "We beat him last time, Emilia and I, because he didn't anticipate that we would work together. What if I got all of you to help me? Simon, Leo, Dan, Tyler, and you. Between us all we can come up with a way to beat him surely?" Ellie stood and began to pace around the room in her dressing gown, wringing her fists together as she worked the idea through in her head. "I need to have the final say with him, but if we worked together. What if we share out everything, the ideas, the plans, and then put it all together between us. What do you think?"

"You mean share out different things between us?" Annabelle asked, sitting up and facing Ellie as she spoke.

Ellie nodded enthusiastically.

"Like what?"

"Well, I need to get stronger physically, Tyler can help me train and work out. Leo and Dan love research, they can do some digging into the stuff that has gone on around the village before. The council, that sort of thing." Ellie beamed at Annabelle, all the pieces were falling into place for her.

"What about me? What do I do?" Annabelle asked, an almost hurt tone to her voice.

"The biggest part of all. You can help me practice the spirit energy control, you and Simon."

Annabelle's expression softened, and a smile spread across her face. "How do we do that?"

"You push me, keep me on track. You may not be able to see the energy, but you should be able to see its impact and how I can manipulate it." Ellie moved over to the bed and sat beside Annabelle, taking her hand. "I really believe we can do this, together. All of us, he won't know what hit him."

Annabelle turned to look at her, "Ok. I'm in, let's do it."

"That's great news," came a voice from the stairs.

The girls whirled round to look, Ellie's mother Katherine had arrived and was beaming at the two girls.

"So glad you can join us on our little holiday Annabelle. Hope you have some walking clothes; you're going to need them."

It took some quick thinking, but between them Ellie and Annabelle managed to ensure Katherine was none the wiser to what they had been talking about. Then Ellie needed to explain about the holiday and that she had wanted to ask Annabelle properly, but the conversation had naturally gone towards the Man instead. The positive news though was that Annabelle was on board the holiday and had got permission from her parents almost immediately. That morning, they had planned for dealing with the Man, although they needed to get the others on board as well. Planned for a shopping trip to get some clothes for the holiday and then had chance to get excited about the holiday as well. All things considered it had been a good day so far. Ellie had agreed to speak to Simon first. The girls agreed that if they could get him on board the others would soon follow behind. Before Ellie had chance to talk to him, Simon messaged asking for a chat anyway, Ellie had guessed it was about his mum and carrying on the conversation from the bus.

They had agreed to meet for a drink in a local coffee shop the next morning, Ellie arrived first and ordered their drinks, two extra hot decaf latte's, found a table and sat down to wait for him. Shortly after, he arrived with his usual cheeky smile and grin, he walked over, and they greeted each other with a hug and a smile.

"Morning," Ellie beamed.

Simon smiled, "Morning Ellie, thanks for meeting me."

"That's ok, it's what I'm here for isn't it?" tilting her head slightly to one side she smiled. "So, small talk or do you want to get straight to it?" she took a sip of her coffee and waited for the reply.

Simon's smile faded slightly but did not vanish completely, "Straight to it is probably best I think, is that ok?"

Ellie reached forward and took his hand, "Whatever you want, I'm just going to sit and listen and let you tell your story. No judgement, if you want my opinion then ask but otherwise I will stay quiet and listen. Ok?"

"Thanks. Sounds good," he took a sip of coffee, sighed and began. "This is mostly what mum has told me over the years. I was just a baby, mum told me that she was still off work when it happened. It was a dark stormy night, you know the type. When the rain falls so hard you can't see through it. She told me that I was scared by the storm, the loud rain and thunder meant I wouldn't settle. Mum had been home with me all day; she had been feeling under the weather. Her and dad had been arguing a lot lately. She told me it was because he had gone back to work and couldn't handle not sleeping when I had a bad night. I think the words she used were 'toxic living environment'."

Ellie raised an eyebrow at this but kept her word and said nothing.

"He was never violent, just to make that point," Simon said quickly, keen to make sure she knew that. "He was just grumpy I guess, but when you love someone and live with them that makes it hard. So, I'm told anyway," he added quickly with a wry smile.

Ellie smiled warmly.

"Anyway. She was determined to make it work, she loved him and was sure that he loved her. They had never had any conversations about splitting up, or anything anywhere near that serious. He had been working late, he told her it was because of work but mum thought it was so he could avoid coming home. Spending more time at the office than with his family to avoid the noise at home." He paused and took a sip of coffee, then continued. "Obviously I can't remember, all I do know is that on this particular night, he never came home. According to his office he left at normal time, but he never made it. Mum called everyone she could, his friends, his family. Nobody knew where he was. She stayed up all night looking at the rain, looking and hoping he would come home. Next morning, she called the police to report him missing. They came around, talked to her but as soon as they found out they had been arguing they seemed less interested. At least, so mum says. Days, weeks, and months went by. Nobody heard from him, it was as if he just disappeared. Fortunately for mum, she was the breadwinner, so she could keep the house. Eventually she began to move on with her life. Generally, she did this, but every year about now she starts to find it hard. Every year around September she gets quiet and starts to isolate herself from the world. It's as if she still hopes." He stopped and looked out of the window into the distance.

Ellie sat back and drank some more, taking it all in.

"I still hope too, sometimes," Simon said. "I never knew him, but I see what it does to mum, and I just wish I could help."

He turned back to look at Ellie, "I know I can't help her, I can't bring him back, that's why I do as much for her as I do. I do everything I can to try and help." He took Ellie's hand, "You said the other day that you think I already help, that I already do more than enough. Did you mean it?"

Ellie smiled, "Of course. You do more than most boys would, you stepped up. You're the man you are because of your mum." She squeezed his hand, "Promise."

He grinned, "So, now you know. You know the story of how my dad ran out on me and my mum. Not even sure how it is possible to just vanish like that, but he managed it."

"I guess if you really want to disappear, anything is possible?" Ellie said sadly. "Thank you for sharing with me, I understand so much more now. Your mum is a lovely woman and I love you; you know I do. If ever I can help her or you, let me know."

"How could you help?"

"Well, if ever you want to treat your mum, I hear spa days are lovely and not your thing," she grinned and winked.

He chuckled.

"Sorry, I simply mean if there is something I can do, ask. If I can do it, I will."

"Thank you. It means the world to me."

"Can I ask one question though, if you don't mind?"

Simon smiled, "I'd expect nothing less."

"You don't have to answer, but what was your dad's name? Do you know? I noticed that you didn't once mention it."

Simon sat back, "Fair question."

"Only because I think it may help you move on a little, humanise him maybe? You don't have to tell me."

"Christian. His name was Christian," he looked down, almost ashamed to say it out loud. "Haven't said that name in years, seems silly now," he sniffed, holding back a lump in his throat.

Ellie squeezed his hand, "It's ok, you're still you Mr Lesley. And you carry that name, and yourself, with pride."

For a moment they looked at each other and said nothing, just smiling and sipping their coffee.

"Thank you, Ellie," Simon finally said, "it means so much to be able to share it with someone."

"You're welcome," Ellie smiled.

"Now, I'll get more coffee, then you talk. I'm done and I want to listen."

"Deal," Ellie grinned.

Simon stood, leaving Ellie to ponder what she had just been told, and work out how to explain what she needed from him. Shortly after, Simon had returned with the drinks. And cake. Ellie had reached the conclusion long ago that Simon had a need for sweet sugary things, and this was the best way to get him to agree to anything as well. In many ways this made the next part of her conversation a little easier.

"So, what do you need?" He asked her with a grin, whilst shovelling cake into his mouth.

Ellie smirked, "You have no table manners at all do you, boy?"

He grinned, revealing cake mashed in his teeth.

"Gross. Anyway," Ellie took a breath and steadied herself. "I need to prepare for a showdown."

"A showdown?" Simon asked, raising an eyebrow. "Are we in the wild west now?"

"A showdown against," Ellie paused, lowered her voice to a whisper, then added, "Against him. Against the Man."

Simon stopped chewing, put the piece of cake he was holding back on the plate. He looked at Ellie, all signs of light-hearted joking had vanished from his eyes. He swallowed his mouthful, "Is he back?" he asked, in as loud a whisper as he dared. "I thought you said he dissolved or something last time."

"I don't know is the first answer, and he did is the second." Ellie replied factually, "The third answer, to the question you haven't asked me yet, is because I think he will be back. I want to be prepared."

"What makes you think he will be back?"

"The Guardians said as much, and I have a feeling that it's not over yet." Ellie took a sip of coffee and a bite of cake; she was waiting for the onslaught of questions from Simon.

"Ok, so, you think he will be back. And you want to, what? Take the fight to him or something?"

"Sort of, yes. Every time he has tried one of his schemes,

it has been on his terms; I think the way to beat him is to take the fight to him. Be ready. Stand up to him rather than playing catch up and, let's be honest here, getting lucky."

Simon contemplated this, taking a drink but never taking his eyes off his friend. "Right. You're preparing for a fight. Is that why you are not going to university?"

Ellie had been prepared for many questions, but not this one, not from Simon. "No. Well, maybe. I'm staying home to earn some money at work to then decide what I want to do. It so happens that this means it will be easier for me to prepare for this yes."

Simon nodded, "Ok. I have a feeling you have a plan here, out with it."

Ellie smiled, "So clever aren't you. Well, I want to train to be ready for him to come back and I need help. Help from all of you."

"All of us?"

"Yes. I have already spoken to Annabelle, and we agreed that you would be the best person to talk to next. I need everyone though, I think there is a job for all of you."

"A job? Sounds like you're planning a robbery," Simon smirked, then clearly relaxing, took some cake.

"I think there is too much for one person to learn and investigate, so what I want to do," she corrected herself, "What I want to ask, is for everyone to do a little bit and help me, help me to learn and investigate."

"Investigate?"

"Yes, I can't be the first person he has done this to, I know it. There will be something somewhere that can help us. And don't forget the stuff we found in that box; the compass, the telescope. All of it has come from somewhere and does something."

"Ok, you've got me interested," Simon added, finishing his last bites of cake. "What do you want to do, with who, and when?"

Ellie beamed, she knew she had him interested now and would soon have his full support. "I have split it into three categories, mind, body, and spirit. Here is what I'm thinking. Tyler, he can work with me on getting my body fit. Physically stronger, stamina, ready for the long-haul stuff."

"Makes sense," Simon agreed, "He is a fitness know all after all."

"Agreed. Leo and Dan, I was going to ask to do mind. They are awesome at research, figuring things out, joining the dots, and all sorts. If there is anything to find, they will."

Simon nodded silently.

"That leaves you and Annabelle to help me with spirit. I want you to help me practice using the energy, using the flow, understanding it. Seeing what I can do. What do you think?"

For a moment, Simon said nothing. Then he sighed, puffed out his cheeks and looked directly at Ellie. "I think you're barking mad," he smiled. "But it makes sense, and I agree it sounds like the right thing to do. I'm in."

Ellie jumped up, ran around the table, and wrapped him in a hug that nearly knocked them both to the floor. This of course attracted attention from all over the coffee shop, and they were soon giggling away at the number of eyes that were now looking at them.

Ellie moved back to her seat, wiped the tears of joy from her face and smiled, "Thank you."

"No problem. But how can Annabelle and I help you? We can't see it?"

Ellie grinned, "I think you will be able to feel it. And that combined with me seeing and using it, the energy that is, will work perfectly."

"If you say so. Is this the part where you tell me that I need to help you convince the others to help?"

"You know me so well, yes your help is needed but I am hoping that they will be as willing to help as you are."

"I'm sure they will be, Tyler will be happy to be involved again, he was gutted he missed it all before. Even though technically we all missed it."

There was a knowing silence between the pair, they sat for a moment contemplating the conversations and decisions they had just made. Ellie felt as comfortable as ever, she was scared of course, but having a plan and the support of her two best friends meant the world to her. She truly felt as though she could achieve anything with their help.

Simon broke the silence first, "Only one thing left to decide then."

Ellie looked at him quizzically.

"It's a big one. Do we need a team name?" he grinned.

Ellie threw a napkin at him.

They finished their drinks and left, arms linked, discussing their next move.

CHAPTER 3

Over the next few days, Ellie, Simon, and Annabelle discussed their plans. Annabelle had been right; Simon was indeed the best option to get the others on board. After many deliberations, they agreed to bring the entire group to Ellie's house, so they could investigate ideas together. It seemed fitting to meet here as it was where they had discussed plans the very first time they had faced off against the Man of Mow. It was Sunday, Ellie's parents were out, and they were ready for everyone to come over. The three had planned this down to the minute, Annabelle had stayed over the night before, and Simon was coming around about an hour before the others, so they could ensure they were all aligned. Ellie woke first, got up quietly so as not to disturb Annabelle and went to make tea; mornings were always easier after tea. She stood in the kitchen and sipped her drink for a moment, savouring the silence. Ellie was feeling anxious about talking to her friends, but knew it was the best way to build her confidence. The boost that she had gotten from talking to Simon had pushed her into believing this was going to work. In her mind, it had to. She grabbed some biscuits and went upstairs to wake Annabelle, who it seemed was already awake; sat up with a smile on her face.

"Tea," she stated loudly, or at least as loudly as was appropriate for this time in the morning.

"And biscuits," Ellie replied with a grin. "Can't have one without the other, you know this." She headed over to the bed and they sat on the end of it together, dunking biscuits in their drinks.

"Have we ever discussed our favourite dunking biscuit?"

Annabelle asked, holding up one to the light as if examining it.

"What?" Ellie spluttered, almost choking on her last mouthful.

"Well, it's a serious conversation to have. And I don't think we ever discussed it that's all," she pushed the biscuit into her mouth whole, turned to Ellie and smiled.

Ellie burst out laughing, "Ok, no we haven't, maybe after we have saved the world?"

Annabelle nodded, swallowed, then responded, "Deal."

They finished their drinks with smiles and laughter, something that sometimes was missing from Ellie's life. She was happy, in moments she was happier than she had ever been, but the constant drain on her since they moved to the village of Mow Cop put a grey cloud on her day. Shortly after, they were dressed, downstairs, and waiting for Simon to arrive. As always, he arrived right on time, with sweets. He walked into the house with an unnaturally large grin.

Ellie narrowed her eyes, "What are you so happy about, Mr?"

"Just life in general," he smirked, almost flushed a little red.

"Tell us," Annabelle joined in.

The girls were keen to get any news or gossip out of him before the others arrived. They went into the kitchen, where they had prepared a tray of drinks and snacks for their friends. Simon headed straight for the tray.

"No, you don't," Ellie shouted, moving quickly to position herself between Simon and the food. "No treats until you tell us what has got you grinning like a cat who got the cream," she folded her arms.

Simon laughed, "Wow ok. It's nothing special though. Just that Sophie is coming to stay for a week soon, we arranged it last night and I'm happy about it," he flushed red this time.

Ellie smiled, "Now that is great news. Why would you hide that from me? From us?" she gestured towards Annabelle.

"No reason really, just a guy thing I guess," he shifted awkwardly. "Didn't want to come in and talk about me today. It's all about you and this crazy plan."

Ellie pulled him into a hug and whispered in his ear, "I'll

always have time for you, always." She pulled away, "But still no snacks until the others arrive. That's the rule," she grabbed the tray and hurried out of the kitchen. "Annabelle, keep him there," she taunted. Ellie entered the dining room and put the tray down on the table. She and Annabelle had already got the room ready. On the table surrounding the newly placed snacks, was the contents of the tin from her room they all found a few years back. Letters, a compass that only pointed to the folly and it's energy flow, what looked like a telescope, this had fitted into the rock in the garden and focused the energy. They had also laid out on the walls using tack the paper plans they had created when dealing with the Man recently. Looking at these brought a lump to Ellie's throat. Emilia. She could not help but think of her and no matter what she did it would always be difficult. In the room was everything they had from previous encounters with the Man. It was not much, but it was a start. Her hope was that as a group they could piece some of this together and work as a team to beat him once and for all. Ellie stood in silence for a few moments, taking it all in and thinking about what she was about to try. She scanned the room, not really looking at anything special or specific. Just browsing as if at a museum. Her eyes settled on the compass, and she could not look away from it. She had never really paid it that much attention but for some reason felt it stood out most in this room.

"Everything ok?" came Simon's voice from the door, snapping Ellie out of her trance.

She turned and faced him, a calm expression on her face. "Yes, fine. Just trying to make sense of it all. It doesn't look like much does it? When it's all laid out like this I mean," she gestured behind her at the room.

Simon stepped forward and peered round, "No, but it is better than nothing," he smiled kindly. "And most of all, we have you. He will be terrified of you now, I guarantee it."

"How do you know that?" she asked, curiously.

"Because I would be," he grinned, then shot away before Ellie could give him a dead arm.

It wasn't long before Leo, Dan, and Tyler had joined them.

They were in the dining room, all sat round the table. Ellie at one end, Simon the other. Annabelle to her left with Leo to her right. Tyler and Dan filling in the two places at Simon's end. The conversation was pleasant, everyone catching up and chatting about everything and nothing all at once. Ellie sat back in her chair and watched, observing her friends. She smiled to herself, fully aware that this was what it was supposed to be like. She sat and said nothing for a while, then she caught Simon's eye unintentionally and he immediately stopped talking, staring across the table at her. This in turn led to Tyler and Dan following his gaze, then Leo, and finally Annabelle turned towards Ellie. Silence fell across the group and that broke Ellie out of her focused state. She blinked, focusing her eyes on her friends and bringing herself back into the room.

"You ok Ellie?" Leo asked kindly.

She turned to him and smiled, "Yes, yes I am," she took a deep breath. "I am because all of you are here. I know not all of you know the full details as to why but the fact you are here makes me feel a whole lot better about the situation. So, thank you for coming."

There were responses of general support, "You're welcome," "Anytime," and "Of course," were some that she was able to register.

"Would you like me to say anything, or leave it to you?" Annabelle asked softly.

Ellie had not considered this; she knew that what she was about to talk about was complicated, difficult, and in some cases down right dangerous. But she had not counted on Annabelle's heart and support being so strong as to speak first. She smiled, "No thank you. Not because that isn't wonderful, but I think this needs to come from me is all."

Annabelle smiled back and nodded.

"Ok, this is going to be tough, so I hope you are all fed and watered enough," Ellie joked, to her relief there was a small sound of chuckling from her friends. "I have a lot to say, and some of it is going to be very-" she paused for a moment, trying to get the right word to form in her mind, "Interesting," she tried. Then spoke again. "Different.

Challenging. New. Unusual. Scary. So many different things."
"How about you tell us, then we will help you decide what it is," Leo commented.
Ellie nodded, "Ok. I'm sure by looking around you have all gathered this is about him. The Man," she glanced at her friends, nobody said anything, so she continued. "Well, I have had enough. I have had enough of everything being on his terms, his way, his rules. I want to do something different. I want to be ready," she began to feel her voice lifting and her spirit rising along with it, this helped. "I want to fight, and I want to take the fight to him."
She was greeted with wide eyes from her friends, but still nobody spoke so Ellie continued.
"All I mean, is I want to be ready. To make sure that we are not caught out. I don't want any more pain, suffering, anything. I want it to end."
Ellie sat back, waiting for a moment before saying anything more.
After what felt like an age, Dan spoke, "First question. Is he back?"
This seemed logical and had been what Ellie had expected as the first response.
"No, at least, not as far as I can tell, but that is part of my point," Ellie replied. "He has come after me, us, twice now. Each time has been on his terms, when he wanted, in his way. I have been playing catch up. I want to be ready so that if he does try anything again, I can be prepared to challenge him from the start and maybe, do this properly once and for all."
Dan nodded, apparently satisfied with this as a response.
"Do you think he will be back?" Tyler added, "I'm guessing over the summer stuff just started with him again, so what makes you think he isn't gone?"
"I don't," Ellie replied truthfully, "I have no idea. But I am beginning to think there is no harm in being prepared just in case."
There was more silence, Ellie looked to Annabelle, and then Simon for reassurance. The latter gave a gentle nod, encouraging her to continue.
"I want to be ready, but I need your help. I know I have asked

a lot, and you have all been through a lot, I just don't think I can do this alone," her voice cracked a little at this, her mind had drifted to Emilia again. "I need to do this, for many reasons but I need your help."

Annabelle reached out and took Ellie's hand, "She needs us to help her prepare, in different ways."

Ellie nodded, holding back the tears, squeezing Annabelle's hand as a way of silent thanks for her interruption. "I think there are three things that I need to prepare and I would like to ask each of you to help me with a different area." She stopped, looking around at her friends.

"Well, tell us what you need then," Tyler replied, "No point in keeping it to yourself now is there?" he smiled.

Ellie knew he was being kind, "Ok, three areas. Mind, body, and spirit. I need to work on them all and get ready for this. I have already spoken with Annabelle and Simon, they have agreed with what I want to do," she nodded softly towards them as she said their names. "Leo and Dan, you are the best researchers and revisers I know. I would like to ask you to help me with mind. Can you help me by researching everything that there is on him and what has happened before?"

The boys looked at each other, nodded then Leo responded, "On it."

There was a chuckle around the group, a softening of the air.

"Thank you, I have put around this room everything that we have, take it, and do what you do best."

They smirked at her.

"I have no idea what will be out there but given what he has said about his previous tries, there must be something," she turned towards Tyler, "Tyler, I need to get fit," She smiled as if stating this was enough.

"You mean stronger?" he asked.

"Yes, but also I need to have more stamina and endurance. I need to be ready for a long fight, get my energy up."

He nodded, "I can help with that, you ok coming to the gym?"

"If I have to," she smiled, "Yes of course."

"So, that's body and mind," Leo commented, "That leaves spirt," he looked at Ellie, then to Annabelle and Simon and back again.

"Yes, Annabelle and Simon will help me with spirit. They will help me practice and work on using the ability, power, whatever it is, that he gave me by mistake last time."

"How will they do that? Aren't you the only one that can see it?" Tyler asked.

Ellie nodded.

"We will be offering support and guidance on what we can see, feel, and sense. We will know how she is doing and will help like that," Annabelle replied on Ellie's behalf.

Ellie nodded, "This is not going to be easy, and if anyone would rather not get involved say so, I understand," she waited as silence fell across the room once more.

Nobody said anything, or even moved. Everyone seemed on edge and tense but there was a strong feeling of support in the room. Finally, Ellie spoke again.

"Thank you, nothing else to say but thank you. For understanding and supporting me. I've just had enough of being afraid," Ellie paused, she knew what she was about to say but did not know why, she had no idea where it had come from or what it meant to her, but she knew she had to say it, "Being afraid of everything, means you learn nothing."

Her friends looked back at her, smiling and showing expressions of support, love, and trust.

The next few hours were spent pouring over the contents of the room. Leo and Dan started makings notes on the details from the walls, the items on the table and what they already knew. Before long they had created digital notepads, divided into categories and subsections. The sort of thing any teacher would be proud of if a student made it during revision season. Ellie was in awe of their organisational skills, and it truly amazed her at how quickly they had set it all up. They had made it online so it could be shared with the group, it could be accessed anywhere. Tyler had also been busy creating a training plan that was daunting to Ellie at first. She trusted him to do the right thing, he was a mini expert in that area after all. It would allow Ellie to build on her strength and stamina, allowing her focus on exerting some pressure in a physical way, something that she felt would be very important in the coming weeks and months. Most of the time Ellie spent talking to Leo, Dan, and Tyler. She knew that Annabelle and Simon needed her attention too, but they were also discussing their own plans between them. Of all the people in the room, they knew the most about her plan before today. She listened as Leo explained the colour coding of their research storage system and nodded tentatively when Tyler explained why he had put in the activities he had, listening to every word even if it did not make much sense to her in the moment. The friends chatted and planned through the day and into the afternoon, until eventually they agreed they had done all they could for the day, and so arranged to get some food. After much debate, indeed more of a debate than discussing the plans for dealing with the Man, they agreed on pizza.

"It is everyone's favourite after all," commented Simon, much to the combined amusement and annoyance of the others. Especially those that wanted a curry. They all agreed that they should have one last night off before getting to work the next day on Ellie's plan. Tyler had already set Ellie up with the gym to get her started. Leo and Dan had also agreed between them that they would meet up to get to work on researching and exploring. There was almost a festive cheery mood in the room as they ate and drank. So much so that when Ellie's parents got home they just saw it as Ellie having fun with her friends. No questions were asked, and they were left to it.

Gradually the friends said their goodbyes, Tyler, Leo, and Dan were the first to leave; Tyler leaving with a promise that she would be picked up at ten AM sharp the next day to go to the gym. Simon and Annabelle hung back, wanting to make sure that Ellie was truly ok after the long day they had.

"I'm good, really good," Ellie said with a soft smile. "You are all just, you know. I couldn't do any of this without your help and support, I know I have that and we will do this."

"We will," Annabelle replied, warmly.

"We are all with you," Simon added, hugging her goodbye.

"Whatever happens," Annabelle added, with a kiss. "Now go and get some sleep, sounds like you have your work cut out for you this week."

"Thanks, I know. Tyler is going to kill me I think," Ellie replied with a grin.

With that they left, Ellie closed the door and leant on it for a moment. She then went to see her parents and say goodnight.

"Had a busy day?" Nicholas asked, looking at his daughter.

"Yes, just been chatting, planning, gossiping, you know. The usual."

"Well, I'm glad you're all ok," he replied, turning back towards the TV.

Ellie looked at him, then at her mother. She loved her parents with all she had but she knew that she could not share what they were planning with them, not yet. She would wait until they were in a position to deal with it fully and then tell them. With this decision silently reached in her mind, she said softly, "I'm going to bed, long day and a long week ahead I think."

She kissed her mum and dad goodnight, who muttered words of goodnight in return. After getting a drink Ellie went upstairs and before long was in bed, ready to settle down to sleep. Lying in bed she could not help the plans and thoughts of the day spinning round in her mind. All she could keep saying to herself was that 'this time, it would be different.' Eventually, Ellie drifted to sleep, with thoughts of her friends, family, and their plans all spinning in her mind.

CHAPTER 4

Ellie's dreams were always vivid and bold lately, as if playing a high definition computer game. She had often thought to herself that it was better than any virtual reality software, except the fact that most of the time it scared her as it was too real, and often came true. Tonight was no different, Ellie was seemingly outside of her house at night. The sky was a deep purple with the silver spackle of stars all over. Looking around Ellie was satisfied that this was a dream and there was nobody around. She decided to walk, without any real purpose or direction, just walk and see what happened and where she ended up. Ellie walked, enjoying the peace, quiet, and familiar surroundings of her village. She moved along roads, over fences, and paths. Before she knew it, she had reached the peak of the hill by the folly. She paused to look at it, it's appearance in the dull light of the moon made it appear grey in colour, as if a shadow of its former self. Ellie had not chosen to walk to the folly but seeing as that was where she had ended up she decided to explore a little. She walked up the crest of the hill along the single wall towards the tower. The same tower that she had trapped the man in all those years ago. As she reached the iron gate and peered through, nothing.

"Hello," she called into it for no apparent reason. She scolded herself for expecting there to be a reply but found herself amused at the echo that came back to her.

She turned and sighed as she walked back down the steps to the hilltop. Once at that level she turned to face the folly with an incredulous look. As if it was to blame for everything and it was its fault that she was there right now, confused, and perplexed.

"What does this mean? What am I missing?" she asked herself out loud. She puffed out her cheeks and clicked her tongue. "Not giving anything away are you?"

She moved on, deciding to look elsewhere. Without really thinking about it, she headed towards the pile of rocks that made up the Statue of Mow. Before long, she was close, and was standing in front of the rock pile. Looking at them gave her a feeling of sadness and loneliness. Ellie had never really got over what had happened with Emilia. She knew it was not her fault, and indeed that Emilia had been created by the Man to try and win once and for all, but it still did not help her feeling of guilt. Ellie leant on the fence that surrounded the rocks, looking up at them in the same way that she did the folly. Wondering, thinking, and trying to work out what this particular dream state was supposed to be telling her. The memories of Emilia bringing a tear to her eye, she let it roll down her cheek. Ellie said to herself out loud, "I'm going to beat him, for us, for you, for Annabelle. I'll do whatever it takes."

As soon as she uttered this last word there was a shout of fear and despair, a screech so horrible it cut right through the silence of the hill, right through Ellie's ears and shook her soul. She turned to face in the direction of the folly, where the sound seemed to have come from. With one last look up at the statue she turned and ran back to the hilltop. Ellie kept a solid pace, surprising herself as she did so and thinking that Tyler may not need to work her as hard after all. Ellie was very aware that there was nobody and nothing else here, so whatever had made that noise wanted her attention. Ellie rounded the last corner and could see the folly clearly now but could still not see anything that could have made such a noise. She moved through the paths and climbed the narrow stairs to the hilltop. Once there she turned, looking all around her for the source, still nothing. She took a few steps forward to look down the ridge to the side of the folly. To her surprise, her friends were there. Gathered in a circle looking down at something, she jumped down the rocks and scrambled across to them. She was approaching the group from behind Simon and Annabelle, with the others forming a small circle around whatever it was they were looking at. Just before she got there, there was a blinding flash and deafening bang from above. Ellie stopped in her tracks and turned. The light was coming from the sky, an object floating just above the wall of the folly, floating like a cloud but shining like the sun. She squinted, as she did so she became aware of her friends moving around her to look up in the same direction. They made no attempt to contact, or even acknowledge, she was there. This was a dream after all. As they watched, the light faded, still bright but it was becoming easier to see. Ellie felt a burning rage rise inside her like a fire. The floating object was not an object at all, it was the Man of Mow. Glowing and shining the way he had when he first presented himself to the very first council. Like a shining star of hope.

"Behold," his voice boomed across the hill. "I have returned to exact my revenge and to complete my plan. Nothing and no one will stand in my way. The last of the Guardians are gone, and now you will all perish."

Ellie processed this, "The last Guardian?" she asked herself aloud, "Does that mean he knows how to stop them? Or does he mean me?"

With a sudden surge of fear, she turned and moved through her group of friends. They were all still looking up at the Man, listening and shouting back at him. Ellie could not focus on their voices though, for what she had seen on the floor had sucked the life out of her. She collapsed to her knees, next to her, lying on the ground, still, and cold, was herself. Ellie was looking at her own lifeless body. She let out a wail of pain and fear, stretching her head back to scream out. As she did so the light from the Man became so blinding once again that she had to close her eyes. Screaming, her eyes closed, Ellie had no idea how long she stayed there for. When she next opened her eyes, the hill had gone, so had her friends, the Man, and her body. She was kneeling on the floor of her bedroom, covered in a cold sweat, her heart pounding, with the image of her own lifeless face burned into her mind.

CHAPTER 5

It took Ellie a while to get back to sleep after that, but eventually she drifted off into a restless slumber. She had an alarm set for eight, which she ignored finally moving out of bed around quarter to nine. Knowing that Tyler was picking her up around ten meant that she had almost an hour to get ready and have some food. As she did so Ellie did her best to shake the memory of her dream from the night before. She had also decided not to tell anyone about it, not yet anyway. She sat in the living room drinking a cup of tea in her gym gear when Tyler rang the doorbell.

"Morning sunshine," he beamed at her when she opened the door.

"You are far too energetic, Mr," Ellie replied. "I'm a morning person but that is too much."

"We will soon have you at my energy levels," he smiled, "Ready to go?"

"Yup," Ellie replied excitedly. She was genuinely interested to see what Tyler had in store for her and going to the gym to get fit would not be a bad thing at all. She picked up her bag and headed out, Tyler leading the way to his car.

"So, what's the plan then? You going to go easy on me?" Ellie asked as they got in.

"Sort of. I've got you a day pass to get in, we should be able to do that most times, so you won't have to pay."

"So far so good," Ellie grinned.

"I have a gym program for you to follow," Tyler responded as they pulled away. "A simple set of things for you to do in the gym that if you do them repeatedly, and up the intensity, they will boost your overall cardio and stamina. Then, we can move onto strength."

"Wow. Intense."

"You'll be fine, you're in my world now, I'll look after you."

The journey was a quick and simple one, the gym where Tyler was currently working was about twenty minutes away. Ellie knew of it, but had never been. When they arrived, she was pleased to see that it appeared to be a friendly gym, meaning that she did not feel intimidated at all when she walked in. She did not need to get changed of course but locked her bag in a locker along with her coat, keys, and phone, before leaving to meet Tyler once more. He was where she had left him, chatting to the receptionist.

"So, this is Ellie, my friend who I am giving a crash course in training today." Tyler said, turning to introduce her, "Ellie, this is Lois, she is another trainer here."

"Nice to meet you," Lois said to Ellie. She was a fair skinned girl with ginger curly hair and a beaming friendly smile.

"You too, can I trust him?" Ellie asked, nodding towards Tyler.

"Yeah he's ok, but if you want another opinion, let me know," Lois teased and winked.

"Ladies I am hurt," Tyler interrupted, "For that I'm adding an extra few things for you Ellie. Come on let's get cracking." He turned and led Ellie up the stairs, explaining as they went. "You can see the pool through the window here, in there you also have the spa's, sauna, and steam room. A good way to finish a workout is with a swim."

"I'll bring my stuff next time," Ellie commented.

At the top of the stairs, he turned and led her to a room that Ellie recognised as a gym room. It was full of treadmills, bikes, rowing machines, and more equipment that she did not immediately recognise.

"For now, I'm going to stay with you and work with you on the program, show you the equipment and how to use it. Then I can leave you and you can repeat it and increase the intensity for as long as you think you can. That ok?"

Ellie nodded, "I remember some of this from my sporty high school days." She replied. It was true, Ellie was no stranger to gyms but had not been in one since leaving school, so a little guidance was appreciated.

"Ok, let's get to it then. I have printed your program, but I will email it to you as well. Next time you come on your own you can bring your phone and listen to whatever gets you pumped up." He handed Ellie a piece of paper, she took it and looked at it.

Ellie's get fit quick gym programme

Warm up (Some simple stretches will do)

Treadmill walk 5.5 speed, Incline goes up every 2 mins 3%, do this for 10mins

Stair master 5mins level 6+ (increase it if you wish)

Rower on level 8, Sing row row row your boat 20 times really loud then you can stop.

10 press ups

10 sit ups

10 squats

10 burpees

10 Russian twists

Repeat increasing time on certain activities, quantity of others, and difficulty of the rest

Ellie looked up at Tyler.
"You have questions?" he asked her calmly.
"A few. What is a Russian twist? And is singing really necessary?" she asked, a small smile creeping across her face.
"No, but it is good fun and is a good timing measure. The less out of breath you are, the quicker you can sing it," he winked. "I'll show you a Russian twist later, now come on, stretch."
He led Ellie over to a matted area of the gym and they spent a few minutes stretching. After this, he set her up on a treadmill.
"Here is where you set the speed," he indicated a switch on the left. "And here is the incline, once you have started, the

clock will count for you. Every two minutes increase the incline by three percent. This will make it harder on your legs without increasing the speed. Ready?"

"One way to find out," Ellie replied.

He pressed the start button, and the treadmill began to move, Tyler set the speed and showed her how to adapt it as she needed to.

Ellie spent about an hour with Tyler working through the programme he had given her. She had to admit, he knew what he was doing. By the end of it she was exhausted and had worked up quite a sweat.

"So, you want me to do that over and over?" she asked, gulping water down as they sat on some benches near the top of the stairs.

"Yeah, the idea is it will get easier, the more you do it the easier it will get and the quicker you will get. Once it gets easy, and you're not feeling the pain, we will change it up."

"Right ok," she gasped, taking another gulp.

"I would suggest bringing stuff to go in the steam room next time, maybe even go for a swim after."

Ellie nodded, "Thank you, Tyler. Really appreciate you trying to kill me, saving him a job and all."

She winked and punched him on the arm. It was only a soft punch though; she had no energy for anything more serious.

"No problem. Happy to help. I need to go though, start work in ten minutes. You going to be ok from here?"

"I think I can find my way to the changing rooms," Ellie replied.

He smiled, they hugged and then he stood and left.

Ellie sat there for a few minutes gathering herself. She did feel good if exhausted, it had helped her clear her mind a little as well. Ellie smiled to herself, she was pleased that she had done this, and felt that this was the first of many steps needed to carry out her plan. Eventually she decided to move, heading downstairs to the changing rooms to shower and change. About half an hour later she was done and walking out of the changing rooms back past the reception. She smiled kindly at the receptionist, a different person this time, and went through the barrier. Ellie knew that Tyler was working so would not be able to see her right now, so she walked out of the gym and towards the bus stop. Before long she was sat halfway down the bus on her way to work, feeling very pleased with herself. The positive energy that flowed through her after exercise was strong, and with a grin to herself she was gently reminded of what it used to feel like working out on a more regular basis. She had missed it. It also felt like a step forward in her plans and this made her very happy indeed. When she arrived at work, she sent a message of thanks to Tyler as well as a promise that she would be back and that she was also going to start running around the village. Ellie locked her things in her locker and got to work. Throughout her shift she had a smile on her face, the positive energy was flowing, she felt confident, strong, and brave. Everything she needed to be.

The next day Ellie woke early and did as she had promised herself; she went for a run. It was a grey morning. Not too cold, but cool enough to make her pick up the pace early on in order to keep herself warm. She had no plans to set any speed records but wanted to keep her heart rate high to push herself and her body. After about twenty minutes she stopped for a drink and a little break, taking note of her rather cloudy surroundings as she did so. Looking out over the surrounding areas she could see the clouds; she was level with them. Even though not in them, seeing them around the hill gave her a sense of isolation. Weirdly, she quite liked it. After a few minutes she decided to head back home again, wanting to see if she could get home quicker than she got where she was now. It was her favourite type of competition, against herself. Fortunately for Ellie, she did manage to beat her time by ten seconds. This meant she had earned, in her eyes, a celebratory hot chocolate and an omelette when she got home. Her parents were at work and she had nothing to do but get ready for work herself, so she took her time over breakfast. Whilst eating, she also messaged her friends to let them know she was still going along with her plan and had a few replies of support and love. At the same, she asked Tyler to get her another day pass, so she could continue to push herself at the gym once more.

This was the pattern for Ellie over the next couple of weeks. She would either be working, at the gym, or running. To her surprise she very quickly was able to go for longer or faster, just as Tyler had promised. Progress was being made. Ellie woke on a Thursday after a couple of weeks of exercise and pushing herself. To say that her body ached was an understatement. She knew that this was part of the process though and so was pushing through the barrier. Today was a day off, no gym, no work, and no running. As much as progress was good, she was aware that a rest day would do her some good too. After going to the bathroom, she checked her phone and saw a message sent the night before from Leo.

"Ellie, we have found out a fair bit. Can we come around tomorrow and go through it with you?. You can get a head start if you want, we have put most of it in our online notebook. Let me know. L x"

Ellie smirked to herself, she loved the way he finished messages off with an 'L', always amused her for some reason. She sent a reply immediately.

"Sure, I'm in all day so let me know when and I'll put the kettle on. Will wait for you to get here to walk me through it all though! ;) E x"

She went to make herself breakfast, and as she was eating a reply from Leo arrived stating they would be there around lunchtime. Ellie spent the morning sorting out a few things around the house and generally busying herself. She even did a bit of cross stitch although she had not really done a lot of this lately. She was working on a design of a cottage, the sort of cottage that she hoped to live in one day with a thatch roof and a beautiful garden. The morning passed quickly and before she knew it there was a knock at the door. She opened it to be greeted by the beaming faces of Leo and Dan.

"Afternoon boys," she smiled warmly, "Come in, tea?

Biscuits? The usual?"

"Yes please," Leo replied.

"Can we set up in the dining room?" Dan added.

Ellie looked at him, "Set up? Set up what?"

"Our findings," Leo replied.

Ellie smiled, "You two are incredible. Yes, the dining room is fine. You go in and make yourselves at home, I'll be in soon with refreshments."

They did, and Ellie went to make drinks. Shortly after she walked back into the dining room and almost dropped the tray. The boys had gone all out, they were leaning over a laptop which Ellie had expected. What she had not expected was them to return with the original plans and flip charts, all the contents of the box, every note they had ever taken, and have them all laid out, colour coded and coordinated ready for review.

"What's all this?" she asked, a shocked tone to her voice.

"Everything," Leo replied without looking up from his screen.

"We needed a system for getting all of this logged down and done, so we made one."

"Wow. Just, wow. Ok. I get it, I think," Ellie replied sheepishly as she really did not have a clue, putting the tray down. "Drinks are here," she added and took a seat, "Am I ok sat here?"

Leo smiled, "Yes of course silly." He turned to Dan, "Dan, whilst I finish this bit, can you explain what we have done and how all this works, then maybe it will make more sense?"

Dan nodded and turned towards Ellie. "Ok, we needed a digital way to log and track all of this," he gestured around the room. "Doing so would allow us to search, link, and reference all of it wherever we are. We started doing it on Leo's laptop, then we made it cloud based. Also means you can read it yourself."

Ellie looked down at the table, feeling a little ashamed that they had put all this effort in and she had not read any of the stuff in the links they had sent her so far.

"I can tell by your lack of response that you've not read any of it yet?" Leo commented, still not taking his eyes off the screen where he was typing feverishly.

Ellie shook her head, "No, sorry."

"That's ok, I think that will change after today." Dan replied excitedly, "Here is what we have done." He took a step around the table towards Ellie. "We colour coded everything, splitting out things that we have all seen or know, from things that you alone have seen or know and then finally things that we have been told, including you. With me?"

Ellie said nothing but raised her eyebrows.

"Ok, example. We all know the Man wants to destroy our world, so that is coded red because we all know it. You know that he can manipulate energy and the stuff around it, that's blue. We have all been told he has tried this before so that is yellow. Not the best examples but does it make sense now?"

Ellie nodded, "Yup, red, blue and yellow. Got it."

"There is more than that though. We have also coded things that we have as physical items."

"Green," Leo shouted.

"Maps and references," Dan added.

"Orange."

"And finally, theories."

"Purple."

Ellie looked at them, a look of astonishment on her face. "You have given everything a colour?"

"Yes, or in some cases more than one," Dan replied, moving to sit by Ellie. "This means we can track everything. If there is an item where you know what it's for and we don't, it is green and blue. Or if there is a theory that we all know."

"Purple and red," Ellie interrupted.

Dan beamed, Leo even looked up from his laptop.

"By George I think she's got it," Leo exclaimed.

"I think she has," Dan added approvingly. "So around us, you can see that everything has a coloured mark or block. Online, we add tags or labels of the colour."

"You are two geniuses, you know that?" Ellie added in admiration of their skills.

"Not really, but we do like to organise," Dan replied, standing and moving back to Leo's side.

"So, what have you actually found out then?" Ellie asked,

taking a sip of tea afterwards.

The boys looked at each other, then back at Ellie.

"Lots of everything, and nothing, all at the same time," Leo replied.

Ellie gave him a puzzled look.

"What I mean is that we have found out lots, but this is still a work in progress. We have made some connections to other odd things that have happened in the village before."

Ellie nodded, "Ok, I'm listening. Lay it on me."

Leo stood, "The main thing we have tried to focus on, is what the energy actually is. We figured it must have been tracked or noticed by someone somewhere before. Where does it come from? How does it work?"

Ellie sat back, intrigued.

Dan took over, "We think it has appeared in history, in different cultures from the very beginning through to now. Never really known or recognised, but always there. Varying from people who claimed to have magical abilities, to fortune tellers, people who conduct seances even."

"Right the way through to those with awesome imaginations," Leo added. "We think it has always been there, for all of us, but only a few can actually see it or use it."

"Like me?" Ellie asked, more to make sure she was following than anything else.

"Yes, like you," Leo confirmed. "We think the spirit energy is what drives our subconscious or is at least channelled by it. And the more susceptible you are to it, the easier it is to see, use, and control. And those that can do this get to use its full range of abilities."

"You've got my attention, are you saying that there have been others like me? Others that have tried to do things and failed?"

"Sort of," Dan replied. "We have found six different instances in the last fifty years, where people have developed an-" He paused, looking at Leo as if waiting for the right word.

"Ability," Leo helped.

Dan nodded, then allowed Leo to carry on.

"Six different people, from different backgrounds, families, everything. No connection that we can see. Until they disappear."

He stopped, and a silence fell over the room as if someone had let all the air out of it.

"Disappear?" Ellie asked, shakily.

The boys nodded.

Leo continued, "Each of the six instances we found, they appear to have an ability of sorts. Nothing major, we aren't talking superheroes here, but they seemed to have demonstrated the same things that you have told us about. Being able to see light that isn't there, feeling energy like it is water, that sort of thing."

"Then, after a varying period of time, nothing. They just vanish. No more anything," Dan added.

"What do you mean?"

"Well, the most recent was about eighteen years ago, way before the time when social media would have meant we could say for sure. So, when we say no more anything, we mean it."

The boys looked at each other, and Ellie had a feeling there was more. The looks on their faces suggested that they had more to say but were unsure how to.

"What is it?" she probed. "Tell me what you are both trying to work out whether or not to tell me."

"Well, five of the six people were all much older, they lived alone in the village, kept to themselves so when they vanished, and houses went up for sale, nobody really questioned it," Leo added, looking at Ellie directly.

"Ok, and the sixth?"

"The sixth, was younger, had a family. People that would miss them. Indeed, his partner filed police reports and all sorts."

"What happened?"

"Because as a couple they had been arguing a lot, after the birth of their first-born child, it got marked up as he just upped and left. On his own."

"It is as if nobody official cared he had gone," Dan commented. "Except his partner who put up posters and everything."

Ellie sipped her tea, processing it all, "Where did you find all this?" she asked.

"Archives mostly, newspaper archives at the library. Not much to search online from that long ago," Leo replied.

"Ok you think that the energy is channelled by our subconscious, and that is why some of us can use it? And create vivid images in our minds, feel it and see it? Have I got that right?"

They nodded.

"We have also gone through everything that happened with Emilia," Leo stopped, realising as he had said it he had not prepared Ellie for it. He looked at her, "Sorry, I didn't mean to just drop that name in like that."

She smiled warmly, "It's ok, I know what you mean, and I can't hide from or change it. Go on, what have you found?"

He smiled back, then continued, "Well, he had a plan. A plan that he was convinced would work because he thought that you, or rather the negative part of you, would not want the glory and attention anymore." He picked up the piece of paper upon which was the names of the six people to go missing, "Each of these people had something they weren't happy with, whether it was an issue at home or a failed relationship. They all had something they would want to change. What if he tried that scheme with you and Emilia. Instead of using you, he tried to make a version of you that would do what he wanted? Removing the idea of choice from his victims?" he stopped, as if waiting for her approval and agreement.

Ellie nodded her head slowly, "That does make sense actually. He knew I was headstrong and stubborn."

"We all know that," Dan added, cheekily.

Ellie mockingly scowled at him, "So maybe you're right. Ok, what else?"

"We also think there is more to this," Dan picked up the compass and slid it to Ellie.

"We have gone through everything that was in that tin we found in your room. The telescope thing we think did what it needed to do that night when you helped focus the energy stream to the folly. But this, feels like it should do more. It is very well made and completely sealed. But it has no markings on it, nothing that identifies where it came from or anything."

Ellie picked it up and turned it over in her hand; she had never paid it that much attention before.

"We just think, that if it was a purchased compass, it would have markings. And why would someone make something that doesn't add anything? If it can only point to the folly, why?"

Ellie nodded, "It is odd when you put it like that I agree," she put it down.

"We think you should carry it with you, all the time," Leo added.

"Why?" Ellie asked, puzzled.

"If we are right, and it does do more, then we need to expose it to as much as possible to see what happens. If you keep it with you, it may suddenly do something one day."

"And if we are wrong, you get to always know where the folly is," Dan added with a grin.

Ellie smiled, "Liking this boys, really am. My notes so far; subconscious. Six missing people. And I need to carry the compass. Anything else?"

"We know the necklace got destroyed, so we are assuming that has served its purpose?" Dan added.

Ellie shuddered a little, though he did not notice. The necklace she had worn the first time against the Man had indeed been destroyed, but she also knew where there was another one. She had kept it secret from everyone as that was the item that had really upset Simon when he had seen it at the Halloween party all those years ago. "Yes, that makes sense I suppose," she replied, hoping it was enough to stop any further investigation.

The three of them continued into the afternoon, Ellie taking it all in and getting her head around what the boys had done for her. She was truly in awe of it all. They had copied all the written notes online, colour coded, labelled, and tagged everything to make it as neat and tidy as possible. When they had exhausted everything they wanted to go through, they began to pack away, and Ellie promised that she would keep up to date with their online records. She had also promised to read up as much as she could to ensure she was taking advantage of their efforts. They left with some final words of support late in the afternoon, before Ellie took herself for an evening walk and then waited for her parents to come home from work, so they could all have dinner together. Just like before, Ellie felt like progress was being made, and that made her very happy indeed. There was a niggle that she could not shake though, a niggle around the necklace, and the story of the sixth missing person. She knew there was a connection somewhere, she just could not see it.

The weekend arrived, one that Ellie had been looking forward to with a certain level of cautious optimism. She was spending most of Saturday with Simon and Annabelle to try and crack the spirit side of what she wanted to do. The excitement she was feeling was down to being able to use and manipulate the energy flow around her, the anxiety was due to the fact that she was not sure if she would be able to do it at all.

"You've done it before, you can do it again," she would say to herself when she was feeling positive. But then it would change to, "You've never tried to control it like this," when she was feeling a little negative about it. Simon and Annabelle were keeping her focused and honest though. She had already received messages from them both offering support. The pair had arranged to meet by the village hall, Ellie had no idea why, but they had insisted. After eating some breakfast, she got ready and began walking around the village to the hall. It was not far, but the last and only other time she had been there was when she had first met the council. As she walked, she thought about that night and what could have been. She concluded that everything happened the way it did for a reason, and whilst in general there had been more negative impacts than positives, there were some great things that had happened to her. Ellie smiled to herself. Through everything she knew that her friends were with her and would support her fully, none more so than her two best friends. As she rounded the corner she saw Annabelle and Simon waiting for her by the gate, wrapped up warm against the bitterly cold wind.

She waved and quickened her pace a little, "Hi," she called once she was in earshot of them.

"Morning," Simon replied, greeting her with a hug.

Ellie turned to Annabelle who hugged and kissed her in welcome too, "Morning lovely."

"It's too cold. Can't we do this indoors?" Ellie pleaded softly.

Annabelle and Simon looked at each other, then back at Ellie and shook their heads.

"No," Annabelle said, "You need to be outside with living things remember. We have a plan though," she smiled softly.

"Ok, let's get going then, why here?" Ellie asked.

"We needed somewhere outside, so you have access to as much living energy as possible," Simon replied.

"But also, somewhere hidden enough that we wouldn't be disturbed," Annabelle added.

Ellie raised an eyebrow and looked around, "You can see this big road that we are standing on, yes?"

They grinned, "Yes we can, that's why we are moving," Simon smugly commented. "Follow me." He moved past Ellie and led them a short distance to a path that led through the trees and bushes away from the road, "This way.".

He led them up the path which was reasonably overgrown but not impassable. At a fork he turned left and kept going. They had risen a little now and had walked with the hall on their left almost in a circle. The path straightened out and began to get a little wider.

"Not much further," Simon called back to the girls.

Almost immediately, Ellie caught a peek over his shoulder of where they were going, and a spark of excitement ignited in her.

"I didn't think this was a real place?" she asked them, "We've never been here before, but I have heard people talk about the field."

"We know, it's perfect for what we need today," Annabelle agreed.

Simon stopped at a white rail, Ellie moved to his right and Annabelle to the left. They were looking at what was once a small village football pitch surrounded by high trees and bushes. The rail ran about chest height all the way around, enclosing the playing area. It was very overgrown and would not be useable as a sports field for some time. The grass and weeds were above waist height and the ground visibly uneven after years of clear neglect. The goal post, for there was only one on the right, had rusted and started to bend. To anyone else in the village this field was useless and in need of some serious care and investment. But to the three friends, it was perfectly beautiful for what they needed.

"Quiet," Simon stated.

"Hidden," Annabelle added.

"Alive," Ellie finished off, excitedly looking from the field to her friends. "What do we do first?" She bent under the bar and led the way into the middle of the field, Annabelle and Simon following just behind her.

"Well, we figured you needed space, somewhere to focus and think. So why not just try and see if you can feel anything here?" Annabelle asked, stopping as she did so with Simon. "We will wait here, you try, and then we will go from there."

Ellie stopped and turned, she was a few steps in front now, "I don't know what to try though."

"Anything," Simon offered, "Just try to clear your mind and feel the stuff around you."

"Stuff?" Annabelle asked, turning towards him. "That's very helpful," she smirked.

Ellie chuckled, turned and took a few steps further away then stopped again and closed her eyes. Taking a deep breath, Ellie cleared her mind, focusing on nothing but the ground beneath her shoes and the breeze in her hair. Although she could hear the rustling of the trees, they sounded more distant than they were as if she was standing miles away from anything. Another deep breath, she tried to clear her mind and think of nothing.

Silence.

Nothing happened, Ellie opened her eyes to make sure nothing had changed, it had not so she closed them again.

'Come on Eleanor,' she berated herself internally, 'you can do this, clear your mind, focus on the energy. You have felt

it before, imagine it flowing up from the ground into your fingertips.'
Ellie was not sure if telling herself off like this was going to help, but it felt right as she stood there in front of her friends with nothing happening.
Still nothing.
She knelt, immediately feeling the damp ground through the knees of her jeans. She bent forward slightly and rested her palms on the soft wet ground. Still with her eyes closed, she tried once more to imagine the flow of golden light reaching up from the ground to her hands.
Nothing.
Taking more deep breaths she pushed herself hard, almost reaching desperation levels of wanting something to happen.
Fear started to spread through Ellie now, a real fear that she could not do this and that the efforts of her friends were going to be wasted. Fear soon turned to panic, and before Ellie knew it she was breathing fast and hard almost hyperventilating. She tried to lift her hands, but she could not, they were stuck. She was stuck in a bent over position unable to move and breathing faster by the minute. Ellie opened her eyes and looked down at her hands, there was nothing there. Nothing visible that was holding her in place. In desperation, unable to move she decided to call out, "Help," she called at the top of her voice, but there was no sound. She tried screaming with all the power of her lungs, nothing. It was as if there was no air to carry her plea for assistance. The panic was real now and looking down at her hands once more she could see strands of light starting to web their way over the top of them. This was different to last time, they were not golden in colour and did not fill her with warmth and energy. The strands were purple, a similar colour to that of the realm where the Man was imprisoned and that she had visited many times before. Ellie was weakening, she could feel the energy leaving her body rather than flowing into it. Her eyes were closing, not through choice or wanting to focus but through exhaustion, Ellie felt as tired as if she had just run a marathon. It was all she could

do to keep herself awake. Before long she could not do that either. Her eyes closed, and she felt her body slipping to one side. Her hands released from the ground and she fell into a heap on her right.

Simon and Annabelle started to move towards her the moment she started to fall but could not get there in time. Within seconds her head had hit the ground with a thud, Ellie lay still with her eyes closed and only just aware of the thumping sound of her friends' boots running towards her. Then nothing.

"Eleanor," Simon yelled, as he and Annabelle ran forwards.

"Ellie," Annabelle called out.

The pair raced over to her, slid to her side, and rolled her over. Ellie's face was pale, and her skin was cold as ice.

"What happened? What do we do?" Annabelle asked in desperation. She moved slightly and lifted Ellie's head onto her lap. "Do something," she yelled at Simon who seemed to be stricken with shock.

This snapped him out of it, and he reached into his pocket for his phone.

Annabelle moved Ellie's hair out of her eyes. "Ellie, come back, come back," she balled, tears and sobs fully formed in her throat making her choke on the words. She reached down and stroked her cheek. What happened next was so fast and was so astounding none of them really knew it had happened. The instant Annabelle touched her, Ellie gasped for breath with colour returning to her cheeks. She sat bolt up right at such a speed that Annabelle was knocked backwards, and Simon's phone was nudged out of his hand. Ellie sat there, breathing fast but slowing down gradually.

Annabelle and Simon looked at each other, a look of panic mixed with relief on their faces.

"What happened?" Annabelle asked, pulling herself to her feet and wiping tears from her face.

Ellie turned and looked at them both, "I have no idea." She stood, "I couldn't feel anything, then I couldn't move, and I started to panic. I called for help."

"We didn't hear anything," Simon interrupted.

"I guessed," Ellie replied, "I couldn't hear myself either. Then

I tried to move again, but a real feeling of tiredness came over me. I couldn't keep my eyes open. The last thing I remember is falling to the floor before I heard you running over."

"We ran as soon as you started to fall, but we couldn't get there I'm so sorry Elle," Annabelle sobbed, rushing over to wrap her girlfriend in a hug.

"It's ok, I'm ok. What happened when you got to me? How long was I out?"

"Seconds," Simon commented, "I didn't even get chance to get my phone out to call for help."

"You had your head in my lap, I didn't know what to do," Anabelle sounded desperate and would not let go of Ellie's hands as if doing so would mean she would lose her again.

Ellie pulled a hand away and touched her cheek, "Is this where you touched me?" she asked.

Annabelle nodded.

Ellie's eyes lit up and she pulled Annabelle into an even bigger hug, "I felt that. That is where the warmth came from, that is what woke me up – if we can call it that." Ellie said, positivity returning to her voice a little.

"Really?" Annabelle asked, a little confused.

"Yes."

"So, does that mean, Annabelle saved you?" Simon asked, a look of soft amusement on his face.

"I think she did, yes," Ellie beamed.

CHAPTER 6

The next couple of days were spent trying to understand what had happened to Ellie in the field, and more importantly, if it would happen again. Unfortunately, none of them could figure out the answer to this. Ellie continued with her physical workouts, she even increased her run frequency in order to keep her physical strength up. She also dedicated more time to looking over the work that Leo and Dan had done, it was extensive and deserved more of her time. The other thing that needed more of Ellie's focus was her family holiday, indeed it was only a matter of weeks away now.

"Make sure you have everything you need," Katherine had reminded.

"Yes mum," had always been Ellie's reply, when in fact she had not done anything.

They had rented a caravan in the Welsh mountains for a week. It would be October so would not be the warmest but the clean fresh air, peace, and quiet would be just what Ellie needed. The fact that Annabelle was coming was a huge bonus as they would be able to spend some quality time together. It also presented an opportunity to shop, after all, Ellie and Annabelle needed new outdoor clothes for all the walking they would be doing. They had arranged to catch the train to Manchester to get what they needed; boots, coats, and the like.

Shopping day arrived, and Annabelle met Ellie at the station ready to catch the train.

"All set for a shopping adventure?" Annabelle asked as they collected their tickets from the machine.

Ellie smirked, "As I can be. Not really sure this will be that much fun you know, hardly fun items, are they? Outdoor clothing."

"Maybe not, but shopping is. And with you it's even better," Annabelle beamed.

"Cheesy," Ellie mocked.

They walked through the ticket office and over the bridge to the platform where the trains to Manchester stopped, it was due in a few minutes, so they would not have to wait long.

"I know I need boots, and a coat. A good waterproof coat. The kind I can wear layers under," Annabelle stated. "What about you?"

"I have boots and my coat is pretty good, maybe just a few layers or something?" Ellie replied. "Then can we go eat?"

"You and food," Annabelle rolled her eyes, "Yes I will make sure you are fed and watered. Any more thoughts on the field stuff, what happened and everything?"

Ellie shook her head. "No, nothing, it has really scared me though, put me off trying again."

"I bet. It was scary just watching what happened to you. Don't let it put you off trying though, Simon and I will be with you. I'm sure you will be fine, how's the rest of your plan going?"

"Really well, have you seen the stuff Leo and Dan have done? It's insane the detail they have gone into with it."

"I had a look, it confused me so closed it again," Annabelle grinned. "And I can see Tyler is keeping you in shape you gorgeous girl you," she pulled Ellie in for a kiss.

Ellie chuckled, "Again with the cheese," but kissed her back all the same.

The train arrived, it was relatively quiet, so they found a seat easily and sat down facing forwards. As the train pulled away, they could see the folly out of the window, standing proud over the hill.

"It really annoys me that I don't see that the same as everyone else now," Ellie commented.

Annabelle said nothing but took her hand and gave it a squeeze.

Ellie rested her head on Annabelle's shoulder whilst the

rumble of the train gently rocked them as it picked up speed.
"I have a plan of attack for our shopping order," Annabelle exclaimed.
"Of course you do," Ellie said, rolling her eyes as she did so. "Tell me what it is then."
"Well, we can start by walking to the main shopping centre, it isn't that far and will give us the best choices and options..." Annabelle began.
Ellie listened but was also staring out of the window, it had started to rain, and the sky had turned a shade of grey so dark it was nearly black. The rain fell on the train and was making streaky marks along the window as it moved along the line. Soon the sky was now so dark that everything outside of the window seemed to be invisible. Ellie sat up and looked out, she could not even make out the trees speeding past now, it was as if they were in a tunnel, which was impossible as the rain was still falling and streaking down the window.
"Can you see anything outside?" Ellie asked, but there was no reply. She turned to look but Annabelle had gone. In fact, everyone in the carriage had gone, Ellie was completely alone. In an attempt to remain calm, knowing that panicking would not help the situation, she stood and moved into the aisle facing the direction the train was travelling. She could see nobody in any of the carriages in front of her, turning, she saw it was the same behind her. She appeared to be completely alone on the train, with nothing but darkness outside. Ellie took a step forwards, towards the front of the train, but as she did so, it appeared to move further away again. Another step, the same thing. Then she tried making several quick steps, but each time she moved forwards the train carriage appeared to get longer, meaning she could never get close to the door at the end. Turning, she tried the other direction, but the same happened. Ellie could move her feet, but it was as if the ground was a treadmill and she could not move in terms of distance. She whirled around, looking for any sign of what was going on, but all that was there was the train carriage, rattling and rumbling as it had always done. She faced forwards once more, peering through the glass in the door into the next carriage, but it had vanished.

All she could see was black nothingness. Nothing but black, except a tiny pin prick of light. Ellie focused on it, trying to reveal what it was and draw it into her vision. As she did so, it got bigger, the way the light gets bigger as a train reaches the end of a tunnel, but Ellie knew this was no tunnel and she was beginning to think that the train was not moving at all. She stared at it, fixated, unable to take her eyes away from the white spec that was growing in front of her. As it got closer to the door, she shielded her eyes from the brightness as the shape moved into the carriage in front of her. It kept advancing towards Ellie at the same speed, she was unable to retreat away and so could only wait for whatever was going to happen next. The white shape started to twist and change in front of her, manipulating its shape and form in front of her very eyes. Ellie lowered her arm, removing its protection from the light as it had begun to fade, allowing her to take in the shape that was now forming. The white spec had molded and shaped itself into something she recognised. Immediately Ellie felt a surge of rage and fury, unable to advance nor retreat all she could do was stare. Scowling into the blank empty face that was now looking straight back at her. The face, of the Man Of Mow.

"Troublesome child," his soft voice commented, carrying solidly over the rumble of the train.

"Child? Really?" Ellie replied defiantly. "Are you really happy calling me a child? Admitting that you have lost twice, to me, and therefore a child? That can't be good."

He chuckled, a chuckle that Ellie knew all too well, "I see nothing has changed."

"One thing has changed," Ellie interrupted. "I want to ask the questions now, this is on my terms." She was surprised that she had the confidence and strength to be so bold so early in her latest confrontation with him. After all, all she had done so far was some revision and gym training.

"Really, is that so?" his soft voice replied. "Ok, enlighten me. What are the questions you wish to ask, I am listening?"

Ellie gulped, even though she felt brave she had not been prepared for him to accept her statement so easily.

"Firstly, what is going on here? Why can't I move? Where is

Annabelle, and everyone else from the train?"

"I have frozen this moment for everyone except us. I am powerful enough to do this now, you see."

"How? How are you more powerful than you were before?"

He chuckled once more, "Who said I could not do this before?"

Ellie frowned.

"I have been, assimilating, as they say."

"Assimilating? Like absorbing you mean?"

"Yes, in primitive language, absorbing. You see, you and that fiendish counterpart of yours Emilia did destroy me. You scattered me into the ether, dissolved me into countless pieces of an infinitely small size."

The mention of Emilia's name sent a shiver down Ellie's spine, but she did her best to hide it from him. She did not want to give him the satisfaction of affecting her in this way.

"I was dissolved in spirit form but not in mind, my soul lived on and part of me was able to grab hold."

"Grab hold?"

"Yes, grab hold of one of those infuriating Guardians."

Ellie's face changed ever so slightly, she tried to hide it, but the Man noticed at once.

"So, it is true, you have met them. Did they fill your head with ideas of grandeur that you can help them?"

Ellie said nothing.

"No matter, I am sure it will come out eventually. Anyway, I was able to grab hold and my spirit was able to grow and take over that one Guardian. This in turn allowed me to take over another."

Ellie did some quick maths, there were four and they had asked her to be the fifth. That meant there were only two left now.

"Once I had absorbed them," there was a tone to his voice that suggested he did not like using, as he put it, primitive language. "I was able to draw in my spirit from all over your world where it had been scattered by you. It did not take long but I am now back to full strength and then some."

"So, is that your plan then? Absorb them all?" Ellie was enjoying making him use her words now, she could tell he was pained by it ever so slightly.

"Partly, yes, you are bright really aren't you girl?" the Man mocked. "I will get them out of the way, but my plan is still the same, only this time..." he paused, clearly for effect. "This time I will be channelling the energy myself. There are others in my world who will support me and together we will achieve my goal, we will destroy your world."

"You know this is getting old now don't you?" Ellie commented casually once again. "I mean, I have heard you say that so many times now it is beginning to sound like you don't believe it. Like when you say the same thing over and over, just becomes noise really."

"Oh, I believe it, and it will become true. Now, did you have other questions?"

This again took Ellie by surprise; it was as if he had decided to soften her up with kindness rather than outright rage and fury as per usual.

"You say there are others, others from your world that want what you want?"

"Yes, there are."

"Why have I never seen them? Why aren't they here fighting and helping you as you say they want to?"

"They cannot travel here. Yet. But soon they will and then it will be too late for you, and your world."

Ellie pondered this, so they are not here yet. That means there is something missing, something he needs. She thought to herself, but what?

"Does that mean if I can stop you absorbing the other Guardians, and destroy you again, that they will never be able to get through from Imaginari?" It was not the best question, but Ellie figured it may buy her some time to think.

"You can try," he stated calmly, "But you will-"

"Not succeed. Yeah, yeah, yeah," Ellie interrupted, cockily. "Heard that before too."

"Can I ask a question now?" he mused, a slight tone of frustration entering his voice.

Ellie said nothing.

"Very well, the other day you tried to control the energy, yes I am aware, I tried to drag you into my world, into the realm where we became such good friends."

"That was you? You made me black out?"

"I did. But I could not draw you in, something held you back and pulled you away from me, breaking my hold on you. What was it?"

There was a real anger building in his voice for the first time, and Ellie got the feeling this had been a big thing for him. He had clearly planned on doing something to her there and then. Ellie thought for a moment, the truth was that she did not know; the only thing she remembered and knew was Annabelle touching her face.

"And before you insult me," the Man broke Ellie's line of thought, "It was not Annabelle. She could not pull you away, she does not have the skill, power, or understanding to do so. The very idea that her touching your cheek could snap you out of my grip is laughable."

Ellie thought for a second or two more, she had no choice though, she needed to be bold.

"I did it. I pulled myself away from you," it was a lie of course, but she wanted to see what his reaction would be and try to see if she could scare him a little.

For a moment, he said nothing. Then his soft voice rang out across the train once more. "You did?" he asked, "You are mastering the skills needed and have developed the strength to beat me?"

Ellie nodded, thinking she was onto something.

"You have mastered the spirit form and believe you can manipulate it enough to control it in order to beat me?"

There was a moments silence, then something happened that Ellie had never heard before. The Man burst out laughing, not a cackle or a chuckle, but an evil laugh that boomed across the carriage.

"Impossible, just impossible. The very fact that you thought you could do so is laughable, girl. No human can master the power, you can feel it and use it maybe a little. But master it? Never."

Ellie clenched her firsts, furious at his gloating laugh but still unable to move.

"Amazing. That tells me one thing girl, well a couple of things actually. One, you have no idea what you are doing and the times you used the energy before have been luck. Two, you have no idea how you were saved from me days ago. Three, I will beat you this time and there is nothing you or your pesky friends can do about it. And as for those Guardians, well, let's just say their days are numbered."

Ellie was raging with fury now, "If you're so confident, take me on here and now, come on, let's just do this once and for all."

She knew it was foolish, after all she knew she would be outmatched but felt going on the offensive was the only way to go.

He chuckled, "There will be a time for that, but not right now, I must wait for the right time to destroy you, and your world. That time is close, but it is not now."

Ellie shifted her weight and adjusted her feet into a more stable stance, she was ready to fight.

"So brave. So brave. It is a shame really, but your time to die will soon come."

This phrase instantly shook Ellie as the vision from her dream of her limp, cold body on the hill came rushing back. She still had not told anyone, but from what Simon and Annabelle had said it matched what they had seen in the field when she fell to one side. Her face had clearly changed to register these thoughts, as the Man noticed instantly.

"See, you know it, you have seen it. Maybe you do have more power after all, that could be a small part of the explanation. We shall see," he mocked. "We shall see," As he said this he faded away.

The moment he disappeared the carriage started to return to normal, the colour outside returned and whilst it was still raining, Ellie could see trees flying by once more. She looked around, the other carriages and passengers had returned as well, including Annabelle.

"How did you get there?" Annabelle asked, a look of shock on her face, looking up at Ellie standing in the aisle.

"What?" Ellie asked, catching her breath and only just realising that she was still standing up.

Annabelle stood, "You look like you have seen a ghost. It was him wasn't it? What happened?" She took Ellie's hand and guided her to sit once again. So many questions were pinging around Ellie's head.

How can she help the Guardians, if there are none left?

What did he mean that I had seen it? Was my dream true?

If he didn't know what saved me from him in the field, then what did?

Ellie looked at Annabelle, "He is back," was all she could manage before bursting into tears.

Annabelle pulled her into a hug, "Tell me everything," she said softly.

It took Ellie a few moments to compose herself, wiping the tears away from her face on Annabelle's shoulder as well as a tissue or two. When she had calmed down, she told Annabelle what had just happened. The darkness, the inability to move in the carriage and the Man's arrival. Ellie focused on the stuff he had said about the Guardians but avoided anything relating to her dream and vision he had referenced. She did not want anyone to know about her fear of it becoming a reality.

"You mean it was him that tried to do something when we were in the field together?" Annabelle asked, after allowing Ellie to explain everything.

Ellie nodded, "Yes, he was trying to drag me in again. Something happened though, something stopped him, and he didn't know what it was, he thought I did."

"What do you mean?"

"Something stopped him getting me into the prison realm again, he thought I knew. I thought it was you touching my cheek, but he told me it wasn't, that it couldn't have been. So, I don't know what it was." Ellie wiped her face once more. "What is going on? I feel like there is so much we don't know."

Annabelle nodded; she did understand but also did not know what to say, "I still think you can do this. You still have a chance and you should carry on."

Ellie smiled, "What makes you so sure?"

"Honestly, I'm not. But what I do know is that not trying is not an option for you. I know you. Whatever happens we are with you, and if you fail, nobody will know for very long anyway," Annabelle smirked.

Ellie smiled, though deep down this stirred something in her. She knew that Annabelle meant well and was being her usual self. But the thought of sacrificing herself for her was still very much in her mind. If her visions were true, then there could be only one way to beat him.

"Ok, shall we try and make the most of our day? You still want to buy me some new clothes, yes?" Annabelle asked with a smile.

Ellie tapped her gently on the arm, "I'm not buying you anything. You should be treating me for everything I'm doing."

They giggled and any tension between them lifted immediately before the conversation moved onto shopping. Annabelle had a skill for bringing out the best in Ellie, looking after her, and making her feel better. This was put to the test today though. Annabelle knew that Ellie would be troubled by everything that was going on, who would not be? But she also knew that the best way to look after her right now was to keep her focused on the here and now. Throughout the day Annabelle led them on a quest of her own, a quest of shopping and eating. Before long they had bought everything they needed and had eaten their fill of burgers, cakes, and doughnuts.

"How do you do that so easily?" Ellie asked as they collapsed on a bench surrounded by shopping bags.

"What do you mean?" grinned Annabelle.

"Shopping. I mean, I don't mind it but you're on another level."

Annabelle swished her hair over her shoulder, "You have your skills and I have mine."

Ellie rolled her eyes, "What's left?"

"Dinner and home," Annabelle beamed, grabbed Ellie by the hand pulled her to her feet and led the way.

It was dark by the time they had caught the train home, and soon after it had left the station the weather turned. In the space of a few minutes it went from dark and calm to downpours and gale force winds. Ellie fell asleep on

Annabelle's shoulder as the train gently rocked. Annabelle was playing a game on her phone, occasionally looking out of the window as the rain continued to batter against the glass. Her mind wandered so she stopped playing and closed her eyes, allowing the gently swaying of the train to clear her mind. She pondered the day, pleased with their shopping exploits but also concerned about the girl that she loved. Annabelle was desperate to help Ellie but did not know how to do so. She squeezed Ellie's hand, reassuring herself more than anything that she was still there. She opened her eyes and looked out the window once more. She must have drifted off at some point on the journey because they were nearly home. The faint outline of the hill and the folly was now outlined against the black sky. The train stopped, which according to the announcement this was because they were waiting for another train to move on up ahead. The jolt of the train caused Ellie to stir out of her sleep.

"Nearly home," Annabelle said softly, "Time to wake up, sleepy head."

Ellie sat up, "Sorry, didn't mean to just nod off like that."

"It's ok," Annabelle smiled warmly.

They both looked out of the window at the pouring rain.

"Wow that's horrible," Ellie commented, "Do we really have to get off in that?"

Annabelle nodded, "Fun," she mused.

As they watched there was a bolt of light that tore across the sky. The light it created lit up the folly and the hill as a silhouette. The light made the rain sparkle like diamonds and for a moment time seemed to freeze. Ellie watched and saw something that filled her with fear and dread. In the sky, directly above the folly was a silver shape. The formation of it was unmistakably a face. A silver shining face with two silver eyes and one black hole for a mouth. Ellie recognised the face; it was much larger of course but was unmistakably the Man of Mow. It was huge and looked like it was about to swallow the top of the hill whole. As she watched, a silver line of light emerged from the mouth and twisted its way down to the tower on the folly. The moment it made contact with the structure there was another bolt of light and it vanished as quickly as it had arrived. Ellie looked at Annabelle; she was fixated by the folly as well and Ellie knew that she had seen the same thing.

"Was that what I think it was?" Annabelle asked, almost choking on the words as she did so.

Ellie nodded, "Yes, that was him. I don't know what he was doing, but it was him."

"How did so much happen so fast? I thought it was less than a second?"

Confusion was etched in Annabelle's tone now, and Ellie completely understood why.

"He can do that. He has a way of slowing things down so that he can let you see what he wants you to see. I think he is using the weather to hide whatever he is doing. But it's getting worse."

Annabelle nodded.

Ellie thought for a moment, "He is waiting for the right time, what if it is the same time as when he tried before? The first full moon of winter? It fits. He said to me earlier that my time would come, and he would fight me, but not until the time is right. What if he needs that night to complete, whatever it is he is doing?"

Annabelle turned to look at Ellie, a look of wonder on her face, clearly speechless.

"What if we can't beat him?" Ellie asked.

Annabelle took Ellie's hand, "I believe we can."

"But what if-" Ellie tried, but Annabelle put a finger over her lips, stopping her mid-sentence.

"I believe. So should you. Carry on doing what you are doing, work hard, push yourself. Simon and I will work out a way to help you and push you with the energy, I don't know how yet but we will solve that, together. Ok?"

Ellie smiled. She truly felt lost but with Annabelle being so positive she could not allow herself to think on it too much.

"Ok. Will you train with me on holiday? Walk and run and stuff?"

"Of course," Annabelle replied and pulled Ellie in for a hug.

As they hugged, the train jolted and moved once more, carrying them towards their stop. For Ellie, it was the metaphor of her life. It was a moving train that she could not control, she could decide which carriage to be in, and which way to face the danger and challenges, but that was it. All she could do was work hard, focus, and do her best. She pushed the vision out of her mind, closed her eyes and breathed in the smell of Annabelle's hair. Comforting as always as the train rumbled into the station.

CHAPTER 7

When Ellie and Annabelle explained what they had seen to their friends, they were met with reactions of shock and fear – but not surprise. Ellie had reached the conclusion that her friends, like her, could no longer be shocked by what happens in her life. Tyler had carried on pushing her and working with her, she had shaved seconds off her personal bests and had now reached a point where she felt physically stronger and able to sustain herself during long runs. He had mentioned that she would soon be in good enough shape to take on a marathon, which Ellie had laughed off saying that if they survived all of this then they could talk about long distance runs. Leo and Dan had continued their great work, Ellie had even taken to reading through their notes online at night instead of reading a book or scanning social media on her phone. They had not found a solution though, they had not yet found anything that would help Ellie. But they believed and said they would continue to work on it.

Ellie and Annabelle were packing for their trip, something they would normally be very excited by. For different reasons, this holiday had given them both mixed emotions. On the one hand the break would be good for Ellie, allowing her to clear her mind and be herself for a while. On the other, Ellie felt guilty that she was doing something so trivial whilst there was imminent danger to herself, her friends, and her family. They were leaving early on Saturday morning, aiming to be at the caravan her dad had rented by lunchtime. They were staying for the week and it would be a lot of walks, games, food, and general relaxing. In truth though, the thing the girls were looking forward to the most was not having phone signal. They had been told that the caravan was in an area where there was no coverage meaning they could switch off and enjoy each other's company with no distractions.

At seven in the morning, the Fields family car was packed and ready to go. They had loaded it with everything they needed, from warm clothes and boots, to food and games. They set off just after seven thirty, Nicholas driving with Ellie and Annabelle in the back already nodding off. Ellie woke after about an hour and a half and looked out of the window. She was delighted to see the view had completely changed. They had arrived in Wales and the view was simply breathtaking. Rolling hills covered in green grass and trees. Lakes and streams flowing with crisp clean water that sparkled in the sunlight. She knew it was cold, but the blue sky and sun made it look deceptively warm and pleasant. She smiled to herself, it was trivial, but she immediately felt her mind relaxing. After a little while, they stopped for a break and Annabelle woke just as the car came to a standstill. The girls got out and headed towards the garage to find a drink.
"Only five minutes, ladies," Nicholas shouted after them.
"Ok," Ellie replied.
After getting a drink and using the toilet they were leaning on a wall by the road, looking out over the scenery around them.
"Beautiful, isn't it?" Annabelle asked.
"Yeah, have you ever been here before?"
"Wales? Yes, but not where we are going, I'd never heard of it until you mentioned it. I know it is near Snowden though, I've been up there."
"Really? To the top?"
"Yes, it's really, really far," Annabelle commented with a giggle.
"You mean you didn't know it was a mountain before you started?" Ellie asked with mocking tones of curiosity and surprise.
"It wasn't my idea to climb it, anyway, what are we going to do on this holiday?"

"I did some reading…"

"Of course, you did," Annabelle interrupted. "You always have a plan and an idea, come on then."

Ellie stuck her tongue out.

"How rude," Annabelle scolded.

"Anyway, the village we are in has three rivers that meet in the middle. It has a few pubs, an ice cream shop, and a fudge shop that are all meant to be lovely."

"Sounds good so far," Annabelle added with a smile, "Food is good."

"There are loads of walks we can do, dad has a book with some in, but from what I read it is quite easy to make up your own. So, we can just wander, take in the scenery and see where we end up," Ellie smiled.

Annabelle smiled back, "Perfect."

"Oh, and I am also going to beat you at every board game we play, just so you know."

"You can try," Annabelle replied, pushing Ellie off the wall.

They giggled at each other.

"You two ready?" Katherine shouted over from the car.

Annabelle helped Ellie up, and the two girls headed back to the car to complete their journey.

Everyone was awake and taking in the scenery now, commenting on the hills and water, it comforted Ellie to have conversations and thoughts about normal things for a short while. They arrived at the final turning for the caravan late morning, just as they had planned. Driving up a very steep hill, around a small bend and towards a gate in the rock wall. Katherine got out to open the gate and allow the car through. It was a small set of caravans that had been set up in a farmer's field on the side of a hill. There were ten in total and they were staying in number seven, so Nicholas drove the car down and pulled up in front of number seven. They got out of the car and walked towards it together. Nicholas had the key and went first to open the door, as they all piled in behind him. It was a standard static caravan, but felt like it could be home from home soon.

"Ok, let's unpack and get our bearings then we can go for an explore. Nick, can you turn the gas and power on, girls get the bags and I'll put the food away. Ok?" Katherine instructed the others.

They all nodded, following Katherine's lead and did as she had asked. It did not take long to do everything. Ellie's parents had the main master bedroom with Ellie and Annabelle in the other smaller room. They unpacked as much as they could and then went into the living area.

"Need any help, Katherine?" Annabelle asked.

"No thank you, all done, and you can call me Kath you know, Annabelle."

"Sorry, I just like being polite and formal," Annabelle replied with a blush.

Ellie smirked to herself, she loved it when Annabelle was a little embarrassed. She thought she was beautiful all the time, but especially liked it when her face turned a faint shade of pink.

"Are we going for a walk to explore a little then?" came Nicholas' voice from the bedroom.

They turned to face him and burst into laughter.

He was standing in the doorway to the bedroom, wearing his walking boots and trousers, his new fleece and waterproof coat, holding his gloves. The thing that made them laugh though, was the fact that he had his hands on his hips, a beaming smile on his face and a novelty woolly hat depicting a moose on his head.

"I'm not going anywhere with you whilst you're wearing that hat, dad," Ellie exclaimed between cackles of laughter.

"Tough," he said, turned and walked out of the door.

After a few moments, the three ladies had composed themselves, put on their walking gear and headed out of the caravan. To the sound of chuckles and teasing, the four set off to see their surroundings.

They did not go far, as autumn had started creeping in by the time they had left it was going to be dark in a couple of hours, so they only did a short walk down the hill and along the river before heading back to the caravan. Nicholas had been calling it base camp much to the amusement of his daughter.

"Dad, we are in a caravan in Wales, not in a tent halfway up Everest. Base camp is a bit much don't you think?"

"Certainly not. We are walking, we are exploring, each day we will come back to our caravan, our base if you will. And caravanning is a form of camping, so base camp works for me."

Ellie and her mum shook their heads in mock disbelief. Before long they were back and in their comfy clothes drinking tea. Katherine had started dinner; she had brought a lasagne with her, so it was bubbling away in the oven whilst they sat and chatted. Between them they had agreed to share the cooking and washing up for the week. They would spend some time all together, but Ellie and Annabelle would also be doing their own thing on some days. That evening they chatted, ate, and drank before playing some games and going to bed reasonably early, it had been a long day after all. Ellie and Annabelle got settled and soon had drifted into a deep sleep.

They all woke up early the next day having slept very well, Ellie in particular was pleased with how well she settled and slept; she had not woken up once. Over breakfast they discussed their plan for the day. They were going to go for a walk together and do some exploring; all wanting to cover more ground than they did the day before. It did not take them long to get ready, they packed some snacks in a bag and set off once again, this time towards the village. They walked down the hill, over the road to the river and then followed it in the direction it flowed. The path was not wide enough to walk side by side, so they were single file. Nicholas leading the way, followed by Ellie, then Annabelle with Katherine bringing up the rear.

"Do you think it's possible to ever get bored of surroundings like this?" Annabelle asked.

"Not for me," Katherine said from the back.

"Nor me, I love this kind of place," Nicholas agreed, "So clean and fresh."

"That's why I like our hill so much," Ellie added, "I know it doesn't have streams or anything, but it is gorgeous at the top, so peaceful and stuff."

They all pondered this; Ellie was surprised at herself that she was able to say something so positive about the hill. She meant it, she did think it was beautiful, but the connection to everything else that had happened up there was also very strong and negative. The group kept going, and eventually reached the little village where another river joined the one they had been following.

"Shall we keep going and then come back to the village?" Katherine asked as they huddled round to decide where to go. "I'm thinking if we do that, we can have some lunch there or something, a longer walk to build up an appetite." She looked at the others, who nodded in agreement.

"Only if I can snack on crisps now," Ellie stated with a grin, "Annabelle, let me get them out of your bag."

They carried on, Ellie munching on crisps whilst they walked along the riverside as it moved through the valley floor. They crossed a railway line and could hear the sound of a train in the distance.

"It feels old world doesn't it, hearing a steam train like that," Nicholas commented, much to the amusement of the others. They walked, took pictures and selfies as they moved along the riverbank. In some areas they needed to scramble over rocks and help each other along as they did so. Eventually, they realised that the riverside had defeated them and agreed to turn back towards the village. By the time they had made it back they had all worked up an appetite so quickly agreed to go in the first pub they saw and get some food. It was good pub grub, and they all devoured three courses with ease whilst chatting the afternoon away.

After eating, and staying for a drink or two, they began to walk back up the river towards the caravan. It was only forty five minutes or so and was pleasant in the afternoon sun, which had started to set behind the hills now though and the shade was a getting cool. They walked along the river once more, back over the road and up the hill to the caravan site. Ellie and Annabelle walked a little slower, rather Ellie was walking slower and holding Annabelle back a little. She stopped by a wall overlooking the valley below and pulled

Annabelle to her side.

"I like it here, a lot," Ellie stated factually.

"Me too."

"Do you think the world would notice if we just came here and hid from it?"

Annabelle chuckled, "The world wouldn't, but our friends might."

"True. I could learn to make new friends though," Ellie joked; she did not mean it of course.

"How are you doing?" Annabelle asked, a concerned look on her face.

"I'm good, really good," Ellie replied confidently, "I feel like we should go on an adventure tomorrow though, are up for it?"

Annabelle nodded, "Absolutely."

They grinned at each other and turned to head into the caravan with Nicholas and Katherine.

The next day, Ellie and Annabelle got up and made breakfast for them all, another fry up that would last them into the afternoon. As they were eating and drinking, they discussed the plans for the day.

"We are going to go over the hill we are on," Ellie stated, "Apparently there is a nice walk there and then down past some waterfalls and stuff. Then we may go into the village again."

"Sounds good," Nicholas replied. "I think we are going for a drive, see where we end up, go on an adventure as it were."

Ellie and Annabelle looked at each other, smirked then returned to their food.

"We won't be able to contact you today if you're staying around here, will you girls be ok?" Katherine asked.

"Yeah, we will be fine," Annabelle replied before Ellie could say the same thing.

"Well, then, that's settled. Dinner tonight around six. I will put a casserole on, so it is ready for when we get home," Nicholas commented after a mouthful of mushroom.

They all nodded and offered words of agreement. The rest of breakfast was spent discussing the weather, the film they

would watch that evening, and who would do the washing up. Ellie and Annabelle volunteered to do the washing up whilst Katherine prepared the casserole. About an hour later, everything was ready, and they were all leaving the caravan. Nicholas and Katherine hugged the girls goodbye as they got in the car and then drove away. Ellie closed the gate and turned to face Annabelle who had walked up behind the car.
"Ready for an adventure?" Ellie asked with a smile.
"With you, always," Annabelle beamed.
Ellie turned and headed away from the gate up the hill. The path she was following led past the caravan at the end of the field and into tree cover. It got very steep and very overgrown quite quickly, and before long they were forced to walk single file behind one another through plants and weeds over waist high.
"This is a good path," Annabelle shouted.
"I think it will clear up soon," Ellie replied. "I hope anyway."
They pushed on a little further into the tree cover, and sure enough the path did spread out a little more. When she reached the top of that part of the hill, Ellie stopped and waited for Annabelle.
"I think we go left, all the way to the top of the peak up there," Ellie commented, pointing to a crest of the hill that was hidden by trees. "Then we come back and head down that way, that's where the waterfalls are I think."
"Lead on," Annabelle replied.
Ellie turned to the left and they walked up the hill through the trees. The path was a little muddy but not too bad, their boots were serving them well. There was a gentle breeze flowing through the trees and the crisp clean air was refreshing for them as they walked higher still. They had to scramble over a few rocks and had to use trees for support in some places, but eventually they reached the crest of the hill. The full view of the valley below came into focus as soon as the trees cleared. It revealed itself to them as if a curtain had been lifted as they reached the top. They stood in silence side by side holding hands taking in the view for a few moments, eventually Ellie spoke.
"Beautiful. Like you," she said, resting her head on

Annabelle's shoulder.

"Again, with the cheese," Annabelle mocked. "But you are correct so thank you."

They giggled, hugged and turned to take some selfies and pictures of the view from the hilltop.

"This is amazing," Ellie said, beginning to relax into her holiday.

Annabelle smiled in agreement, Ellie looked into her eyes just as a gust of wind blew from behind Annabelle and covered her face with her hair. This sent Ellie into hysterics of laughter as Annabelle fought to get her hair back under control.

"You should keep it like that," Ellie exclaimed between fits of laughter.

"Hmmmmmm, you can go off people you know," Annabelle replied with a cheeky grin. "Shall we get off this hilltop now?"

Ellie nodded, took Annabelle's hand and led her back the way they had come. When they reached the fork again, the girls followed the other path as it twisted down the back of the hill, climbing over walls and skipping over streams as they did so. Soon the path levelled out and they were able to walk side by side again. As they moved on along the bottom of the hill into a valley where it met another hill, they could hear the unmistakable sound of a waterfall getting louder as they walked. After a short while they rounded a corner and stopped to take in the view. They had reached the waterfall that was flowing torrents of water down the hillside into a stream. The waterfall was made up of lots of different streams, gathering in a pool at the top before tumbling over the edge to another larger pool. From there it flowed further down the hill towards the main river and village. The girls stood and admired the view.

"Wow," Annabelle commented.

Without saying anything, they took out their phones and took some pictures of each other as well as some more selfies. They needed to cross over the stream to carry on, which gave them an opportunity for some good angles on the waterfall as it tumbled into the pool. Annabelle crossed first and turned to take some pictures of Ellie. As Ellie smiled for the camera, she noticed something behind Annabelle. A rock, but it looked out of place, as if it had been placed there deliberately. After Annabelle had taken some pictures, they swapped places and Ellie went to take some of Annabelle, ignoring the rock as she did so. She took the pictures, "Done," She called to Annabelle, who turned to look at the waterfall facing away from Ellie. Ellie turned to investigate the rock, she felt like she had seen it before but could not place where or when. She walked over to it and the closer she got the more she felt that it looked out of place, unnatural even. Upon closer inspection, it looked like an old worn seat. Without thinking about it, Ellie decided to sit on the rock. She turned and positioned herself ready to sit. It would have given a perfect view of the waterfall and would probably have prompted Annabelle to take some more pictures of Ellie. They did not get the chance though, for the moment Ellie sat on the stone, everything went black. To Ellie's shock and immediate fear, the ground vanished, the waterfall disappeared and so did the hill side, leaving Ellie alone sat on a stone apparently floating in black nothingness. She tried to stand, but could not, she was unable to move as if she had been glued to the surface of the grey stone. After a few seconds, Ellie treated this as a mini blessing as the fear of standing up onto nothing took over. Would she fall? Could she fall if there was nothing to fall from or to?

She called out at the top of her lungs, "Annabelle!" Nothing, she had vanished as well. There was no echo, nothing at all. Just Ellie, a stone seat, and pitch blackness. She closed her eyes and tried to focus, willing herself to be brave and not panic. Then, there was the soft whisper of a voice, but she could not work out where it was coming from. Ellie opened her eyes and looked around, still nothing. To her right she heard the whisper once more, this time more audible and she recognised the word that was being said.

"Eleanor," in a quiet soft voice, as if being spoken on the top of a hill miles away.

This realisation sent a shiver of fear down her spine; she remembered where she had seen the stone before. She had seen it in her dream, the one where Annabelle woke her

before it finished. Sure enough, just as Ellie registered this, a thick heavy looking cloud appeared forming right in front of her eyes. Once again Ellie tried to move but she was held fast.
"Eleanor," the soft voice called, clear now as the cloud moved ever closer.
Ellie faced it, knowing that all she could do was wait and see what was going to happen, to let it happen and pray that she was able to handle it. The cloud was almost on her now, inches away from the stone seat that was holding her fast and tight. Her heart was pounding so hard she thought it was going to burst through her chest.
"Eleanor," the voice said again as the cloud reached the stone. Ellie took a deep breath and closed her eyes, waiting for something to happen. Nothing did. She held her breath for as long as she could, but eventually had to exhale and then breathe in again. Ellie expected the air she breathed to be different, to taste or feel like smoke. But it did not. She gently opened one of her eyes to peek at what was going on around her. The darkness had been replaced with grey smoke, and she concluded that she was standing in the cloud. There was no noise now, no voice saying her name over and over.
"Hello?" she croaked, her throat dry with fear.
"Hello, Eleanor," the voice replied. "Do not be afraid, we will not hurt you."
Ellie looked around, trying to find the source of the voice. Without realising, she had turned so far her legs had automatically stood her up from the chair. The moment she did so the stone vanished into mist leaving Ellie surrounded by grey cloud.
"That would be easier to believe if I could see you," she stated calmly.
There was no reply, Ellie continued to turn slowly, scanning the scene for anything that could give her a clue as to where she was or what may help her. After a few rotations, Ellie noticed that the cloud was swirling in a different way in one specific place. She stopped and focused on it. As she did, it began repeating the new pattern in a second place, right next to the first. The cloud was spiralling, the way water goes down the plug hole in a bath but it was swirling up as if being

pushed out from beneath. As Ellie watched, the two circles of cloud took form, and began to rise. She took a step back in fear, not knowing what was happening. The two shapes grew larger and were soon the same height as Ellie. Two swirling spirals of cloud in front of her, which as she watched, began to change once more. The parts nearest the ground split into two, the area in the middle expanded outwards with the area at the top narrowing. As Ellie watched, the shapes twisted and swirled into the unmistakable shape of people. Two human shapes forming out of cloud as she watched, open mouthed. After a few moments more, the swirling stopped, the cloud calmed, and the shapes became perfectly visible. They were wearing long robes that covered them from shoulder to foot, their hands clasped in front of them. Their faces were neutral, in that they had perfectly formed eyes, ears, nose, and mouth but they looked identical. The way that dolls look the same on a toy shop shelf. Ellie gathered herself and stood as tall and proud as she could.

"Who are you?"

Neither of them moved their lips, but a soft voice replied, "We three, are the last Guardians of Imaginari."

CHAPTER 8

Ellie stared at them, waiting for more words of explanation. None came.

"Sorry, we as in you and me?"

"Yes," came the voice, again without an apparent owner.

"And we are Guardians of-"

"Imaginari," the soft voice finished off for her. "Imaginari is the world we call home, the world you have heard so much about. The world whose energy and powers you are only just beginning to understand."

"Why can't I see your faces? How do I know which of you is talking?"

"We communicate by transmitting our thoughts and words directly to each other, we do not speak or hear as you do. Even now, our thoughts are entering your mind and your own brain is making them seem like normal words. When in fact this place is completely silent. As is our world."

"Silent? Imaginari is silent?"

"Yes. We do not have physical presence, so we do not need sound either; we can transfer thoughts, images, ideas, anything we need to by thought alone."

"Should I be scared by that?"

"No. We will not harm you. We are on your side, but we do not know for how much longer we will be able to help."

"What do you mean?"

"He is hunting us, he has already killed two of us; we are the last. We three are the only Guardians left now."

"You keep saying that, but I am not a Guardian, I'm not strong enough or.."

"Yes, you are," the voice interrupted, still in the same calm tone. "You always were, and you always will be, what you choose to do with the gift is your choice, but it is still your gift to have."

Ellie frowned at this, "Ok, so, what do you want?"

"We want to tell you everything we can, share all we know, show you our world, you must help protect it in order to protect your own. He must be stopped."

"I know he needs to be stopped, and I know that saving your world also protects mine, but how? I can barely feel the energy never mind use it."

"That is because you are asking the wrong questions, you must ask yourself the right question in order to succeed."

"And what is the right question?"

"We do not know."

"Brilliant," Ellie snapped.

"We do not know because it is always different, and you are the first from your world to be able to use our energy properly. This is new, we have no reference for this."

"You said use energy properly, does that mean people have tried before?" Ellie asked quizzically.

"Yes. He has tried many times to carry out his plan, he believed that there would be some of you that could help. Most importantly would be willing to help. He has tried over the centuries, but each time has failed because the person was wrong, they did not understand nor ask themselves the right question. So, it failed, he killed them or trapped them for failing him. He believes that he is the one true ruler of both worlds."

Ellie stood, looking at the two figures, taking it all in.

"We met you before, when we were stronger. We showed you the previous events, yes? Do you remember what happened when we nearly destroyed all life on your world?"

"You mean when you showed me the dinosaurs? Yes, I remember that. You tried to stop him, but he pushed on and it wiped them all out and scattered you all throughout my world and yours."

"Correct. After trying many times through the centuries, he found you, or rather, you found him. The descendant he needed, the bloodline was right, but you were not willing.

You fought him. He could not understand why you would not fear him and do his bidding; he lost. Then he tried with you once more, but he made another version of you."

"Emilia," Ellie interrupted, a lump in her throat. "Her name was Emilia, and she was the bravest of both of us."

"Yes, she was. But remember, she was made from you, her bravery came from you."

"So did her anger," Ellie added.

"Again, yes, she was made from you. All that was good came from you as did all that was bad. Do not forget the good, for there was more of that. He thought that making a bitter, sour, and resentful version of you would be what he needed. A version that would work with him, but he did not think of you being able to work with her. He did not plan for the two of you to be able to focus on that which is good to work together to achieve a goal. You destroyed him and scattered his spirit across the worlds."

Ellie grinned, she liked hearing that part.

"He's back now though, isn't he? I've seen him. He gloated over me again."

"He is, and he did. He is getting stronger, stronger than we have ever seen him and we fear that there will be only one chance to stop him. He will eventually be too powerful, and it will be impossible to stop him. But he does not have or know everything, which is why he is waiting."

"Waiting? Waiting for what? He said something about wanting to wait for me to be ready to die before he killed me, but didn't say anymore than that."

"He fears you, Eleanor. He has lost to you twice and each time has been because he made a mistake, and you worked out how to take advantage of that mistake. He cannot afford to make another one, so he is waiting for the right time to strike. As he does so, he is gathering strength, taking our spirit forms to build up his own energy and power. You must be ready."

"I'm trying," Ellie shouted, indignantly. "I'm doing what I can, but I can't work out how to use the energy, I tried but then he tried to kill me again."

"We know, we know. You are doing well. And the incident in

the field is a mystery to him, and us. If you figure it out, you must keep it a secret from him still as that could be the key."

"Ok, I'll bare it in mind," Ellie commented with a smirk. How am I meant to figure it out? she thought to herself.

"We are sure you will," came the voice.

Ellie's mouth dropped open.

"We can see, and hear, your thoughts remember."

Ellie blushed, realising that if they had expressions, they would probably be laughing at her a little right now.

"So, what do we do now?"

"We want to show you our world, we want to show you Imaginari, so you can see what it is like with your own eyes, we hope this will allow you to unlock the power you have and use that energy to beat him once and for all."

"Now? I can't, Annabelle will be worried and waiting for me," Ellie said.

"Time moves differently in our world; you will be back before she knows you are gone."

Ellie sighed, "Ok, let's go."

"Remember, our world is silent if you want to ask anything, just think it. Your mind is powerful, and once you are there it will be even more so. Be careful. We will be with you the whole time, as will the other members of our world. They will not harm you, but know this, they will fear you as a physical being. The Man is on his own, but he does have some supporters."

Ellie nodded, "I'll be polite, promise."

"Our world is different to yours, but it is driven by it, you may be surprised as to how this will look."

Ellie readied herself, braced for whatever may happen. Moments later, the cloud around them began to move. Ellie immediately had the feeling of being in a lift, a huge cloud like lift that was hurtling downwards at terrific speed. What made the feeling even stranger was the lack of sound or air; there was nothing. After a few more seconds, the clouds stopped moving and faded completely, leaving Ellie and the two Guardians standing in a grey scale street, with high buildings either side.

Ellie turned, taking it in. It looked like a street, with buildings reaching as far as the eyes could see in all directions. They were joined together at intervals by what she assumed were bridges. Around her, spirits moved as if she was not there, moving through her and her Guardian guides. If she did not know better, Ellie would think she was in a black and white, grey scale version of a city from her own world. It was mixed up in terms of time though. She saw modern cars as well as Victorian carriages.

"What? How? It makes no sense?" Ellie said aloud and instantly regretted it.

Until now she had not registered how quiet it was; there was no noise at all. Nothing. Her voice boomed across the street the way an announcement does at a stadium. Except there was no background noise to absorb it, so it was deafening. For a brief moment, every spirit around her stopped and looked at her, in the direction of the noise that had infiltrated their world. In that moment Ellie felt as small as she has ever felt, she was still unclear as to how much of a risk she was taking by coming here. To her relief, after a few more seconds of silence and staring; the spirits began to move once more and the world returned to how it was before her blunder.

"Remember to just think, Eleanor," her spirit guide said softly.

'Sorry, old habit of talking and all that,' Ellie thought.

"We understand."

'How does this work? It is, I mean just, well, look...' Ellie was struggling for words to think of to find out how this world worked. As she looked around, it made no sense to her at all.

"Follow us, and we will explain."

The two spirits turned and began to float away, Ellie quickly followed.

"Our world is created by the energy of yours, everything that is living, however big or small, has a consciousness. That consciousness drives the energy here, where it is then turned into what you see around you. Most of the energy, from things like plants, is turned into the standard shapes that you see around you; buildings, roads, the things that we have created over the centuries to try and replicate your world. Because we have longed for it for so long, we have tried to copy it."

'So, all this is being made by energy from plants?' Ellie asked.

"Mostly. Nearly all plant-based energy creates static objects here. None have a physical form of course, but they are what you would call inanimate objects."

Ellie nodded, taking it in, 'What about the rest of it?'

"The rest of what you see, what you would call people, the moving objects, more unusual things, are created from energy from sources with imagination."

'Imaginari,' Ellie thought, without realising it.

"Yes, Imaginari is named after imagination. Nearly everything that can be imagined by someone, or something in your world, is created here. Somewhere."

'You mean, when we dream, that dream becomes real here?' Ellie asked, astounded.

"Simply put, but yes. We are driven, created by, and controlled by the imaginations of people, and animals from your world."

'Animals?' Ellie asked, confused.

"Have you not ever seen a dog dreaming? Or wondered what a lion thinks as it sits atop a rock in the savannah? All those things are created here."

'Wow, that must mean this place is huge.'

"If it were real, as in physical, it would take up more space than your Earth's universe, it is vast. But because it is not real, and can be manipulated and changed at will, it is only a little bit larger."

'Sorry, I don't know what you mean.'

The spirits stopped and turned to face her. Ellie found this amusing as they were not talking to her from their faces anyway.

"Look up, you can see the building line, yes?"

Ellie looked and nodded.

"You can see that it is what looks like a normal building, connected in a few places by bridges and walkways. Watch."

Ellie did, and after a few seconds the scene changed completely. A huge gaping hole appeared in the building to her left, and as she watched a giant whale came swimming out, swimming in what would be the air in our world. After it had fully emerged it turned upwards and disappeared, a train appeared with track coming into view beneath it as it moved along. It had lots of carriages and travelled across what was eventually a bridge to the other building where a second hole had appeared, as if it was traveling between two tunnels over a ravine. As soon as the last carriage had gone into the hole in the second building, the first hole closed. Then came a ship, an old galleon style ship that Ellie recognised from films and TV. It swooped down the side of the building and then levelled off at street level to sail past her as she watched. It was being crewed by spirits, lashing sails and carrying barrels. Ellie watched open mouthed as it floated up the street and out of sight. The most astounding thing though, was that it was all happening in silence. There was not a single sound from any of it.

'What was that?' Ellie asked in her mind after a minute or so.

"That was the result of many different thoughts and imaginings from your world all happening at once. They appeared now because we were shielding you from it until we were ready to show you, when you were ready to see."

'So, someone thought of a whale, and a train, and then a pirate ship?'

"Not someone, many people, or creatures that can imagine. The energy flow groups them together and allows them to take form. The more thoughts that are grouped, the larger and more detailed the imaging."

Ellie was in a state of shock, it was breathtakingly beautiful and stunningly silent. 'You mean if I ever daydreamed about flying?'

"Yes, you would have created a spirit here that would have been lifted up into the sky and flown around."

Ellie had no words, no thoughts, to describe how she felt about this.

"Same as if you imagined winning a race, or flying a spaceship, if more people were thinking the same thing, then it would create a full detailed image like you just saw."

'That is incredible,' was all Ellie could manage.

"The relationship is a special one, it will become clear to you. The key though is to understand that the worlds are linked, and we need yours to survive. The Man does not understand that, never has, and he will stop at nothing to achieve his goal."

The spirits turned and moved on, Ellie following behind.

'He wants to take all the energy in one go, from my world, to make yours real. Is that even possible?' It seemed a logical question to Ellie, having seen what she had seen she knew that such things would not be possible in our world, the real physical world.

"Our world is already real; he wants to allow us to have physical form and to be able to touch. He wants us to feel and to have things that exist for us to use. This world is not enough for him, it never will be."

Ellie pondered this; she could not understand what he had hoped to achieve. There was no way that what she was seeing would be possible in a physical world.

'Does everyone here know him? Do they agree with him?'

"Yes, everyone knows him, but no, very few agree with him. Most of us are happy with our form and the way our world works. They like the connection and the balance between the worlds."

They had reached the end of a row of buildings and were now at a crossroads between four streets. The streets all looked very similar, and now Ellie had seen the whale, train, and ship, she was fully aware of the other weird things going on around her. There were creatures she did not recognise, creatures that would be the stuff of nightmares walking down the path. Ships and vehicles flying through the air, some looked normal others looked outrageously creative and to Ellie's eyes, impossible. There were gaps and holes appearing with people moving through them appearing and disappearing at will. So much activity.

'How many are there of you?' Ellie asked as she watched a group of spirits move together up the street, before being covered by a bus that suddenly they were all sat in as it sped them away.

"The same as there are of you."

Ellie whirled round to face them, 'What?'

"The spirit forms you see, the people here, are matched one

to one with people from your world. It is the same with animals; there is a one to one relationship with every living thing in your world to a spirit here. When you are imagining, dreaming, or creating, your spirit is more active here. When you are not it simply moves about doing what it wants to do."

'You mean, I have a spirit here?'

"Yes, you do."

'Can I meet it, her?'

For a moment there was no reply, then a shadow started to appear in front of Ellie. Within a few seconds it had formed into the shape of a spirit, the same as the others.

'Is this it? Is this, me?' Ellie thought.

"I am," Came a reply.

Ellie jumped a little, she still had not got used to the thinking way of talking.

"Here, the world is connected, and we know who we are conversing with, and who they wish to connect with."

'You just know?'

"Yes."

"Eleanor, try and imagine something, give it a go and see what happens."

Ellie thought for a moment, and to her amazement, the spirit changed in front of her. it was wearing what appeared to be a space suit, and it floated up into the air. Moments later, it shot into the sky like a rocket and was soon out of sight.

'Wow,' Ellie thought, 'That was amazing. And everyone can do that?'

"Essentially, yes. You are the first to know of the true impact of their imagination though, maybe you will consider this when you next daydream?"

Ellie nodded; it was food for thought indeed.

"This is also how the power works in your world. When you have controlled the spirit energy before, when you used Emilia's spirit to destroy him. You pulled it out of this world into yours and sustained it long enough to use in battle."

'Will I need to do that again?'

"We believe so. But that was different, you had help, you had Emilia pushing and fighting with you, you must find a way to do this yourself."

Ellie sighed, 'Has anyone else been here? Has anyone even come close to knowing about this?'

"Only one who remained in your world. A man who believed that there was an energy, something that could be used to create magical things. He was a member of the council. A true fighter and believed that the Man was evil. He wanted to protect your world at all costs."

Ellie tried to think of who it could be.

"He tried to convince people in your world that there was a greater power, that he may be able to control it to help."

'And could he?'

"No. He was not from the bloodline, your bloodline. But he was right about the energy and our world."

'Who was he?'

"One who was taken by the Man many years ago. The man who lived in your house before your family."

Ellie froze.

"You did not know him," the voice continued, "But we believe you may know of some of the things he made."

'The telescope, the compass?' Ellie thought, a million questions racing in her mind.

"Yes, we believe he discovered something that even we are not aware of; you will need to investigate this and see if you can understand anything further from his notes and designs."

Ellie digested all of this, it was almost too much to take in.

'I will, my friends and I will do what we can.'

"You will need your friends before the end, more than you will ever know."

The spirits turned and began moving once again, Ellie following behind. As they moved along the street, it changed many times over. Ellie was staggered at the rate that the world could change around her. She saw planes, trains, and cars from all eras, some that she did not even recognise. She saw animals walking tall and wearing clothes boarding what she assumed were buses. The road became a river, with fish and other sea life jumping out of it as they passed, then it became a smooth racetrack as some cars sped by. All still without a sound, Ellie could not recall the last time she had been anywhere this quiet, or indeed been this quiet for so long herself.

'Why does everyone look human here, but the Man chooses a more ghostly look?' Ellie asked, it had been bugging her for years why he presented himself the way he did. She had presumed that it was the way his world was but clearly this was not the case.

"He believed that it would be more intimidating for your people. When he first revealed himself to Abijah and wanted his service, he wanted to present a look that would insight fear. He assumed that fear would drive loyalty."

'It worked, didn't it?'

"It did work, most of the time, yes," they agreed. "But not with you, and not with everybody. He tried to trick you and it failed, remember."

Ellie found this statement to be a little insulting, how could she forget the terror and fear she had gone through soon after moving to the village.

"We meant no offence," they added, clearly reading her thoughts once again.

Ellie smirked at herself, she really needed to stop thinking things that she did not always mean.

The spirts stopped, Ellie was not concentrating and ended up walking through them both and having to turn around to face them once more.

'Sorry, my bad,' she thought with a small giggle.

"We have one more thing to share with you, Eleanor, then we must get you back and leave you to your battle."

'Ok, what's that?'

"As well as being linked to energy, and directly with people and animals, the power we have here is not just limited to imagination and creation. We also have the ability to see the future, in small glimpses."

'You can see the future?' this piqued Ellie's interest.

"In a manner, we can see glimpses, wisps, fleeting moments of time that may come to pass, or that have already passed. When this is revealed in your world, it is seen as dreams, or ideas, forward thinking."

'You mean when people picture themselves winning a race,

and then they win the race? That sort of thing?' Ellie asked, trying to make sense of it all.

"Close enough. We believe that part of the power imprinted in you has led to this ability also being in you."

'You think I can see the future?' Ellie was a little shocked at this.

"Maybe, think about it, have you ever seen or dreamt anything that has come to pass?"

Ellie thought, and she had two thoughts that came to mind.

"So, you saw us coming to greet you on that rock in a dream, before you even knew the rock, or the waterfall existed?" they asked, reading her mind once again.

'Yes, in a dream a while ago. It was the night after I had decided to come to Wales. Annabelle had to wake me, I thought it was just a part of the other stuff that goes on around the Man.'

This was all true, Ellie feared she had just been having a nightmare.

"But it is the other one that you fear the most is it not?"

Ellie shuddered.

"The one you have seen, but have not yet experienced that is bothering you?"

Ellie nodded. 'I saw the Man, over the folly. He was gloating over my friends, saying he had won. They were gathered around my body, it looked so cold and lifeless. As if...' she stopped, unable to think it.

"As if he had killed you where you stood, in front of your friends?" they asked, finishing the sentence for her.

'Yes,' Ellie replied in her mind, holding back the tears as she did so.

"This is an example of potential foresight, it may not come true, it may be nothing."

'Or it could be everything,' Ellie commented.

"Indeed, it could."

'Are you saying I need to die? Or is that a future where I lose?'

"We do not know. It could be that you lose. Or that the way to beat him is to die. Or it may not come true at all. It is not set, there are many possible outcomes. But know this, nearly everyone in this world does not want what the Man wants.

They long for physicality the same as he does, but they better understand the balance between our worlds. If yours is gone, ours will follow soon after no matter what he or any of us do to try and prevent it."

'You mean, I now have to worry about all of these people relying on me as well?'

"No, do not worry about them, know that they are on your side, if sides and lines are to be drawn they believe what you and we believe. Harmony and balance are the only ways to survive."

Ellie sighed, 'This is a lot to take in, you know.'

"We understand, and we wish we could do more. But now, we must get you back and go ourselves, we have lingered for too long."

'What do you mean? There is so much more we can help each other with,' Ellie asked desperately.

"He is hunting us, if he finds you here as well then he will no doubt strike hard and fast. The longer we stay together, the greater the risk on us all."

Before Ellie could say or think anything a cloud of mist had started to form around them. It completely hid from view the world that she had been exploring and now all she could see were the forms of the two spirits in the mist. As soon as it had enveloped them, it started to move, giving Ellie the sensation of moving up in a lift the opposite to how she had felt when she was arriving here. It got faster, moving at such a speed that it was now just a blur. Ellie closed her eyes as it was starting to make her feel sick.

"Remember," the voice spoke to her again. "Be strong, be brave. Find your question, learn, practice, investigate, and do not fear what may come to pass. You will succeed if you push beyond what you know, what you believe, and what you feel. You are a Guardian, and as such you can do whatever you want to do."

Before Ellie could respond, there was an ear shattering bang, then the sound of a waterfall with birds chirping and the wind in the trees. She opened her eyes to find herself sat on a rock, looking towards Annabelle who was admiring the waterfall. Exactly as she was before she left.

CHAPTER 9

Ellie sat in silence, staring at Annabelle for a moment whilst her eyes and ears adjusted to the light and noise of the world. The walk had seemed quiet and peaceful before, but after the silence she had just experienced in Imaginari, the waterfall and breeze were deafening to her. She shook her head gently, trying to focus her senses a little.

"Are you ok?" came Annabelle's concerned voice from the rock pool.

Ellie looked up and attempted a smile to try and stop a flood of questions coming her way. It did not work.

"What's up? Did I miss something?" Annabelle asked as she quickly moved over to Ellie and put her arm around her. "You're shaking. Are you cold?" Annabelle asked, squeezing Ellie in close.

"No. I'm terrified," came Ellie's shaky reply, moments before bursting into tears. She turned and buried her face into Annabelle, she just wanted to hide away and hope that everything would be ok.

"Ellie, what happened? Tell me. Was it him again? I didn't notice anything."

"Because you can't," Ellie shouted, lifting her head up and pulling away. "Nobody ever does, it is just me, always me having to deal with all of it and it's not fair."

Ellie stood up and looked away from Annabelle towards the waterfall, anger flowing through her now.

Annabelle was speechless, "Ellie, I..." she paused, trying to think of the right words to say. "I just meant that I hadn't noticed anything, I didn't mean that nothing had happened. I know there is only so much I can do but I am on your side, one hundred percent I am on your side." Her voice cracked a little - the outburst from Ellie had hurt Annabelle deeply.

Ellie softened and allowed the calming sound of the water to enter her mind. She immediately felt the anger fading and calmness returning. She turned to Annabelle, despite her anger fading there were still tears flowing down her face.

"I'm so sorry, I didn't mean that. I'm just so scared, and I don't want to lose you. I don't know what to do," she collapsed to her knees, holding her face in her hands.

Annabelle rushed over to her, pulling her to her feet into a hug, holding her tight, "I know." She whispered as she stroked her hair. "I know, I'm here to help, you won't lose me, and I am always on your side."

Ellie sobbed, she could not think of anything to say. She felt that the outburst was needed for her to release some of the pressure and tension in her mind, but also that a lot of what she said was not true. She knew that Annabelle was with her and would help in any way that she could. It was also not fair to attack her the way that she had, and Ellie knew that. "I'm sorry," she managed to mumble through her coat.

"It's ok. I have no idea what it feels like, but I am here to help," Annabelle pulled away and lifted Ellie's head with her hands, holding her face in her palms. "You're wonderful, amazing, and cute when you cry," she said with a grin, it was intended to bring a smile to Ellie's face. It worked.

Ellie chuckled and wiped away some tears, "Thank you."

Annabelle kissed her, a final attempt to restore some calm and love back to the conversation.

"What did I do to deserve you?" Ellie asked.

"It must have been something really good," Annabelle replied, amused with herself. "Now, are you going to tell me what happened as we carry on walking?"

"We need to get into town, I need phone signal, so we can let the others know as well." Ellie surprised herself at how quickly she was able to say something so decisive and direct.

"Ok, we can do that."

Ellie nodded.

"Let's get walking then," Annabelle gestured to the path they were following, took Ellie's hand and led her away from the waterfall.

Ellie explained, in detail, everything that had just happened. To Annabelle's credit, she just listened, astounded that her girlfriend had just visited a world made up entirely of dreams and mist. Ellie covered the silence, the creation of anything from trains to spaceships, as well as the fact that she was one of only two people to have gone there and survived. Annabelle listened as the Guardians fate became clear to her, the fact that the Man was hunting them down to achieve his goal. Feeling particularly brave, Ellie also told Annabelle about the fact that she may be able to see a version of the future. She was proud of herself for doing so, she still had not revealed the dream that scared her so much, but it was a step forward.

"What do you think?" Ellie asked, after explaining as much as she could. They were nearly at the village now; the walk had taken some time, but the conversation had passed it quickly.

Annabelle thought for a moment. "It's a lot to take in, how long do you think you were there for?"

"I don't know, it must have been an hour or more easily."

"So, time does move quicker there then, as I said, I didn't even notice you had gone anywhere. As for what you learned, wow, it's incredible."

Ellie smiled, "The world you mean?"

"Yes. The fact that whenever we dream or imagine it actually comes true somewhere is amazing."

Ellie nodded in agreement.

"It's scary too, but amazing. It makes sense that he is hunting them down though. The Guardians I mean."

"Because they are his biggest threat?"

"Sort of, but I think it's something else. I think he needs them out of the way, not because they are a threat but because he needs their power. You said there were some people that supported him in his world?"

"That's what they said, but we didn't see anyone or anything whilst I was there."

"What if, he needs the Guardians power to handle what he is trying to do? What if he needs it to open up the energy between worlds?"

Ellie considered this, "That makes sense."

"Then he can use that power to take out his biggest threat. You."

Ellie looked at her with a wry smile. "You don't need to say that," she mused.

"I'm serious. Think about it. We know he has tried this a few times, and you are the only person that has beaten him not once, but twice. He must fear you."

"What do you mean?" Ellie asked.

Annabelle stopped walking and turned Ellie to face her, "Just listen to me. The only time the Guardians were able to stop him was way back when they all wanted the same thing, yes?"

Ellie nodded, staying silent.

"Right. He tried to use Abijah and the first council, but he failed because he made a mistake and in doing so created the chance for you to stop him, yes? Assuming the bloodline thing is true."

Ellie nodded again, paying close attention now.

"He tried a few different people, all from the village, all of whom failed for different reasons, but he never actually lost. It just didn't work. Then you came along. He tried to trick you the first time, and you beat him."

"That's true," Ellie added, "He expected me to be scared and just let him win."

"Exactly. Then the second time, he tried to make a version of you and change time so that you would back down to him. But the good in you broke through. That is why you are his biggest threat. You have already beaten him, he knows it. So next time he faces off against you he wants to tip the scale back in his favour. Using the Guardians power to do that, and if he has enough to pull the entire world through-" Annabelle stopped, realising what she was about to say.

"He may actually beat me," Ellie finished for her, solemnly.

"Yes, but I don't think he will, I'm just trying to understand and make sense of as much of it as I can."

"I know," Ellie noted. "You could be onto something there, that makes sense. What do I do?"

Annabelle took her hands. "You keep doing what you are doing. Yes, he is trying it his way, but remember, you beat him with minimal preparation. This time you are preparing yourself, he won't be ready for that."

"He already knows," Ellie tried to explain.

Annabelle put a finger over Ellie's lips, "I know, I think that scares him. Keep doing what you are doing, we will help, the boys will find something, and then we can try. He won't be expecting teamwork again."

Ellie welled up, she really did not know how to process this level of love and support. "You really think we can do this?"

"I really do," Annabelle replied, "It will be tough, and we have lots to do but I think we have a chance."

Ellie smiled, nodded, then turned to carry on walking, "Ok, we should let the others know, then we can enjoy the rest of our holiday together. Deal?"

Annabelle grinned, "Deal."

They walked into the village, hand in hand, Ellie feeling brave and defiant once more. Once there, they headed into the pub where they'd had dinner the day before. As soon as signal arrived Ellie shared the updates with the group via their chats. She told them there was a lot to go through and asked for no replies or questions until she was done. They did as she asked and read her messages. Once she was done, the replies started to come through.

'We got this,' was Dan's comment.

'You're stronger than all of us, he won't know what has hit him.' Tyler added.

'Dan and I are still working on it, but we think we will find something,' Was Leo's addition.

Simon's was more simplistic, and for some reason meant more to Ellie than the others combined, *'We love you Ellie, whatever happens, we are with you x'*

"Mushy soppy boy," Annabelle commented with a wry smile. "He knows you're with me, right?"

The girls chuckled.

"Yes, he does, he loves us both you know," Ellie added.

They all agreed to meet and discuss properly when the girls were back from holiday. Ellie and Annabelle stayed in the village and had some food. They also took the opportunity to plan some other days for their holiday. For a brief moment, Ellie felt like a normal person, having fun with the one she loved. Always in the back of her mind though, was what she may have to do or sacrifice to keep her safe.

CHAPTER 10

The holiday continued as any normal holiday should. There were walks, nice meals, sightseeing, and most importantly, positive memories of time well spent with family and friends. That is how Ellie saw it anyway, there were no other interruptions from spirits, no weird dreams, or anything remotely close to that. The thoughts and fears she was facing did not fade though. Ellie was all too aware of the pressure she was under, and the impending fate that waited for her was never too far from her mind. Leo and Dan had asked to meet Ellie and Annabelle by the folly.

"We don't need wall space this time," Leo had joked when they discussed where to meet.

They had agreed to meet the day after the girls returned from holiday, Annabelle was staying over with Ellie again anyway. They woke up, had some food and got ready, then began walking up to the folly.

"Do you think they have anything to help?" Ellie asked, with more desperation than she would care to admit.

Annabelle took her hand, "I'm sure they have." She comforted, "And if they haven't, we will keep trying."

Ellie smiled. It was a clear but cold day, a nice way to ease back into the village after their week of near solitude. "It is nice here, isn't it?" Ellie asked, looking out over the landscape around them.

Annabelle nodded, "It is. It has a feeling of being more remote than it actually is if that makes sense?"

"It does," Ellie agreed with a grin. "It would be better if we didn't know what we know though."

"Very true," Annabelle concurred.

They walked up the path, their coats rustling as they did so. Eventually they reached the peak of the hill, where the folly stood. There were a few other people on the hill, looking out over the views around them, blissfully unaware of the meaning and power that existed here.

"I can feel, all of it," Ellie commented.

"What do you mean?" Annabelle asked quizzically.

"I can feel all this around us, the grass, bushes, all of it. It's like it is buzzing around me, it feels electric."

"Have you ever felt that before?"

"Sometimes, I noticed it when we were on holiday, maybe I am getting more familiar with it?"

Annabelle smiled, "Maybe."

Ellie took some steps towards the folly, "I still remember it you know."

"What?"

"That night, the night when I faced him up here for the first time."

"I remember that night too, for a different reason."

Ellie looked at Annabelle, who had a big grin covering her face.

"Yes, I remember the kiss as well," Ellie commented with a grin equally as broad. "But it was also the night everything changed for me I think, in many ways."

She walked on, over the top of the hill towards the peak, Annabelle followed. They stopped in front of the tower, the gate still guarded by the metal grill.

"You never told me what it was like?" Annabelle asked, moving alongside Ellie.

"Terrifying," Ellie answered, simply. "I remember standing right here when he merged into one, in that moment I thought we had lost, it completely shocked me."

"Then you went and lay over there?" Annabelle gestured to the arch.

"Yes, that is where you found me as well," Ellie blushed.

"Do you think we need this place again?" Annabelle asked, looking up at the tower. "Can we trap him in it again?"

"I don't think so. I think it lost that ability when I beat him before. It was destroyed spiritually that night." Ellie

looked up too, "The power that passed through this place was incredible, and I had no idea how powerful it could be then." She touched the stone, feeling its coarse sandpaper like surface with her fingertips.
"Can you feel anything from the stone?"
Ellie shook her head, "No, it is only living things I can feel."
"Then how did this work?"
It was a good question, and something that Ellie herself had pondered over. "Honestly, I have no idea, I've tried to figure it out but never have."
She pulled her hand away from the stone, turned and walked back down the steps alongside the wall, Annabelle followed behind.
"Maybe you'll figure it out one day?" she offered hopefully.
Ellie smiled, appreciating the positivity, "That will have to wait for now though, look." She nodded down the crest of the hill to the small car park for the folly, Dan and Leo were just walking up the path towards them. Annabelle caught up with Ellie and stood next to her.
"Ready?" she asked.
"As I'll ever be," Ellie took Annabelle's hand and gave it a squeeze.
"Hi there," Leo called as they got within earshot.
"Morning," Annabelle replied.
"Not been here long, have you?" Dan asked, a small amount of concern in his voice.
"No, we've just been walking and reminiscing a little," Ellie replied, looking at Annabelle and smiling. "What have you got then? Anything new?"
"Straight to it as always, eh?" Leo commented, "Firstly, how are you? Sounds like you had a rough time away?"
Ellie replied sharply, "Not at all, holiday was amazing with one little blip in the middle. I'm determined not to let him ruin our lives, you know."
Silence fell between the four of them for a moment, nobody knew what to say.
Eventually, Ellie decided to break the silence, "Sorry, didn't mean to snap, I just want to get this over and done with."
Leo nodded, "We know, Ellie. We know." He smiled kindly

and the tension was lifted immediately.

"Ok," Dan jumped in enthusiastically, "We don't have news, but we do have a theory, follow me."

He walked past Ellie and Annabelle, leading them back up the hill to the crest where the folly sat.

"We were just up here," Annabelle commented.

Dan stopped and looked at her, a wry smile on his face, "But I bet you didn't look with your soul as well as your eyes, did you?" he winked.

Annabelle frowned, "What?"

"Let's let the boys have their fun," Ellie interjected with a chuckle. "Go on Dan."

He grinned, turned and carried on up the steps to the gate. Once there he stopped and turned quickly to face the other three, his arms outstretched.

"Let me take you back, to a time before time," he shouted, as if greeting audience members at a show.

Ellie and Annabelle sniggered. Leo rolled his eyes.

"He has been practicing this you know," he whispered to them.

"I heard that. No talking in the back please," he bowed slightly, "The performance is not necessary, but it is my bit of fun. Indulge me."

With a gentle shake of the head, Annabelle stated, "Ok, we will. Go on."

"As I was saying, a time before time, the phantom world now known as Imaginari was strong and was built on the foundation of power from living things here, in our world."

"He knows his stuff," Ellie added with a knowing look and nod.

"Five Guardians came, they tried to steal the energy from our world but failed. Four decided to live in harmony, but one craved power. They tried to stop him and in so doing wiped out the first sentient life on this Earth, the dinosaurs. The Man, the one who stood alone to try and destroy, was lost and vanished for a millennium. He returned, he challenged and bullied the first villagers on this very hill to build this monument." He slapped his hand against the stone of the tower, "He told them it was to act as a lock, that the five stones around it would act as keys to keep evil at bay when in fact it was going to open up the portal between worlds and allow him to steal all of the living spirit energy from our world in one go. It failed, not through bravery or skill, but by poor judgement on his part. He needed a willing soul to open a portal. This again destroyed him, and he was forced to wait until the right moment came along. He tried a few times, taking people in varying stages of life and circumstance, each was wrong, for he could not find the right person to help him."

"Enter Ellie," Leo added from beside the girls.

"Indeed. Enter Ellie. He needed you, he tried to trick you and tempt you into doing his bidding. You resisted and eventually beat him, here, on this very spot."

Ellie felt a small swell of pride, nobody had ever spoken about what had happened like this before.

"Then, after losing to you once, he returned sending you flying through time with another, another that he made from you in the hope that it would be the worst of you. Emilia. That plan also failed because he had not counted on you working together with her, to beat him. He needed her to be the worst of you and to use that anger to tear open the sky. It nearly worked. It was only because of some quick thinking between you that you were able to stop him. You used his own creation against him to absorb and dissolve him and his power, scattering him across both our world and his." He paused for effect, as there were no questions or response, he continued, "Now he has returned, we do not know what his next plan will be, or what he wants to do. But we know more now than ever."

"Tell us then, show off," Annabelle called out, "We already know all this."

"I know we do," Dan retorted, "I needed to explain that bit first." He looked at Ellie, "These are the new bits, the things that we know now that we did not know when you beat him before. Number one, he stands alone. Almost. We now know that he may have some followers but generally his world is against him. Two, he needs you," he pointed at Ellie. "He knows you are the key to his success, but also the biggest chance of him failing as well. What he will do about this, we don't know, but we know we need to be ready."

Ellie shifted slightly on the spot, even though she technically already knew that, hearing it spoken in such a factual way was hard to digest.

"Three," Dan carried on, apparently unaware of Ellie's sudden unease, "You can control the same power he wants to harness. Yes, not as strongly or as well as he can at the moment, but we believe you can master it."

"Four, the compass," Leo added, almost making Ellie and Annabelle jump, they had forgotten he was there for a moment.

"Yes, the compass," Dan continued. "That was made by someone that had tried to use the energy, the previous owner of your house was one of the people that the Man tried to turn, tried to use to achieve his goal. He is also, we believe, the only other person to have seen Imaginari."

Ellie looked at Dan, astounded. "What?" she managed to stutter out.

"There was something you said, about when you were with the Guardians. They said that you were the first to truly understand the impact of your mind, or something like that. But also, that there was only one before you who had been to their world and returned, a member of the council who believed the energy could be used to make magical things."

The realisation of what he was saying hit Ellie like a tidal wave, she almost fell to her knees as the energy was drawn from her by it, "The compass? You think he made that, using the energy?"

"It is a working theory, but yes, we do," Leo confirmed.

"How?"

"We don't know, but we are certain it will be able to help you."

"Again, how?" Annabelle asked on Ellie's behalf.

"Look, all we know is that the compass should do more than it has so far, it makes no sense. We are also hypothesizing, guessing, that the previous owner of your house, who was a council member, and more are all connected."

"We could be wrong," Leo added, "But we do think we are on to something. It all fits."

"It does," Ellie agreed with a solemn tone. She had so much going around her head in that moment. It did make sense to her, it was possible that the previous person who went to Imaginari was the owner of her house, and that he had figured out a way to create the compass to serve a higher purpose. But what?

"Do you have the compass with you?" Annabelle asked, snapping Ellie out of her deep trance.

Ellie said nothing but nodded and pulled it out of her inside zip pocket and held it in her hands in front of her. She held it tight in her palms, the way you would hold a hot drink in winter to warm your fingers. Without her realising, the others gathered around her, creating a circle around the battered looking compass. The needle was still, pointing towards Dan. There were no markings on the face, nothing to indicate any kind of direction.

"Is it working?" Leo asked.

Ellie shrugged.

"Turn it, see what the needle does," he offered kindly.

She did so, the needle stayed balanced and true, pointing at Dan.

"Why is it pointing at me?" Dan asked, a small amount of shock in his voice.

"It's not," Ellie replied, "Move aside and I'll show you."

He did, he moved to the right but the needle stayed put, pointing at the tower of the folly.

"See," Ellie stated, "It is pointing at the folly, not you."

"Ok, let's test that," Leo added. "Follow me," he turned and headed back down the peak to the crest of the hill. "Keep an eye on it, let's walk around the folly and see what it does."

Ellie followed, with Annabelle and Dan behind her, all the time keeping one eye on the compass in her hand as she did so.

When they reached the bottom of the stone steps, he turned to his left and headed down the steeper stairs to the lower level of the top of the hill. Halfway down, he stopped and turned to Ellie.

"Well?" he asked.

"It's turned," Ellie informed them, Annabelle and Dan had

caught up now too. "The case has turned but the needle is still pointing at the folly."

"Ok, let's keep going," Leo turned and walked down the remaining steps, at the bottom he turned left again keeping the folly above them and to the left. After a short distance he stopped again.

"Same," Ellie called out to them all, before anyone could ask, "Still the folly."

They gathered around her, creating a circle around the device once again.

"Can I ask a sideways question?" Leo asked, looking at Ellie.

She raised an eyebrow, "Go on."

"When you use, or feel, the energy around you, how do you do it? Do you have to focus? Think? How does it work?"

"Honestly, I'm not really sure. When I used it to fight him, with Emilia, it was out of desperation and instinct I think. It just sort of came to me, as if the adrenaline was carrying it or something. Other times, it has been when I have had to really think on it, honestly it's exhausting."

"Ok, maybe try that with the compass?" he added, softly.

The other three looked at him, the look on Dan's face suggested he was not aware of where this was going either.

"What I mean is, maybe the reason it is doing this now is because that is what it has been programmed to do. But, if it could be changed or recoded using the energy, it may behave differently?"

They stared at him, then there was a general feeling of optimism that spread amongst the group.

Annabelle spoked first, "Makes sense to me."

Ellie puffed out her cheeks. "Ok, I'll give it a go. Just don't laugh at me."

"We won't," Dan comforted, putting an arm around her.

"Ok, give me some room."

They stepped back, not far, but far enough so as not to crowd Ellie whilst still being able to see the compass needle. Ellie closed her eyes, and for a moment all she could think about was how silly they would all look to anyone nearby. She smiled and chuckled to herself. Focus, Ellie berated herself. You can do this. Think of the compass, the energy, the energy going into the compass, so it points at, what? Ellie stopped her train of thought. She could not continue because she did not know what it was supposed to be pointing at. As soon as her mind reached this point, she was unable to move on from it, stuck in a rut of thought that was keeping her mind locked still. Ellie could feel herself getting angry, almost shaking with rage as she squeezed the compass in her hand, willing it to do something different. After a few desperate moments, she relaxed and opened her eyes with a defeated sigh. She looked at the compass needle to confirm her fears. It had not moved. She looked up at her friends, taking in their hopeful faces and gently shook her head. "Nothing."

They moved towards her, "No drama, no problem," Leo comforted.

Annabelle took her into a hug, "You'll get there, besides, they could be wrong." She buried Ellie's head in her hug, hiding her face from the boys as she could feel her shaking and beginning to cry. 'I think you are right,' she mouthed to Leo and Dan.

They nodded in acknowledgement, 'Ellie does too,' Leo mouthed back silently.

Annabelle nodded.

"What if I can't do this?" Ellie asked, her voice muffled by tears and Annabelle's coat.

They did not say anything, Ellie knew there was nothing they could say but their silence was telling.

"Maybe that's enough for today?" Annabelle offered; the boys nodded in agreement.

"We only wanted to help," Leo said, shakily.

"I know," Ellie said, still muffled. "You did, you do," she pulled away from Annabelle to look at them, her eyes red and puffy. "You are all doing so much, and I just don't want to let you down."

Dan raised a hand, stopping Ellie in her tracks. "You will never let us down. You will do this. We know it," he smiled warmly.

Ellie walked over and hugged them both, kissed them on the cheek and said, "Thank you."

They blushed a little, which amused Ellie to the point of

smiling a little.

"We'll go then, leave you two to it," Leo said.

With a hug for Annabelle, they left, leaving the girls at the foot of the folly, Annabelle holding Ellie tight to comfort and shield her as best as she could.

CHAPTER 11

Late autumn arrived with a flurry of golden colours from the trees, strong winds, and longer nights. In a weird twist of irony, Ellie felt that it reflected her mood, strength, and focus. These thoughts only crossed her mind when she felt deflated though. Nearly two weeks had passed since her meeting on the hill with Annabelle, Dan, and Leo, and she had not forgiven herself. Ellie had gone for more runs and pushed herself to the point of exhaustion when it came to practicing with the energy flow. She had tried different approaches and tactics, ranging from doing it at different times of day to doing it immediately before or after physical exercise such as a run. Nothing was working. To her frustration, the more she tried, the further away she seemed to be from achieving anything significant. The problem was this just made her try harder and exhaust herself further, thus Ellie found herself in a spiral of self-perceived failure, pressure, and isolation. The isolation was driven by her, not her friends. Annabelle in particular was extremely worried about Ellie as she had never seen her like this. Being driven and passionate about something is one thing and is a trait to be admired, but not to the point of shutting out the rest of the world. Ellie had not quite gone that far, yet. She still spoke to and saw Annabelle, but her other friends were hearing less and less from her. Annabelle had decided to act and had arranged with Simon for them to go to Ellie to try and see if they could help her. The goal being to see if they could do anything to help get their plan back on track. Initially Ellie had not been receptive to the idea. Fear of failing in front of her friends again was daunting and scary, but she soon warmed to the idea after Annabelle explained that nothing would change their opinion of her. Today, Saturday, was that day.

When Ellie woke up and looked out of the window, it was the sort of day that reflected exactly how she felt. It was grey, clouds covered the sky with a foreboding dim gloom that made her want to crawl back into bed and pretend that the day had not arrived. The thought of Annabelle telling her off for thinking like that gave her a small warm feeling along with a little burst of energy, and almost hope. They cared about her, she knew that, and they were not going to judge, they were going to help. Ellie had agreed to meet them at the disused football pitch they had been to before, the place where she had nearly been drawn into the prison realm by the Man had it not been for, as far as she was concerned, Annabelle. Ellie decided to run there, so she got her gear on and headed out. She took her normal route, up the roads and through some paths and fields to allow her to clear her mind. It was pleasing for her to know how much she could focus when she was running, the feeling of leaving her worries behind and clearing her head was significant and she only hoped it would be enough today. She had to master these skills, she did not know why she knew but there was a feeling deep in her soul that there was something building. The sort of feeling you get when a storm is brewing above, tension, pressure waiting to burst, and she knew the Man was up to something. Something big. It did not take long for her to arrive at the white rail surrounding the overgrown pitch. She stopped at the rail and looked around, Annabelle and Simon were not there yet.

"You guys here?" she called out, just to be sure.

Nothing.

"Ok, Eleanor," she said to herself out loud, "Let's try this before they get here."

She moved into the middle of the field and knelt, the ground was soft and cold on her knees, but she did not mind. Ellie took a huge gulp of water, got the compass out of her pocket and held it in her hands the way she had before. Closing her eyes, Ellie focused on her breathing to slow it down, her heart was still racing after the run, but it did not take long for her to calm herself and focus. First, she listened to nothing but the wind in the trees, she concentrated hard to tune out any other sound. Then, holding the compass tight in her hand, she began to think.

What are you here for?

Do something. Please.

Show me this isn't all for nothing.

She opened her eyes and looked at it, nothing. It still pointed straight ahead, the direction of the folly on the hill. She shook her head, "Come on Eleanor," she scolded. Closing her eyes once more, she focused. Her breathing slow and steady, her hands clasped tightly around the cold metal casing.

I need help.

I need strength.

I can't do this on my own, my friends are doing what they can, but I don't think we are enough.

Give me guidance, something.

This last one took Ellie by surprise, even though she was thinking it, it surprised her that she had used the word guidance. The more she thought on it, the more it felt curious to her.

Guidance? she asked herself. Is that what this is? I suppose a compass is a type of guidance.

To Ellie's surprise, she felt a tingle in her palms and fingertips, a small spark of something that made her open her eyes and immediately look at the compass. She was speechless, the compass was no longer pointing forwards to the folly. It was pointing to the right, between two and three if it were a clock face. In a state of shock, she looked up in the direction it was pointing, across the field and straight into the puzzled faces of Annabelle and Simon.

"It worked," Ellie shouted at the top of her voice excitedly, in an instant her mood had changed to one of excitement and hope.

Annabelle and Simon climbed under the barrier and hurried over to her.

"What do you mean?" Simon asked.

"I got here early," Ellie answered, getting to her feet. "And I decided to try again before you got here, I just cleared my mind and thought of what I wanted it to do and, look-" She indicated at the compass. "It's not pointing at the folly anymore."

They looked, Ellie looked, and was immediately dismayed.

"It wasn't," to her horror, the needle was once again pointing in the direction of the folly. She looked up at Simon who was standing opposite her. "I swear it wasn't," she pleaded.

"We believe you, Ellie," he said kindly.

"We do," Annabelle agreed, "Why not try again?"

Ellie, defiant, immediately got back down on her knees and closed her eyes. "Ok, give me a minute, just stay still and don't say anything. Watch over it and take note if it moves."

Annabelle and Simon looked at each other and shrugged, all they could do was support and do as she had asked.

Ellie cleared her mind once more, focusing on the sound of the wind in the trees and the thoughts she was sure had moved it before.

Guidance. I need guidance. Give me something.

She thought hard, harder than she had ever thought of anything. It felt odd to sit and think of guidance, but it felt right to her, she did not know why. After a few moments, she felt the tingle in her palms and fingertips once more, out of excitement she opened her eyes. Nothing, it was still pointing the same way, towards the folly.

"It's still pointing this way," Simon said, almost embarrassed to say it.

"I felt it," Ellie muttered.

"Felt it?" Annabelle asked.

"Yes, I felt the same tingle and spark that I felt before when it moved, when it pointed at you two over there," she gestured towards where Simon and Annabelle had come from.

"Try again," Simon suggested.

"I just did, and it didn't work," Ellie shouted, anger seeping into her voice once more.

"I know, I have an idea, just try again. Please."

Ellie looked at Annabelle, who in turn looked at Simon with a look of confusion and desperation.

"Fine," Ellie snapped, closing her eyes.

As soon as her eyes were shut, Simon gestured to Annabelle that they should move sideways a little, creating a gap between them. This meant that from Ellie's position, the folly was at twelve o'clock, Annabelle at ten, and Simon at two. Annabelle figured she had guessed Simon's train of thought but kept quiet just in case.

Ellie focused and cleared her mind again, it was harder this time, her blood was boiling with rage and her breathing was elevated once more. But she did it, slowing her breathing and focusing on the sound of the trees.

Guidance, she thought to herself, guide me, help me, give me anything. Please.

The tingle came back, stronger than ever this time so much so that she was scared to open her eyes and look through fear of failing again. The tingling grew stronger now, the way pins and needles spreads down your arms when you shiver, a small spark of power flowing from her hands into the compass.

"Ellie? Are you ok?" came Annabelle's voice, concern etched through it.

"Yes. I'm ok," Ellie replied, then thought about it. "Why? What can you see?"

Without thinking, she opened her eyes and looked down. There were two things immediately visible to Ellie that had not been there before. First, she was drawn to the purple strands of light that were covering her palms, the same strands that had appeared the last time she was in the field. At that very moment, panic set in and then she registered the other new thing. The needle of the compass was no longer pointing at the folly. It was pointing at Simon. Before Ellie could say anything to get this across to the others, there was a blinding pain in her palms. To Ellie it felt as though the compass was on fire. She tried to drop it, but her hands would not let go of the burning metal. She closed her eyes and screamed out in agony, there was a loud bang and then silence. Total silence. So much silence Ellie thought she had died, until she opened her eyes to see nothing but grey mist and cloud as far as she could see. She immediately knew where she was.

CHAPTER 12

Ellie took a deep breath, the sound of it was deafening in the silence. As she watched, a world appeared around her, created from the mist as she knelt there speechless. She was back in Imaginari. Ellie was not sure if she had got here on her own or if she had been pulled back in. The memory of the purple strands of light over her palms made her look down, she was still clutching the compass, but it was no longer burning, and the light had gone. Standing, she put the compass back in her pocket and looked around. The world was forming steadily, but it did not match what she had seen before. At first, she assumed this was because she was in a different part of the world, but then remembered that as it was always created from imagination and thought, it may be different every time anyway.

"Correct," a soft female voice said in her mind.

Ellie whirled around, expecting someone to be behind her, but no one was there.

"Don't be alarmed, I shall not harm you."

Ellie went to reply, then stopped herself and thought instead, 'Where are you?'

"Well done for remembering to think, and not speak," the voice said. "I am here, and nowhere at the same time. You can hear me, I can hear you, let's leave it at that."

'Ok, it makes it hard for me to trust you, or know what you want.'

"Why?"

It was a good question, and Ellie did not have an immediate response to hand.

The voice continued, "Why do you need to see me in order

to trust me? My ideas, thoughts, and advice are what matters are they not?"

Ellie nodded, 'Yes, I didn't mean to offend.'

"You did not offend me," the voice responded. "I was simply curious as to why you need to see physical form in order to trust someone. No matter."

'What do I call you?' Ellie asked.

"You can call me Sybyl," she replied.

'Sybyl?' Ellie asked, immediately thinking of an old lady in a chair.

"Yes, Sybyl, I am old though Eleanor you are correct. I was not given that name, but I have chosen it. I come from an ancient past, it is short for Sibylla, a name from what you would call ancient Greece, a legend as it were. I am here to share, help, and see what can be done about that which may or may not come to pass soon."

'Did you bring me here?'

"No, I did not. I felt your arrival and came as soon as I could to try and help."

'What do you know about the Man? And how can I beat him?'

"Direct I see, I like that," Sybyl replied. "I know much about him, but I do not know how you can beat him, only how others have failed before. You have succeeded, twice, have you not?"

'Depends. Technically yes, but he has also come back twice,' this was true Ellie had often wondered the value of victory if your enemy kept returning.

"Sometimes you need to lose some battles, to win the war."

'What do you mean?'

"You have seen the future with your power, haven't you? Have you not seen what may come to pass?"

'You mean when I die. Yes, I remember that.'

"That is only one future, but maybe to win the war with the Man, you must lose a battle with him."

Ellie pondered this, not really knowing what to say and wished the conversation would move on.

"You need to expose him, draw him out, but you doubt yourself and your ability?"

'Of course, I do. I don't know what I'm doing.'

"Doubt is the beginning of most failures, be brave, be strong."
'People keep saying that,' Ellie commented, 'It's not that easy you know.'
Silence.
'Sorry, it's just hard to deal with, the pressure I mean,' Ellie added, sheepishly.
"I understand. But know that this world, Imaginari, is on your side. We believe in balance and harmony, only one, the most powerful of us, wants to destroy."
'The Man is the most powerful of you all? How?'
"He is one of the original Guardians, one of the first spirits to exist in our world. As such he has learnt much and has kept his power to himself and built it up. He is older, and angrier, than most. He believes that it is not fair, he believes that we are the more advanced world and as such should have a right of rule over yours."
'He wasn't alone at first though, was he?' Ellie challenged.
"No, he was not. The other Guardians did indeed want to create the same as he did, but as soon as they saw the cost, the destruction of your world, they changed their minds and tried to stop it. They did stop it, sacrificing themselves in the process. The worlds have existed in harmony ever since."
'Are you all made from imagination?'
"No, only some are. The majority of us have existed as a part of the energy flow since your world was formed. We gained consciousness, developed thoughts, and then began to use the extra energy, from imagination as you say, to better our world."
'Has anyone else been here before? From my world I mean,' Ellie reached down and felt her pocket that contained the compass.
"And returned safely?" she asked, "Only one, and he made that compass in your pocket."
'It's true?' Ellie asked, a small spark of excitement in her heart that they may be onto something.
"It is."
'What does it do?' Ellie asked, getting it out and holding it once more. The needle was holding firm and pointing to her left.

"I do not know."

Ellie's heart sank a little, 'How can you not know?'

"It is the only thing we know of to have been built in your world that can be altered by energy from ours. We have had no dealing with using the energy with physical objects, this is the one and only, as such we have no idea what it does or how it does it."

'Before I got here, today, now, I think I made it point at my friend Simon.'

"Interesting. Do you know what you were thinking of when it did that?"

Ellie wracked her mind. 'Guidance,' she recalled. 'I was asking lots of questions, but the one that stuck and made it shift was when I wanted guidance and help, I think.' She looked back down at the device in her hand, 'Is it strange for a physical item to be here in this world?'

"Very, I think this is the first time it has happened."

Ellie pocketed it and sighed.

'What now then? Can I look around? Is it safe?'

"It is safe, you can go where you please but remember you are physical, you have presence, be aware of your surroundings when moving through our world."

'I know, I was here before.'

"I know that also, but you are here alone now."

'Aren't you coming with me?' Ellie asked, rather more in hope than anything else.

"I will be nearby, but will leave you to explore on your own, I think that is best and you may find more answers that way."

Ellie smiled, 'Which way?'

There was no reply, but a small shimmer of light moved to Ellie's left, rippling away from her the way a pond ripples when a stone is dropped through it. She followed it.

Ellie moved through the mist as it took shape around her. There were no tall city buildings this time, just rolling hills of grey topped with trees and shapes that Ellie assumed were houses or similar buildings. There were also small ones of animals, it was as if she were walking amongst farmland. Apart from the silence and lack of colour, Ellie concluded that this could be the countryside pretty much anywhere in the world. She found it peaceful and strangely tranquil, even though she knew that there was something sinister at play around her. No matter what she thought or was told about the world of Imaginari being on her side and against the Man, she could not help but feel as though she was being watched or observed. She did not know by who. Ellie assumed that if the Man were here he would have shown himself by now but she still could not bring herself to relax too much. Ellie moved along the road, looking at the scenery rolling by as she did so. The world seemed more stable than before, there were no random trains or shapes appearing. Ellie felt completely alone, wandering through a grey scale silent countryside. That changed suddenly when she rounded the next corner, where she was greeted by a number of spirits heading straight for her. Ellie immediately stopped in a state of shock and surprise, they were about twenty paces in front of her and moving steadily. Just as quick as they had appeared, Ellie felt a searing pain in her head as it became flooded with voices all whispering to her at once. Some male and some female but all at once made them a garbled noise that was deafening. Ellie could only make out a few of the voices and what they were projecting to her.

"She is here."

"It's her, she is really here."

"Is she a Guardian now?"

"Why are you here?"

"How did you get here?"

Ellie covered her ears; it was a move based on instinct though and made no difference.

'Please, stop,' Ellie thought, pleading as best she could. To her surprise, all the voices stopped at once.

The spirits advanced and spread out around her, encircling her. Ellie looked around, desperate for a way out but could not see one, she thought she would be able to run through them if she needed to but that would be a last resort. Deciding to open a dialogue, she reached out.

'Hello, I mean you no harm, my name is Eleanor, my friends call me-'

"We know who you are," a strong voice shouted, cutting her off. "We have been watching you, ever since he told us of you, we have been watching."

'You can see into our world?' Ellie asked, confused. She knew that they were aware of the world and what went on in it but had not considered how they may be doing this.

"Foolish girl, of course we can. We can see anything we wish."

'But can you travel to my world?'

"No, only those that are most powerful, the Guardians and such, can do that. They get their power from us. They take it from us."

'So, the Guardians get their power from you? Does that hurt, make you weak?'

"It makes us weaker, not so weak that we cannot move, but weak enough to keep us under control."

'I thought the Guardians were good, and on your side of peace of stability?'

"They are," one voice said.

"They were," added another.

"Most were and still are," came a third opinion, confusing Ellie even more.

'Sorry, I don't understand,' she asked, meaning every word.

"The first Guardians, the Five, created a way to draw power from other spirits in our world." A voice explained, calmer this time, "They did this by connecting to us all in equal amounts, focusing on us. This was manageable, each of us giving a little is better than a few of us giving a lot."

Ellie registered this, it made sense so she let the story continue, all the while turning slowly around looking at the spirits that had surrounded her.

"They wanted to explore, to see if there was a way to improve our world, the ultimate goal being to make it physical."

A different voice added, "They were the ones that discovered the extra energy we get from imagination and living things in your world. They discovered it and wanted to enhance it, grow it, and allow it to flow freely into our world."

The original voice took over once more, "Their plan was accepted by all of us, they could have some of our power in exchange for finding a way to improve our world, make it physical. They broke through into your world."

A female voice continued, "This was many millennia ago. When they tried to take the energy, it became clear very quickly that it would destroy your world. As I'm sure you know, four of the five Guardians tried to stop. One continued."

'I know that. He is the one I am trying to stop now,' Ellie thought, assuming they were all listening to her. She was surrounded by six spirits, and she did not know how to project to that many minds at once, so she carried on thinking as she always had in this world.

"We know," a voice snapped back at her, "He knows. He knows everything and will stop at nothing."

"He wants to break the oath that the Guardians took. The original bond of protection and growth."

'I want to stop him, I am trying to,' Ellie added, desperation in her mind.

"You will lose," came a cold male voice.

Ellie did not appreciate it, even though it may be true and indeed had been reflected in her own thoughts and mind, hearing it made it even worse. 'Maybe I need to lose a battle in order to win a war,' this was as defiant as she dared to be.

"Fool," came the single reply.

Ellie ignored this and decided to try and take control of the situation as best she could. 'You said you have been watching me, why? For how long? How?'

There were some inaudible mutterings in her mind that she could not quite make out, Ellie assumed that they were discussing this amongst themselves, then a voice spoke in her own mind.

"He revealed you to us. Ever since you became important, he has not stopped following you. Watching, always watching, waiting for the opportune moment to strike."

This sent a chill down Ellie's spine, 'What is he waiting for?' she asked.

"The moment to be right. Timing is everything. Do you know why you are integral to his plans?"

'No, only that it is something to do with my bloodline. Being an only child or something?'

"Correct, but you do not know why your bloodline?"

'No,' Ellie answered.

"It is because of one of the Guardians, one of the original four. When they went as a five to your world and failed, one Guardian tried to create a bond to trap the one you know as the Man forever. His final act was to create a new spirit rule. You are familiar with this?"

Ellie hesitated; she was not sure if she was.

"You have used them yourself. You changed and manipulated a spirit rule when you and Emilia beat the Man before."

Ellie's eyes widened, 'A rule?'

"Our world does not physically exist, so the laws that govern your world do not apply. Rules such as gravity."

"Cause and effect," added another voice.

"Those things have to be created here, they have to be set and governed, this was the primary function of the Guardians. As such as a final act, one Guardian sacrificed nearly all their energy to dispel and enforce a new spirit rule."

"It was an attempt to stop the Man and protect both our worlds, and it held true for millions of years, until your world changed."

'What do you mean?'

"You know when the five tried do you not?"

'Millions of years ago, the time of the dinosaurs,' Ellie confirmed.

"Correct. Then all creatures that could fuel our world were born in groups, pods, large nests of eggs that would hatch together. No single generational line would be created."

Ellie processed this, trying to take it all in.

"The Guardian in question created a rule, knowing that the Man would try again. It stated if anyone tried to use a spirit from your world to open a portal to ours, it must one; be willing, and volunteer itself. And two; the first time this happened would only set the code, the family DNA that would be needed. This means the first time would never work, no matter who was chosen."

A female voice added, "Finally, third, that the DNA from that family line must be from an only child, a single generation-"

'Hang on,' Ellie interrupted, trying to make sense of it all.

CHAPTER 12

'You mean that the rule was set so that the first time the Man tried, unless they were willing it would fail?'

"Correct."

'And then that person's DNA or bloodline would be the only one that could unlock it, but they must be from a single generation? No siblings?'

This began to make sense to Ellie now.

"Again, correct," multiple voices confirmed.

'So, if dinosaurs, animals, or anything other than humans had carried on being the main living species on our planet the protection would always have worked?'

"We believe so, yes."

'Right,' Ellie concluded, things beginning to fall into place. 'Let me see if I have this right. When the five fell, one of them created a spirit rule to try and protect both worlds, this held firm until the Man presented himself over the Mow Cop hill to Abijah and the villagers.' She paused, waiting for a contradiction or objection. None came so she continued, 'When he chose the baby Joanna it failed because she wasn't willing, being a baby, she was probably terrified. This then triggered the code and her DNA was locked into the gateway between worlds, meaning it could now only be unlocked by a willing spirit that was an only child. I am the first in that bloodline to not have any siblings, so that makes me the key?' This complete story satisfied Ellie to a point, it did not comfort her or make her feel better in any way, but more understanding was helpful.

"That is correct. If you had not resisted him the first time, if you had shown any inkling of desire to help him, he would have torn your spirit from your body and used it to open the portal, and nothing would have stopped him."

'That is why he created Emilia, in the hope that she would do that. He hoped he could use her instead of me?'

"We believe that was his plan yes."

'Would it have worked?'

"We do not know."

'How do I stop him? How do I beat him?'

"You must stop him using your spirit, you must protect it at all costs. That is the key he needs."

'Doesn't he need it to be willing as well?' Ellie asked, fairly sure of this fact as she did so.

"Yes, but he can manipulate it, and you, to navigate around that rule. It would take him time, but he could do it."

'Is it true that using the energy, the power, can reveal the future?'

"It can," came a single female reply.

'Would that work for me too? Should I believe what I have seen and dreamed?'

"You can believe what you want to believe, what will be will be."

This was not helpful, and Ellie was hoping for something a little more certain from them. Then a question came to mind that she was frustrated that she had not thought to ask before.

'Who are you all?' she asked.

"That is not important, what is important is why we are here."

Ellie frowned, 'Ok, why are you here?'

"We are here because we needed to see you for ourselves, we wanted to see if you were who we had heard so much about."

"We hear from him, we needed to see for ourselves, but we wanted to meet you. We needed to know."

'Know what?' Ellie asked, confused.

"If you are willing to do what it takes to beat him, to win, to save us all."

'Have you figured that out by this conversation?'

"Partially, yes. We have seen your soul and believe it to be pure."

"This matches what we have seen when we have seen you before."

'You keep saying that, when have you seen me? How are you watching me?'

"We can see your world, we can view it."

'How?'

"We will show you, it will take all of us to show you."

Ellie waited, and as she watched the group of spirits all placed their hands on their temples in unison. Within seconds Ellie felt a blinding pain in her mind and she closed her eyes to try and shut it out. Before she could ask for it to stop, or try anything else, it vanished as quickly as it had arrived.

Ellie's eyes were closed, she knew that because her hands were covering them instinctively. But she could see. With perfect crystal-clear vision, she could see Annabelle and Simon, they were standing by her body in the field where she was trying to make the compass work. They looked worried, and as if they were moving towards her, but in slow motion.
'Why is it moving so slowly?' she asked.
"Time moves differently in our world, we view at the speed that is relative, so it appears slow to you, when you return it will be as if you have been gone for seconds."
'You can see anything in our world like this?'
"Yes."
The vision changed, she was now looking at Tyler working hard in the gym, it changed again, this time to Leo who was leaning over a laptop apparently studying something. Then to Dan, who was eating a sandwich whilst looking at his phone.
"We can see anything we like," came a soft comment in Ellie's mind.
"Some we have an easier connection to, but in theory we can see anything we like."
'Do we know when you do this?' Ellie asked, feeling a little uncomfortable.
"No, you are always unaware. The only thing you ever notice is memories of your dreams and imaginations, that you now know Ellie are created here in mist."
The vision changed once more, and she was now looking at the folly standing on top of the hill, clear blue sky all around. Next, on to the Statue of Mow standing proud as it always had. Ellie was transfixed as the images in front of her changed and moved so freely and easily. Then her view went black. Ellie opened her eyes and found herself to be back in Imaginari, surrounded by the spirits that were now lowering their hands.
"We can do that in our own minds at any time, we needed all

of us to push those images to you."

'Would I be able to do that?' Ellie asked curiously.

"No, not yet."

"We do not think so, no."

The mixed replies were starting to irritate Ellie. It was as if they were keeping some information back and that was irritating. She decided to be brave.

'Will you help me beat him?' she asked.

There was a moment when there was no noise at all, the silence deafening to her.

"We cannot interfere with events as they unfold, but if they unfold in the only way where we can help, then yes we will."

'You mean there are many ways this will play out, and you will only help in one of them?'

"Yes."

'But you don't know which one?'

"We know which one, and we know what must happen, but we cannot interfere or tell you as doing so means it would not happen."

'Ok, different question. Can I do it?'

"We have watched, he has made us watch and we have seen your bravery and courage. You have the strength."

"But you must see it through, you must be brave and be prepared for the challenges and decisions that are ahead of you."

'Great,' Ellie added sarcastically, 'Anything else?'

"Our time is nearly up, if everything happens as it can then we will meet again Ellie, but now we must go for he is coming."

'He? The Man?'

"The one who we learn from, the one that introduced us to you, the one that told us to come and find you."

This confused Ellie further, 'Why do you have to leave if you are working with whoever this is?'

"The Man is watching, always watching, we are six, six strong spirits being led by a seventh. If we meet as a seven the Man will sense it, find us and destroy us."

"I fear we have lingered too long, we will leave before he arrives to discuss with you," said a voice, sounding worried but vaguely familiar to Ellie, though she could not place it. It was the first time it had spoken in this meeting as well.

'Why do you have to leave?'

"You cannot be here much longer; your spirit and body are not prepared for it. You must also see him before you leave. When you return it will be like seconds to your world and friends. Much longer here and you will be torn apart."

'There is a limit?'

"Your body and spirit can only take so much, you are doing the right things, but the time is nearing for the main challenge. The biggest test you will face."

'You mean the training and stuff I am doing is right?' Ellie felt a boost of confidence at the thought of this.

"Yes. You are nearly ready, but you will only be certain at the final moment, you will know when."

Ellie nodded.

"Now, we must go."

At this, four of the six spirits faded instantly, leaving Ellie with two.

'Wait, is there anything else I need to know?' Ellie asked in a panic.

"There is much that you need to know, but little that you can know," came a soft reply, again in the voice that she thought was familiar.

'Helpful.'

"Yes, you are."

And with that, they vanished, leaving Ellie in silence once more surrounded by grey mist. She looked around to confirm that she was again alone, then took a deep breath to steady herself.

"Was that helpful?" came the gentle female voice of Sybyl out of nowhere.

'Both helpful and unhelpful at the same time,' Ellie replied, a little surprised. 'Why did you stay quiet? Why didn't you tell me what was going to happen?'

"You needed to explore and discover on your own, I could not interfere with that."

'People keep saying that, it's annoying.'

"I know. I am also here to say that you will miss your meeting with him."

'Who is him? Who is it?' Ellie asked exasperated, 'Why can't anyone tell me?'

"You will find out on your own, annoyingly though, he is over there."

Ellie turned, which was odd considering that she did not know where 'there' was. Sybyl still had no form and was just a voice but somehow Ellie knew where to look. A short distance away was a floating spirit, shining brilliant white.

'That is the one they were all vanishing for?' Ellie asked.

"I am," came a booming reply in her own mind. Ellie did not recognise the voice, but she felt oddly comforted by it. "Alas, they lingered too long and now our meeting will be cut short. I hope it is not the end, and that we get chance to meet once more. The Man is coming, he is nearly ready for you and you must be ready for him."

'I'm not going anywhere until I know who you are. Who those six were and what the hell I am supposed to do now,' Ellie shouted as best she could in her own mind.

"That is not your decision to make. If all goes to plan there will be time, I assure you. For now, though, farewell."

He vanished as quickly as he had arrived.

'What was that all about?' Ellie asked, hoping for a reply. None came. 'Hello?' she asked, 'Sybyl? Anyone?' Nothing, just the silence and Ellie with her own mind and thoughts.

She took a step forward, but as she did so she became aware of a tingling sensation in her palms. She looked down, they were being covered in purple strands of light. Ellie braced herself, she was sure she knew what was coming and she was ready for the pain. The tingle got stronger and became an ache spreading from her hands through her wrists and into her arms and chest. She closed her eyes and waited for the pain to reach her head. Moments later, she fell backwards and crashed into a heap on the floor. The ground beneath her was wet and cold, she could hear the sounds of trees, birds, and far off vehicles once again. All were being drowned out by the sound of her own name, being called out by Annabelle and Simon.

"Ellie," Annabelle shouted, rushing over to her side.

Simon hurried to her other side, both of her friends kneeling on the ground and waiting for a sign of life from Ellie.

"I'm ok, I'm here," Ellie muttered softly. She pulled herself up onto her arms, resting on her elbows. "If I was to ask, what just happened, I think I can guess?" Ellie asked them both, a quizzical look on her face.

Annabelle looked at Simon, who returned the same blank look.

"I bet, I looked like I was passing out or something and I just fell over backwards then you rushed over? Maybe five seconds max?" Ellie stated.

They both looked at her.

"Pretty much, you were trying to get the compass to change, you screamed out in pain and then fell over onto your back," Simon replied. "Why? What happened for you?"

Ellie smiled, "First, I didn't try to make it move, I made it move."

"You did it? That's great," Annabelle exclaimed, wrapping Ellie into a hug.

"Secondly," Ellie continued, in a soft calm voice. "I went back to Imaginari, apparently on my own. Thirdly, I also now know why it is me that is the key to this."

"The bloodline thing?" Simon asked.

"Yes, but I know why now. Why my bloodline."

Simon nodded, "Ok, do you know where the compass was pointing?"

Ellie looked at him, he had a cheeky grin on his face, the same one that he had the day they met. Ellie smiled to herself at the memory of that day.

"Yes, Simon keeper of sweeties, it was pointing at you," she stated with a grin.

"Do you know why?" Simon asked.

"Or how?" Annabelle enquired.

"Shhhhhh," Ellie cut across them. "No and no, I don't know that, but I do know more now, and we are on the right track. I know it. I can feel it. But I also know that he is coming. He is ready, soon the Man will make his move."

CHAPTER 13

They acted fast. As soon as Ellie felt she was strong enough to move again, they got out of the field and headed to her house. Whilst they were waiting and then walking, Annabelle and Simon took the initiative of getting the others up to speed. They could not tell them much, because they did not know a lot, but they arranged for everyone to come to Ellie's that evening to discuss and think of any next steps. They did not need much convincing, and by the time they had walked back to Ellie's they had arranged for everyone to be there in about an hour.

"Just enough time for me to have a shower then," Ellie commented when Simon informed her that she would have company soon.

"I figured sooner rather than later is all," he defended.

"I know. I know," she smiled warmly at him, hugged him, and kissed him on the cheek. "Thank you."

He blushed a little.

"Now, you two go and get some drinks and snacks ready, I'm going to go get sorted. Help yourselves in the kitchen, I'll be down again soon."

They did as she asked, Ellie went upstairs whilst Simon and Annabelle got things ready. They would not be disturbed as Katherine and Nicholas were away for the evening, so the six friends could plan together as much as they needed to. Ellie felt she was sweaty after her run and exploits in Imaginari, all she wanted to do was get clean and relax a little. Knowing that doing so might be difficult, she focused on getting herself ready and had a shower. Afterwards she dried her hair and then headed downstairs. It was odd that she hated the total silence in Imaginari but did not mind the level of silence at home from being in a room on her own. When she got to the kitchen, Annabelle and Simon had been joined by all the others.

"Wow, you're all early. Or was I a really long time?" Ellie asked in a small state of shock.

"We heard there was news and wanted to know as soon as possible," Tyler replied.

Everyone else nodded and stared in silence at Ellie.

"Ok, well stop staring you're freaking me out," she headed to the kettle, "Drink anyone?"

"We all have one," Annabelle replied with a smile.

"And biscuits," Dan chimed in.

Ellie shook her head and chuckled, "Ok, let me make this tea and I'll tell you all I now know."

About an hour later Ellie had explained everything to her friends, who to their credit stayed silent and listened throughout.

"There you have it. Looks like we are running out of time, I have no idea who that group in Imaginari were or how to get them to help us. And the only useful thing I found out was that I need to stop him using my spirit."

"Easy," Simon commented with a sarcastic grin.

Ellie smirked. There was a secret behind the smirk though, she still had not told anyone about her vision, and the fact that with every person that she spoke to it seemed to get closer to being true.

"You mean you can get there on your own now?" Leo asked.

"I don't think so, I think something strange still happened. That purple light stuff, I don't know where that comes from."

"But you can change the compass now too?" Dan added excitedly.

"Yes, it has changed," Ellie got it out of her pocket; she had checked it upstairs and it was still not pointing at the folly. She put it on the table and the needle spun and settled on Simon once more.

"How do we know it is Simon though?" Leo asked incredulously, as if hurt that he had not been chosen by the device.

"Watch," Simon stated, he stood and moved around the room. To the amazement of everyone it followed him in a perfect circle as he moved around them back to his original spot at the table. "See?"

There was a stunned silence, nobody knew what to say or what to make of what they had just seen. Eventually, Simon spoke first.

"The elephant in the room, I have no idea what is special about me."

"We all agree with that," Dan commented sarcastically.

"When did it change? What exactly happened?" Leo asked, as always looking for the logical explanation to anything.

"I was focusing on it, trying to see if I could get the energy into it, thinking of various things. I think it changed when I was thinking about guidance and help," Ellie replied, looking at Simon. "So, any ideas? Guide me oh wise Simon," she smiled and took a sip of tea, amused with herself slightly.

Simon sniggered, "I have no idea. I have nothing to share that we don't already know. Seriously, I have nothing."

This sent a wave of disappointment across the room, although expected it was still a let-down.

"Right," Tyler chipped in, "We know that Ellie can get to Imaginari, we know she can control the energy and the compass, but we don't know why specifically on that last one? Is that right?"

"Pretty much," Annabelle agreed in a subdued tone. "I feel like we are missing something key, but I have no idea what it is."

"We all feel like that," Ellie agreed. "Like there is something huge that we have missed somewhere. Personally, I think we need help from the group I met in Imaginari. They seemed very informative, and most of all scared of the Man. Just annoying that they didn't tell me how to get their help."

"How can we trust people who say they want to help but don't tell us how to get it?" Dan asked.

Nobody said anything, nobody knew what to say.

"Can I suggest a change of tact?" Leo suggested, they all looked at him. "I have a theory on how you may be able to beat him."

Ellie raised an eyebrow.

"It is only a theory, but I've been pondering it for a while now."

"Go on," Ellie stated, "Open to any ideas here, so let's have it."

"Power," Leo said simply, as if it explained everything. "I think you need to overload him with power."

"How do you figure that?" Simon asked.

"I was thinking about the last time you fought him, why he needed the spirit from Emilia and you, to make it work."

"We only know that now because of the DNA from Joanna, my DNA," Ellie tried to correct him. "That is what is connecting me to all of this."

"Yes, I know, but I also remember him saying something about needing the power. I don't think he can do it on his own. I think, he needs the power of the spirit from a willing lone generation member from your family tree. I understand that," Leo seemed pleased with himself, everyone was watching and hanging on his every word. "What I mean is that I think he can't handle the power on his own. Think about it, I know he needs you to unlock the portal, but why risk trying to get you or anyone else to help after that point?"

Ellie considered this; it did sort of make sense, "Go on."

"All I am saying is that he has been obsessed with power, control, and victory. It doesn't make sense that he would risk it all by getting someone else involved. I think if he did it on his own, through nothing but his own spirit, it would destroy him."

"Overload him," Tyler commented, "Makes sense to me, Ellie?"

They all looked at Ellie, who in turn looked at Leo, trying to process it all. "I guess it makes sense. I have no idea how to do that though?" She looked lost and helpless once more, "I only know how to do little things, like make the energy interact with the compass and send tingles through my fingers. I can't do much."

"You have though," Annabelle reassured.

Ellie looked at her.

"Remember? It was you that used Emilia's spirit, you used it to beat him. I think you can do more than you think you can." Ellie pondered.

"You made the compass change after a few tries, maybe you need to push a little more?" Tyler added, and immediately regretted it when he saw the look on Ellie's face. He quickly defended himself, "I simply meant to try, that's all. The compass was made by someone else, maybe that is why it took you longer to figure it out? All I meant was you are stronger than you are giving yourself credit for."

"That's true," Simon chipped in, trying to help him out of the hole he was digging for himself. "The compass was made by the guy who lived here before, we don't even know his name, but maybe he knew more than he let on? Maybe he was a pioneer? Maybe he did more to help you, or anyone that came along, than we know at the moment?"

They all thought on this, "Where do we look though?" Annabelle asked. "We have looked over everything that he left in that tin, the compass, notes, and telescope etc. I'm pretty sure Leo and Dan would have found something with the amount of effort they have put into it?"

Ellie looked at Annabelle, "Say that again."

"What?" Annabelle replied, a little shocked.

"Say that again, exactly how you just said it."

Annabelle looked at the others, then with a puzzled look on her face began again. "Ok, I said where do we look. That we have looked over everything and that Leo and Dan have gone over the telescope, compass, notes, and I would have thought they would have seen something."

"Exactly," Ellie said with a smile.

They all looked very confused, staring at Ellie waiting for an explanation.

"Leo and Dan have looked over everything in detail, including the compass, telescope and notes, right?" Ellie began.

They all nodded softly, very confused.

"But they couldn't change the compass because they can't use the energy like I can, I could reveal more." They were still not following so Ellie continued, "What if I apply the energy to the notes and the telescope, the way I did the compass. What if that makes them change and reveal more information to us? What if he hid more clues right in front of us, but in a way that would never be revealed until someone came along that could use the spirit energy?" Ellie was excited now, blood pumping hard and fast around her body.

"Like you," Leo replied, a small tone of excitement in his voice.

Ellie pointed at him, "Yes. Exactly. It would be the perfect way to protect secrets from anyone that shouldn't see them." Without another word, Ellie turned and left the kitchen, ran upstairs to retrieve the notes and telescope. It did not take her long to return clutching them in her hand. "What if the answers are right here and have been all along?" she put them down on the table, the compass in the middle, telescope on the right, and notes to the left.

"It makes sense," Annabelle commented, "and we haven't tried it yet, so why not?"

Ellie smiled and looked at the others. To her delight, smiles were appearing all around the table, backed up by nods of support and reassurance.

"Go for it Ellie," Leo said, everyone else staying silent.

"Ok, let me think and focus on this, I don't really know what I am doing remember."

They all moved back slightly, giving Ellie some room around the table. She placed her palms either side of the items that sat there, aware that the needle was still following Simon round the room. She closed her eyes and took a deep breath.

"Do you think I should try the same thing as I did the compass?" she asked the room.

"It's a start," Annabelle replied, gently squeezing Ellie's shoulder as she did so, comforting her.

"Ok, here goes."

Taking another deep breath, Ellie cleared her mind. Guidance give me guidance, she thought, The compass isn't enough, we need more help. She focused and tried to will something into existence, she did not know what but was desperate for something to appear to help her and her friends. Please, we are so close I can feel it we just need a little help, she continued to think. Who were the spirits in Imaginari that helped me? Who can guide me? Us? She took some more deep breaths and was about to give up when she heard a small gasp from Annabelle.

"What?" Ellie asked, keeping her eyes closed, "Is everything ok?"

"Yes, we're fine," Annabelle replied, "You may want to look at this though."

Ellie opened her eyes and instinctively looked round at Annabelle. She was white as a sheet but otherwise ok. To Ellie's surprise, the others were all looking past her down at the table, motionless and silent. Ellie turned back to the table, facing the items that her palms had been resting by moments before. The compass was seemingly unchanged, the needle holding firm pointing at Simon. It was the other two items that had drawn the attention of her friends. The telescope was glowing purple, it seemed to be seeping colour onto the table with a faint hum. She was about to reach out and grab it when she noticed the notes. The four pieces of paper were also glowing, although the colour was starting to fade now. The interesting thing however was that the original text and handwritten scrawls they had read years before were fading and were being replaced by four pages of neat and tidy handwriting. Clear as day a new set of words were appearing on the page. Glowing purple at first, but then settling down to be in plain black ink. Ellie reached forwards and nervously picked up them, glancing at her friends who were all wearing the same look, a mix of excitement, fear, and surprise. Ellie gathered them in front of her and began to read aloud. They had now been numbered one to four, so she began with number one.

"If you are reading this then two things must have happened. The first is that I am no longer guarding these pages, the second is that you have mastered the ability to use the energy flow between our world and Imaginari."

She paused, looked up to a sea of beaming faces, her friends had moved back to the table and were now sat intently as if listening to a presentation. Ellie continued.

"These pages have been created and protected in the hope that my information will help in the fight against the Man. Before reading, know this, he is a formidable opponent that has already taken many lives from the village in his desperate attempts to draw power from our world into his. The most recent was that of Christian, the young man in the village who had recently become a father and apparently ran out on his family. I know this not to be the case as I have met him in Imaginari. He was trapped by the Man after refusing to help him, I believe he may be able to help but I have been unable to track him down since our last meeting. I hope that these devices I have made, and the notes I have left about myself, will help you to victory where I have failed. Good luck. Alistair.

Ellie looked up, "That's all the first one says," she checked the back to be sure, it was blank.
"What does the next one say?" Annabelle asked impatiently.
"Ok, here goes," Ellie switched papers and continued to read aloud.

"This compass was once a cheap one from a camping shop, however I was able to take it to Imaginari and work with Christian on it. We were able to tune it using the energy there, and then reset it. This means that the compass will now point to the nearest source of Imaginari energy. In Mow Cop this will be the folly. However, if the energy in the compass is increased, it can be altered. Christian and I set up the compass so that it would point to help and hope, the energy flow would understand the users request for help and point to the nearest source of support. All you need to do in order to access this knowledge, is ask for help."

Ellie stopped and looked up, Simon had picked up the compass and was turning it over in his hand.
"So, you made it point to me, because you asked for hope and help? That makes no sense, how can I help?" he asked.
"I don't know what to say, if what Alistair has written is true, then the compass and the energy determined that you would be able to help me somehow," Ellie replied, feeling sorry for

her friend as she could see the pressure he suddenly felt he was under.

"It makes no sense, I'm not special, I don't know anything," he slid the compass back across the table in frustration. It stopped next to the telescope. "Read the next one," he snapped.

Ellie wanted to say something, to comfort her friend and to try and help, but she did not know what to say. She decided to do as he had asked and moved on to the third note.

"The telescope, like the compass, has two functions. The first will allow you to check the energy flow from the key stone in the garden of this house, and the folly. It should be constant. If you line up the tube with the symbol on the stone, the energy should flow through it and up to the folly. I have never tested it with any other stone but have no reason to believe it would not work. The second function, it will allow you to see into Imaginari from our world."

Ellie stopped, her hands shaking a little.

"What is it?" Annabelle asked, concerned. She took Ellie's hand.

"Seeing into Imaginari isn't meant to be possible, they can see us but not the other way around."

Dan reached forward and picked up the telescope, held it up to his eye and looked. To the others, Ellie included, it looked as though he was looking at Tyler, who waved comically.

"I can't see you, mate," Dan said.

"What can you see?" Tyler asked.

"Grey? Nothing but grey?" Ellie asked, knowingly.

Dan lowered the telescope, "Yes, how did you know that?"

"That's Imaginari. Grey mist and smoke, nothing else."

"That sounds boring," Tyler commented.

"When thought of like that, yes, it is," Ellie agreed. "It's beautiful though, completely silent and has the ability to create anything. Anything at all that you can imagine. A world where you can think and create, enjoy and share memories and thoughts. Anything you want, and it is done, you just can't touch it."

Ellie was staring into space now, it was the first time she had considered the beauty of the place. She had been there twice but had not appreciated the wonder and beauty of it until now.

"Sounds amazing," Leo commented, snapping Ellie out of her trance.

"It is, it's beautiful," Ellie agreed.

There was a moment of silence, whilst they all processed this, and Ellie felt for a moment that everyone was on the same page. They had to beat the Man. Ellie put down the page and picked up the final one, "Shall I read the last one?"

Everyone nodded silently.

She looked down at the paper and began to read.

"Finally, I want to tell you who I am and hopefully explain why you should listen to me. I do not know if listening to me is guaranteed to help. But I do know that not listening to me will definitely not help."

Ellie looked up, "Why can't anyone just talk normally?" She commented, the others smiled slightly which was comforting to Ellie, she carried on.

"My name is Alistair, and I am a member of the council of Mow though I am soon to be removed from their ranks. The reason they wish to remove me is they feel I have taken our tasks too seriously and therefore am now mocking them. This could not be further from the truth – I am actually more involved and have explored and discovered more than any of the previous councils, combined. I was able to travel to Imaginari, explore and bring back the items explained in the previous pages. I took those items to the council, but they simply mocked me and threw me out of the meeting. Since then, I have not been invited back. I have however been tracking the Man and have found what I believe to be a weakness that can be exploited."

There was a sudden sense of excitement in the room, Ellie could sense it even if nobody was saying anything.

"I now know more about him, having spoken to Christian and other spirits in Imaginari and have been piecing things together.

First, the prison realm, the one with all the purple vapor was made by the Guardians to try and contain him. It was built as a holding area and the spirit code around it was written so that he must pass through it in order to move between worlds. Other spirits and I can move directly between Imaginari and our world."

"Is that true?" Annabelle asked.

Ellie looked up, "I have no idea. I have only ever seen him in the prison realm, the two times I have been to Imaginari I have gone straight there. So, I guess?" it made sense to her, but it was based purely on this note and her own assumptions. She looked back down at the paper to carry on reading.

"Second, he must have a person that is an only child from a specific family, their DNA needs to be exactly right, and they must be willing to help him. He cannot force it out of them."

Ellie nodded to herself, taking this as reassurance that all the information about why it was her, and her family, to be correct.

"Thirdly, his power. We know the power from the spirits comes from living things in our world, and from dreams and imagination. But I was trying to work out how he was so powerful here. He is surrounded by living things here, and they all create and push energy into Imaginari, so this could be why he is so powerful? I have followed him, and with the help of Christian in his world, we have been able to identify a weakness. The key stones. The five stones placed around the hill were put there by him before the folly was built. He put them in place to amplify his power and enhance it when he was in our world."

Ellie stopped reading for a second, "That makes sense, he put them there when he bullied the first council, with Abijah. He made those stones crucial to this hill and the folly so that they would always be here to help him."

"Didn't your family try and move yours?" Leo asked.

"Yes, not long after we moved in, it wouldn't budge," Ellie replied. "When I went back to the time of Abijah, I saw the stones get made by the Man, he used immense power to do it, it was insane."

"Does that mean we need more power than that to destroy them?" Annabelle added.

Ellie looked down and scanned the last few lines, "Listen."

"We, Christian and I, believe that if the stones are destroyed he will no longer be able to reform, so the next time he is defeated after that he will be gone for good."

"Right. Destroy the stones that we can't destroy, beat the Man that we don't know how to beat, and get help from those that we can't reach?" Dan commented factually, making Ellie look up from the page, "Sounds easy when put like that, doesn't it?"

Ellie nodded, "That's about the size of it."

She stood and moved to the kitchen window, putting the page down on the table as she did so, looking out at the stone in the garden. It was dark now, night was setting in, but she could make out the cold hard stone in the darkness. She looked in the direction of the folly, she could not make it out, but she knew where it was.

"What do we do then?" Annabelle asked from the table, "Ellie, what do you want to do?"

Ellie turned, but before she could reply there was a blinding flash from behind her friends at the table. They all jumped up and whirled round, now all facing towards the direction of the light. At first, all they could do was shield their eyes, then as they adjusted their eyes, and the light began to fade, Ellie could make out two shapes in the light. Two human shapes, and before they said anything Ellie knew who they were. Ellie took a step forward, putting herself between her friends who had retreated in fear now, and the two bodies of light.

"Guardians?" she asked, semi confidently.

Initially there was no reply from the glowing white shapes. The light had faded now, and they were now just two gently glowing human shapes in the kitchen. Ellie could sense the fear in her friends and desperately wanted to help reassure them, "Everyone stay calm," she said softly, not taking her eyes off the figures.

"Seriously?" Dan shouted from somewhere to Ellie's right, "How can you be so calm?"

"Because this is what I deal with regularly, Dan. Trust me," Ellie stated.

"How do you know it's not, him?" Leo added.

It was a valid question, and in truth Ellie did not have an answer that would have been helpful at this stage. She decided to lie and say something that may help her friends.

"Because if it was, I think we would be dead by now. He is more of a wham bam kind of spirit," she smiled to herself, amused that she was able to say something so casual in a situation that to everyone but her was not ordinary.

"Guardians," she addressed the spirit shapes again, "If I am right and it is you, say something. If you trust me you can trust my friends, I vouch for them. Why have you come?"

For a moment there was no reply, then a voice spoke in her mind, the same as if she was in Imaginari.

"We are here, to warn you."

Ellie looked round, judging by her friends faces, they had heard it too. As if reading her mind Annabelle mouthed 'I heard it.' This fact alone comforted Ellie slightly, they were here to talk to them all, that was a positive step. She turned back to the spirits.

"Warn me about what? I already know that he is preparing himself, and that I am going to have to battle him soon."

"Soon, is sooner than you think," came the chilling reply.

"Tonight," came a second voice, "He is preparing for the final stages of his plan."

"Tonight?" Ellie asked, a tone of panic in her voice.

"Can't Ellie just run?" Simon asked, she looked at him, a look of confusion on her face. Simon addressed the spirits directly, "If she runs, and stays away from him, he can't use her spirit, can he?"

"Soon he will be too powerful for that rule to hold true, he will be able to break down the barrier once he has destroyed you."

"Great. So now even that won't work," Ellie cursed.

"We have been watching, we know what you have discovered

and can tell you we believe it to be true," the soft voice continued.

"What?" Ellie asked.

"The stones," came the reply. "He made them using a mixture of energy from our world and they may hold the key to his survival, and destruction."

"How can we destroy them?" Leo asked, taking the question straight out of Ellie's mouth.

"You can't, not on your own," the first voice replied.

"You will need help; you will need to repeat what he has done in making them."

"That makes no sense," Annabelle stated, Ellie felt the same way.

"What do you mean?" she asked.

"You will need to use many things, the same way he did, to allow you to destroy them," the Guardian replied.

"Time is against you, Eleanor. He is ready, he will soon have taken over us, he has traced us here."

"Here? As in my house?" Ellie exclaimed.

"He will not harm you here, but he will be ready for you."

"Is he going to kill you?" Ellie asked bluntly.

"Yes, he is."

Ellie did not know what to say, before she could though, the Guardians spoke once more.

"We will help you create a tool to destroy the stones, we three must work together to do that. We need the perfect item and the perfect alignment of power and application from us, together."

Ellie was confused, the constant riddles were beginning to become annoying, "What do we need?" she asked simply.

"You need an item that is from your world, that we can relate to the Man, that we can then lace with energy together."

"It will be the last thing we can do before he destroys us, Eleanor. We must act fast."

Ellie turned to her friends, "Ideas?" she asked in desperation. They all had the same awe struck and fearful expressions which Ellie fully understood.

"We need something physical," she said aloud, "From our world, that relates to the man that we can attach a power to."

"We don't have anything do we?" Annabelle asked.

Ellie shook her head but was also searching her mind for any kind of idea, a flash of inspiration. "Think," she said to her friends. "All the conversations we have had, all the places we have been, things we have tried. We must have something?"

"I assume we can't use the telescope or compass?" Leo asked.

Ellie assumed not, but before she could say as much the Guardians spoke for her.

"No, they are already assigned a task, this must be a new item," the voice continued. "It must be something that can form a link, a chain of energy from itself to the stone. Something that can hold energy and deploy it when needed."

"A chain?" Ellie said aloud, "We don't have anything like that, do we?"

She looked at her friends, first at Annabelle, then Leo and Tyler followed by Dan and finally Simon. All had the same blank, helpless look except for Simon. Ellie looked at him, he had the same mysterious look he had the day they had met on the hill.

"What?" Ellie asked.

"Ellie, have you ever lied to me?" he asked bluntly.

This question sent a shockwave of silence across the room, everyone turned to look at Simon.

"Is now really the time, Simon?" asked Annabelle.

"What do you mean?" Ellie asked.

"I can think of one thing that fits the description of what we need, but if you have never lied to me then it is lost already."

Ellie was baffled, "What on earth are you talking about?"

"The first year you were here," Simon explained, "When all this began, at the Halloween party at school, you were wearing something that you took off and threw away in front of me. Did it stay thrown away?"

Ellie froze on the spot, instantly understanding what Simon meant.

"What is he going on about?" Tyler asked of Annabelle.

She shook her head, "No idea. Either of you want to bring us up to speed?"

"He is referring to the necklace, the symbol of Mow necklace that I wore for a while. He made me take it off and throw it away that night."

"Didn't that get destroyed on the hill?" Dan asked.

"That was the one from the tin, the other one, my one, Simon made me throw it away."

"Ok..." Annabelle replied, as if waiting for more information.

"Well, Ellie?" Simon asked. "Did it stay thrown away?"

Ellie did not answer, she turned and left the kitchen calling back, "Nobody move."

They did not.

Ellie ran upstairs into her room and crossed to her jewellery box. She opened it and rummaged right to the bottom. There it was, a golden chain with an 'M' encased in a circle dangling from it. She felt guilty, the instant feeling of shame spread across her body like a winters chill. She had thrown it in the bin that night, but then later on had gone back to retrieve it. She had kept it hidden and secret ever since. She had never known why, but right now she was glad that she had. After another moment she turned and ran back down the stairs as fast as she could. The scene was the same as when she had left it, her friends together facing two spirit Guardians.

"No, Simon," she stated. "It did not stay thrown away."

Simon's face fell, he was feeling a mix of relief that they had something to try, but anger that she had lied to him.

"I'm sorry, I swear I have never worn it."

He said nothing.

"Simon," she said as boldly as she dared. "If we make it through this you can yell at me, tell me off, and whatever you like. But please, help me. Tonight," her voice broke at the end, tears forming in her eyes. She was terrified of what was happening, but the thought of Simon being angry at her was worse than any other pain she had faced today.

He said nothing but nodded and smiled.

Ellie sighed and decided to move on and deal with that issue later. She turned to the Guardians.

"Will this work?" she asked, holding up the chain so the symbol dangled about eye height.

"Yes," came the simplistic reply. "Put it on the floor and stand with us around it."

Ellie did as they asked, she placed the necklace on the floor and stood with the Guardians. They moved slightly, making a circle around the necklace between the three of them.

"Link hands with us, form a circle," they instructed.

Ellie held out her hands and whilst she could not physically grab or feel the Guardians hands, she was aware of a tingle, a static charge flowing through them. Her friends gathered behind her, all wanting to see what would happen but also stay a safe distance as well.

"Relax, say nothing, and trust us," the Guardians spoke softly to Ellie.

Ellie nodded, although she was secretly wanting to scream with fear. For a few moments, nothing happened. Then without warning, the necklace began to glow. The golden chain starting to pulsate with purple light.

"Purple," Tyler whispered, "the same as the prison realm?"

Ellie did not reply, but she was assuming the same thing. As she stood in silence she felt a surge of energy flow up through the floor, into her feet and up through her body. It was a wave of power that made her body feel more alive than it ever had. The energy flowed up, into her arms and out to her hands. The moment it reached them it shot out of her fingertips and down towards the floor, into the necklace. Ellie looked and could see that the same thing was happening between the Guardians. The three of them had created three beams of purple energy flowing into the necklace. It pulsated and shined, glowing on the kitchen floor as if it was about to melt and dissolve. Ellie held on, shaking with energy and exhaustion, it was draining her, but she knew she had to hold strong. The purple light grew stronger, blinding, it reached a point of such brightness she had to close her eyes. Then, it was gone. As quickly as it had arrived it vanished. The Guardians lowered their arms and returned to be side by side. Ellie looked down, as she did so the last shades of purple faded out of the gold chain and into the floor.

"Can I pick it up?" she asked, softly.

"Yes. It is ready."

Ellie bent down and cautiously picked up the chain. It felt normal, no sparks, nothing.

"Keeping it in contact with the stones for long enough will

destroy them."

"How?" Ellie asked, still looking at the chain and symbol.

"It has been laced with the prison realm energy, the purple glow you all saw. When in contact with him, or the stones, it will dissolve them and banish them to the same place."

Ellie lowered her hand that was holding the necklace, "All we need to do, is put it on the stone?"

"Correct," one of the Guardians stated.

Ellie turned to walk to the garden, wanting to try this out right away. She made it to the door, her friends turning to follow behind with the Guardians unmoved in the kitchen. When she got to the door, and could see the stone, she stopped and turned to face the Guardians once again.

"Thank you," she said.

Before the Guardians could reply there was an ear shattering bang and blinding flash. Ellie shielded her eyes from the light. After a few moments, when her eyes had recovered, she could see that one of the Guardians was fading. Fading with a silver glowing hand protruding from their chest. Annabelle screamed, Simon and Leo jumped back whilst Tyler and Dan were stunned into silence. As Ellie watched, the silver hand had shaped itself into a fist and was rotating through the Guardian's fading spirit. Ellie took a step to the side, trying to peer round the spirits to see if the owner of the fist was in the room. There was nothing there. As if to confirm this there was another all too familiar voice now in her head.

"Foolish Guardian, did you really think you would be safe with her? That pathetic girl that you are all laying your hopes on?" The Man's voice boomed across the kitchen directly into the ears of those in the room.

Ellie looked at her friends; whatever relaxation and relief there was before had gone now and sheer panic and fear had set in, taking over.

"Let them go," Ellie pleaded.

As soon as she said it, she realised this was a mistake.

"Them you say?" came the Man's mocking tone. "I did not realise they were both there, they are even more foolish than I thought, staying together knowing that I want them both gone."

Ellie turned white as another hand appeared just to the left of the Guardian he had already caught. He was clearly trying to find the other and knew they would be next to each other. To her surprise though, the second Guardian, did not move, run or make any attempt to protect itself. It simply projected into Ellie's mind one last time.

"Eleanor, you can do this. Believe in yourself, use your physical strength and your spirit power. Create to destroy, follow your heart, your destiny, follow hope."

Ellie wanted to reply, but her throat had dried up and before she could muster anything to say the inevitable happened. The Man's hand shot out of the second Guardian's chest, twisted itself into a fist and began to rotate slowly.

"Finally," his voice, clear as if he was in the room. "I will soon have destroyed you all and I will have the power I need to destroy you, Eleanor Fields, and exact my victory over your world. There is nothing you can do to stop me, I am too powerful, and you are too weak, pathetic human playing God. I am a God, I am a spirit, I can create, and I can destroy. Now with the last Guardian's gone, you will die."

His silver hands glowed bright, strands of light flowed from all over the trapped Guardian's bodies, streaming into the Man's hands. Ellie knew that he was absorbing them and their power, and there was nothing she could do.

"I shall use the stones that have served me well one final time, I shall draw them to the hill, the folly, and use them to amplify my power. You cannot stop this."

There was a rumble from the ground, as if an earthquake was shaking the house and hill. Ellie quickly looked over her shoulder into the garden. The stone was shrinking into the ground, the way a whale disappears beneath the surface of the waves. Turning back to the kitchen Ellie needed to shield her eyes once more. The light grew brighter, as it reached its peak both Guardians let out a shriek of pain. It made Ellie and her friends cover their ears and collapse to the floor. They shielded their ears and eyes from the light and tried to block out the sound. Moments later there was another ear shattering bang, and the light was gone. Ellie opened her eyes and got to her feet, looking at where the Guardians had been moments before. She heard her friends doing the same behind her, but she was in a trance, frozen with fear and shock unable to move or speak.

"I am now more powerful than ever before," the Man's voice rang out, from nowhere in particular deafening the group of friends.

Ellie said nothing, she did not know what she could say. One thought kept revolving around her mind. Tonight, was the night it would all end, one way or another. Tonight, was the night my vision would come true and I will die.

CHAPTER 14

For a few moments, nobody said anything. Ellie was looking into the space where she had just seen the Guardians die, speechless. Her friends were astounded at what they had just seen and did not know how to comfort Ellie, or what they should say next. Ellie took some steps forward and sat at the table, her palms resting either side of the compass and telescope. Her mind was racing in a blur, and she did not know what to do.

Simon broke the silence, "That was a tough few minutes."

It was a poor conversation starter, and it did not inspire anyone else to comment right away.

Annabelle sat next to Ellie, putting her hand over hers on the table. Eventually she asked, "What do you want to do?"

Ellie looked at her, tears rolling down her cheeks, "I don't know. I don't know how we can do this."

"I have an idea," Leo commented.

Nobody responded.

"I'm serious," he replied, a little hurt at the lack of enthusiasm. "Yes, that was a really rough time, but we have a plan and a clear order of actions, don't we?"

The girls turned to look at him, "How can I beat him?" Ellie said, muffled by tears, her cheeks puffy and red. It was truly how she felt in that moment, she had felt lost and defeated before but never like this.

Simon stepped forward, clearly on the same wavelength as Leo, "We destroy the stones, then you take him on."

"How can we do that?" Annabelle asked, knowing Ellie was about to ask the same question.

"We have the necklace," Leo replied.

"But the stone is gone," Ellie shouted, slamming her fist down on the table in frustration.

"I know," Simon said, "That's a good thing." He smiled.

"How. Is. That. A. Good. Thing?" Ellie asked, doing her best to hold back the anger.

"He made a mistake, he has helped us," Leo added, moving to stand next to Simon, clearly wanting to help and support.

There was now a standoff between Ellie and Annabelle at the table, with Simon and Leo standing nearby. Tyler and Dan simply stood and watched open mouthed at what was unfolding before them.

"Waiting," Ellie said, tapping her fingers on the table, anger beginning to take over now.

"He said he wanted to use the stones, yes?" Simon said.

Ellie and Annabelle nodded.

"He wanted all of them, near the folly. Correct?" Leo added.

Annabelle nodded again, Ellie did not.

Leo and Simon looked at each other and grinned.

"He has taken the stones to the folly, they are now all in one place," Simon stated excitedly. "That was his mistake, he has underestimated you again, Ellie."

There was a pause whilst everyone took this in. Ellie softened, processing what Simon was saying.

"He may still be tough to beat, and we are still up against it, but his arrogance again has made it easier for us. They are all together, instead of spread for miles over the hilltop," Leo finished off.

The two boys looked very pleased with themselves that they had figured this out and were like two schoolboys waiting for praise for doing great homework. Ellie wiped the tears from her cheek, sniffed, and stood. Instinctively Simon and Leo took a step back. Ellie was straight faced and looked calm and calculated. Simon shifted slightly on the spot. She took some steps towards them both until she was right in front of them. Looking from one to the other she said, "That is why you bring me hope," she smiled a beaming smile and wrapped them in a hug.

The boys relaxed, relieved that she was not angry with them. Ellie felt a spark of hope; Annabelle, Tyler, and Dan moved over and joined the three turning it into a group hug between all six of them. There, in her family's kitchen, Ellie felt safe, secure, and protected. She had friends. She had hope.

Shortly after, they were set and ready to go up the hill to the folly. They were sat around the table, Simon had taken charge and was explaining a plan to the others, they were all listening intently to him.

"Ellie, you are the only one that can fight him. You need to hold him off and keep him distracted whilst we destroy the stones with the necklace. If we understand the Guardians correctly, he can't die until the fifth and final stone is destroyed."

"Why do you say that?" Annabelle asked, "Surely if she gets the chance to kill him off, she should take it?"

"Normally, I'd say the same-" Simon replied.

Leo interjected, "But the Guardians said the stones must be destroyed before he dies, that was the only way. Could be a language thing but I don't think we can take the risk, can we?"

Ellie nodded, "I agree, we need to stick with what they said as best we can."

"Right," Simon continued. "We need to take everything, the compass, telescope, necklace, all of it."

Ellie patted her pocket, "I have the compass and telescope."

"I've got the necklace," Annabelle stated.

"Ok," Simon looked at his friends, finally resting his eyes on Ellie. "I'm sorry this is all on you, I think I speak for all of us when I say we will do what we can. But I think it is safe to say that most of the pressure here-" he stopped, as if not wanting to finish off the sentence.

"Is on me," Ellie finished for him. "I know, and it sucks, but knowing you all have my back is enough. We have a chance, we have hope." She winked at Simon, "That's good enough for me." She put her fist into the middle of the table, "Lame team fist bump thing?" she asked her friends, a wry smile on her face.

They all smiled, but all put their hands in.

"We are with you, Ellie," Annabelle said.

"No matter what," was Tyler's comment.

"You got this," Leo and Dan said together.

"We love you," was all Simon managed, holding back a lump in his throat.

"Ok. Let's go finish this," Ellie said, defiantly standing up and heading out of the kitchen.

The others followed, and in single file they left the house. They had prepared for the cold winters night, and it was a good job. The sky was clear and there was a bitterly cold wind that had a vicious bite as soon as they left the warmth of the house. Ellie led them on the most direct route, as picturesque as the village and surrounding views were at night, this was not the time for sightseeing. The group walked in silence, in pairs, up the roads and paths of the hill. Ellie and Annabelle in front, Simon and Tyler in the middle, with Dan and Leo at the back. Ellie took the time to focus, she needed to clear her mind and be as prepared as she could ever be. She had done all she could, but she knew that it was going to take all her strength, and an awful lot of luck to beat him. In truth, Ellie was hoping that her instincts would take over and she would know what to do when the time was right. As they walked, she could sense the energy around her. She tried to remember that, imagine channeling it all through her body to use in a fight. It was only at this moment that she realised she had never actually been in a fight. She had come close as many a child does, but she had never actually had to fight anyone. Ellie silently prepared herself for this, she had focused on physical strength and endurance but not any kind of skill. Would that matter? Only time would tell. As quickly as she could she pushed that thought from her mind. She needed a clear head and to be focused on positive energy and her goal. Defeating the Man. They followed the path, the folly in sight nearly all the time. Ellie would occasionally glance up at it, expecting to see the Man's floating figure. There was nothing, no sign nor sound that was out of the ordinary. This was both comforting and distressing at the same time. Ellie felt a weight of pressure building on her, and she knew that soon it would burst.

They reached the top of the hill, the only thing that was higher was the folly itself. They spread out, all looking out over the hillside for anything unusual.

"Anyone see anything?" Ellie called out.

"Nothing here," Simon called back.

"Nope," Leo and Dan shouted.

"Same," Tyler agreed.

There was no reply from Annabelle though, Ellie turned to face her.

"Annabelle?" she asked and headed over to her.

"I'm pretty sure they are new," Annabelle called back.

The others followed Ellie to where Annabelle was. She was looking down the side of the hill towards the car park and pointing to something about halfway down. A small circle of stones, five in total, in a circle.

"That's them," Ellie called excitedly, and immediately ran down the hill towards them, for a moment forgetting everything else.

The others followed and within a few seconds they were all at the circle of stones, Ellie in the middle, the others around the outside of the circle.

"These are the key stones," she said confidently.

"Well, they weren't here earlier," Leo agreed.

"Now what?" Dan asked.

Ellie looked around, "Anyone else bothered with how quiet it is?"

Their silence said they all felt the same way.

"Do we just put it on them then?" Annabelle asked, breaking the silence in the group.

Looking at her, Ellie shrugged, "I guess so. Try it."

Annabelle swallowed, now appreciating that by carrying the necklace up the hill she had volunteered to use it. She reached forward, holding the necklace chain in both hands as if she was placing a medal around the top narrow part of the stone. They all held their breath, Annabelle held the chain over the top of the stone in front of her. When it was lined up, she looked at Ellie, who nodded. Annabelle dropped the chain and it landed around the stone with a satisfying jingle sound, the 'M' landing facing inwards towards Ellie. Instinctively, the group all flinched a little, as if expecting an explosion of sound and light. Nothing happened. For a few moments nobody dared breathe or speak. Still nothing. Ellie relaxed and took a step forward towards the stone that now had the chain around it, the symbol facing her on the inside of the circle. She peered at the symbol, leaning in as close as she dared. She was about to stand up and say something when she noticed the faintest of purple glows emitting from the golden 'M' on the chain. She smiled to herself and lifted herself to her full height.

"Just wait a second," she said, knowing that nobody else had seen it yet.

As she watched, the purple light grew brighter and began to emit not just from the symbol but from the chain itself. After a few seconds, they could all see it. Annabelle had moved around the edge of the circle so as to be behind Ellie for the best view. Dan and Simon had done the same. As they watched, the chains light grew brighter and brighter, and soon the stone began to emit a strong hum through the ground. Ellie could feel the vibrations and hear the sound flowing through her and all around. It grew louder and brighter, Ellie started to squint, but before the light reached a level of blinding the friends, there was an ear-shattering bang. With a flash of light, the stone vanished into purple dust, the necklace fell to the floor with a gentle thud, softly resting on the grass. They stood in silence, watching as the faint purple dust fell to the ground.

"Wow," Annabelle spoke first, "That was, wow."

They all nodded, speechless.

Then Ellie came to her senses, "He will know now. We need to do the others, and fast."

She took a step forward and picked up the necklace. She turned to her left to place it around the second stone. Just as she was about to lay the chain around it there was a blinding light and a blast of air that sent them all sprawling. Ellie fell down the bank, her friends scattered across the hill side, none of them now near the stones. Ellie scrambled to her feet and was instantly aware of two things. The first, she was no longer holding the necklace, she must have dropped it during the roll down the hill. The second was that the Man had appeared, just above the circle of stones. Ellie reacted first.

"Guys?" she called out, hoping someone else had been able to get to their feet.

"Yeah?" Simon called.

"Simon, look at where I am," she needed to get a message to him without tipping off the Man, she also closed her fist as if holding something very important, bringing it up to her chest. "You'll be pleased to know, the thing you wanted thrown away, has been thrown away again."

Knowing instantly what she meant Simon did not reply, he took as strong a mental picture as he could of where Ellie was. The necklace must be somewhere between the stone circle and where she was now, he realised this just in time. For moments later the Man spoke, his voice booming over the hilltop like a stadium announcer.

"Foolish girl. Did you really think I would let you in so easily, you cannot destroy all the stones that way, I shall not allow it."

Ellie remembered the plan, no matter how scared she was she needed to keep him busy and distracted. "Then why not prove it? Take me on," she called back, surprising herself.

"You dare challenge me?" he demanded of her.

"I'm not scared."

"You should be, now you shall die."

Ellie had seconds to take one last look at her friends. They were all on their feet and were watching, helpless at the short exchange. She focused on the one she loved, Annabelle. She realised now that she had not told her that she loved her. Now was the only chance she may get.

"Annabelle," she called out. "I-" but she never got the chance to finish.

Mid-sentence the Man had swooped down and slammed himself into Ellie's chest, the force should have sent her flying backwards, but to her friends, Ellie just vanished. The moment that he made contact with her, the two figures vanished with a flash, leaving the five of them scattered over the hill side.

"No," Annabelle screamed, "Ellie!" she collapsed to her knees, tears rolling down her face.

Simon was the only one who acted. He loved Ellie, but he needed to take over their part of the plan. He needed that necklace.

"Move," he shouted to the others, "We need to find that necklace and destroy these, remember. We don't know how long we have to do this, so move!"

His words seemed to bypass the brains of his friends and go straight to their legs like a command. They immediately descended on the space where Ellie was and began to search for the precious necklace, not knowing how long they had or indeed if they would ever find it.

CHAPTER 15

Ellie opened her eyes and got to her feet as quickly as she could. She had not expected him to attack as quickly as he had, but she had thought he would bring her here at some point. The prison realm, the place she now knew had been created as a way to stop him moving easily between worlds. This was his domain, he felt most powerful here. She looked around, but he was nowhere to be seen. Had he gone back to finish the job, keeping her here and out of the way?

"I know you're here," she said to the open space, it moved in the same way she remembered, purple vapour everywhere, moving the way steam does above a teacup. "Show yourself," it was braver than she felt.

Moments later there was a hissing sound, covered with an evil cackle. As Ellie watched, the Man's form began to take shape in front of her, creating the shining white figure that she knew too well. Ellie took a step back and readied herself, she did not know what she would do, but she knew she had to do something.

"You are getting braver," he said in his cool, mocking tone. "I am impressed. It makes no difference, mind."

"Even though I know your secret, and can destroy the key stones now?" Ellie was not sure if this was a wise move, but she had said it now so needed to go with it.

"True, that was unexpected, I am impressed that you have been able to make such things, even if those pesky Guardians helped you."

There was a tone to his voice when he said 'Guardians', as if it made him feel sick to have the word pass his lips.

"I have told you before, having help is a good thing," Ellie said defiantly.

"Rubbish. I do not need anyone."

"That hasn't gone so well for you before though, has it?" Ellie was trying to use time; she knew that her friends would be frantically trying to find the necklace and destroy the other stones. But how would she know when they had? They had not counted on being separated like this. Ellie knew it would end here eventually, but this was a hiccup in their plan indeed.

"You cannot destroy them whilst you are here though, can you?" he mocked. "And I think your friends are not as faithful as you think they may be."

Ellie faltered, he was just trying to unnerve her, but she needed to stay focused. "You're still not taking me on though, are you scared?"

This it appeared, was a statement too far.

"I do not need to fight you, Eleanor," he boomed. "I am going to destroy you the way you would destroy an ant."

He flicked his wrist, and instantly Ellie was bound tight, her wrists being pulled down forcing her to her knees. As she struggled, her ankles were also forced together and held fast to the moving purple floor. Ellie struggled but it was no use, she was held tight, unable to move, unable to free herself and fight.

The Man moved down to within inches of her face, "You will watch as your world burns," he snarled. He moved away, turning his back on Ellie and holding his hands out to his sides. "I shall create a window to your world, so you can see what happens as I destroy it and all you care for. And do not worry, it will be in real time, not the silly time delay nonsense you see from Imaginari. But do not try and communicate through it, sound cannot travel through this window, only light."

Ellie cleared her mind and relaxed as best she could, ignoring the restraints, she needed to focus and stay as calm as possible. The Man moved to the side to face her, he had created the window, she could see the folly from above and she could see what was happening now.

"You see, girl," he teased her, "You will watch as your friends mourn you and then perish at my hand."

Ellie looked, and instantly had a small spark of hope. She could indeed see her friends, but they were not mourning, they were searching.

"Anything?" Annabelle asked, desperation setting in.

They had been searching the hilltop for what felt like hours with no sign.

"No," came the disappointing replies from Simon, Leo, and Dan.

Tyler appeared over the crest of the hill, "Nothing here either," he added.

"Where the hell is it?" Annabelle asked. "Ok, I'm going to recreate what happened," she walked up the hill defiantly and stood in the centre of the circle of stones, now with a gap where one had been destroyed. "Ellie was leaning over this one, yeah?" she asked.

"Yes," Simon confirmed, as he and the others reached the ring of stones.

"She was facing this way, he then blasted her, us, backwards," she turned. "She flew down that way, didn't she?"

The boys nodded.

"Simon, go down and stand where she was when he took her, let me see the line of sight from here to there."

Simon did as she asked.

"If you had flown backwards, from here to there," Annabelle called out, "It must be somewhere between us, surely?"

"Unless," Leo muttered, turning away and walking at a diagonal from the circle of stones.

"Unless, what?" Annabelle asked, a frustrated tone to her voice.

"Well, she was pushed back yeah?" Leo replied, "So, her arms would have been blown sideways, meaning her wrist could have flicked the necklace over here somewhere."

He was looking near some bushes about thirty meters from the stones, but at an angle from where Simon was.

"How do you know which hand she had it in?" Tyler asked.

"I don't," Leo replied, "But I know I'm right."

"How?" Annabelle asked.

"Because the necklace is right here," Leo exclaimed, turning around with a beaming smile on his face, holding the chain aloft.

Annabelle grinned and clapped her hands together, "Great, now get it up here fast you ninny."

Leo chuckled but did as he was told and moved quickly back up the hill to the stones. As soon as he got there, he placed the chain around one of the other stones, the five friends watched and waited. The same thing happened, after a few moments of nothing, the purple light grew brighter, creating vibrations that moved through the floor like sound through a wall. After a few more seconds, the stone shattered into purple dust.

"Quick, the next one," Annabelle said, reaching down to pick up the necklace and move it along. She knew there was no time to waste.

Ellie had seen the second stone be destroyed, but the Man had not. He had been too busy looking at her, wanting to see a sign of weakness, of desperation, and defeat. She needed to keep him focused on her, to buy her friends as much time as she could.

"What do you want? Do you want me to beg for my life, is that it?" she asked, trying to force herself to cry, to make herself seem weak. "Do you want me to ask that you spare me, my friends, and family? Say that I'll let you win if they can live?"

He chuckled, "My dear girl, I do not want you to live. I want you to die, remember. You and your meddling friends," he started to turn back towards the window.

"Wait," Ellie shouted.

He stopped and looked at her.

"What if, what if I can help you?" she asked, thinking on the spot. Her friends had managed to destroy another stone, that was three of five gone.

"Help me? How? Why?" he asked, clearly confused but keeping his gaze on Ellie none the less.

"I can see now; I see that you will win. You will always win, nothing I can do will stop it. So, maybe if I help you, you'd be willing to spare my friends?" Ellie felt sick to say the words, but she knew she had no choice, all she needed was time.

He cackled, "You think I would do that?" he asked, a cold tone to his voice. "You think that I would allow your friends to live?"

"Maybe," Ellie responded, sheepishly.

"Not a chance, they will die, and for your stupidity I shall ensure that your precious Annabelle not only dies last but gets to watch as your other friends' crumble to dust."

This hit Ellie like a bullet, and she immediately lost her focus. In the split seconds that she had done so the Man turned back towards the window and saw the fourth stone about to dissolve to purple dust.

"What? How is this possible?" he exclaimed, "What did you do, girl?"

Ellie smiled. He may have noticed but her friends had done her proud.

"No matter, I shall put a stop to this," with a wave of his hand the window moved further away and became bigger, it expanded and expanded until it was the same size as the real thing. If Ellie had not been so terrified she would have been impressed, she was now watching a huge window to her world, so big it was life size. She knew that he was about to pass through and she was powerless to stop him. If he made it, her friends would be done for and there would be nothing to stop him. But what could she do? Ellie closed her eyes and tried not to think, she tried to clear her mind of her fears. Ellie breathed deeply, trying to work out what she could do.

What can I do? she asked herself, in her mind.

Ellie tried to recall anything and everything that had been said to her by the Guardians and spirits alike. Then one thing came to mind as clear and loud as a bell on a quiet day.

Find your question.

It was an odd thought, but in Ellie's mind it seemed to carry weight, it seemed to mean something. She went with it, 'My question, isn't to ask for help, or to beg. That's not me,' Ellie thought, 'But I do need guidance. I need someone to show me the way. Just a little extra help,' this seemed garbled, but at the same time as clear as day to Ellie. 'If I was getting ice

cream, I know what I want. I just need someone to show me where it is.' This amused her, Ellie felt a smile cross her face, 'Who can help me?' she asked. To Ellie's surprise, a voice that was not too dissimilar than hers spoke in her own mind.
"I can."
Ellie opened her eyes, there was nobody there, the Man was still moving towards the window and was nearly there. She tried to make sense of what had just happened, 'Who are you?' she thought, keeping the communication in her mind.
"I am you; I am you from Imaginari. I am your spirit to control and command. I am here to help, to help you find your ice cream."
Ellie nearly laughed out loud at this but kept her cool, 'Ok, can you get me out of these?' she asked.
There was no reply, but moments later Ellie felt the restraints release and she was free. She stood, as silently as possible wanting to keep the element of surprise over him.
'How does this work?' she asked.
"We are one," came the reply, "You do not need to talk to me, you can simply act, and I will act with you. I am your subconscious spirit from Imaginari. I am you."
'We can do this, can't we?' Ellie asked, seeking reassurance as best she could.
She did not wait for a reply, she knew she needed to act now as the Man was almost at the threshold of the window. Ellie took a chance. She started to run. She ran to her right and then started bending her run to the left, her idea was that she would meet the man from the side just as he reached the window but doing it like this would keep her in his blind spot. She was banking on him being so arrogant to not check on her, that he was so furious with her friends that he would ignore everything else. To Ellie's delight, moving in the realm was silent, there was no noise of her feet on the floor, all she had to do was keep her breathing as quiet as possible. She built up speed, pushing as much as she could to run as fast as possible. He was about to cross the threshold, three steps away, two, one. Ellie stopped, but in stopping willed her spirit to keep going with the full force of her speed slamming into the Man. The combined force of her run and

the spirit following behind was like a train, the force sent him sprawling sideways to the floor away from the window. Ellie regained her composure and stood tall.

"Going somewhere?" she asked confidently, her spirit returning to her side.

"Impossible," he stammered.

"I'm just getting started," Ellie replied, and with a swing of her arm, sent her spirit towards him once again, slamming through him keeping him pinned down. Ellie glanced behind her at the window, the fourth stone had just vaporised. One more to go. She turned back just in time to see the Man getting to his feet, instinctively she summoned her spirit and it slammed through him from behind, forcing him down once more.

"Remember how I did this before, with Emilia's help?" Ellie teased, "I've got the hang of this now."

She gestured and forced her spirit back towards him again, the Man was ready this time though. He leapt to his feet and reached out a hand grabbing Ellie's spirit by the throat. The moment he did so, Ellie felt as if the cold hand was around her own neck, she clasped at it, unable to breathe.

"Girl, you do not even know the beginning of my powers, or what I am capable of," he moved his arm out to the side, holding Ellie's spirit out by the throat like a doll as he did so. "Do you remember what a splice is? When I made Emilia from you?"

Ellie could not respond, she could not breathe and panic was starting to set in.

"Well, let's do that again shall we, but in a far more permanent way."

He raised his other hand and gave a gentle gesture that Ellie did not recognise. A blue line appeared, joining Ellie to her spirit by the chest, each end being where the heart would be.

"First, a little transfer I think," he made a fist and pulled from Ellie to her spirit.

To Ellie, everything went black. She lost all feelings, sight, and sounds for a second. When she came around, the feeling of being choked was still in her throat, but she was no longer in her body. Ellie was now being held by the throat inches from the Man's face. She looked around, her limp body was now only being held up by the blue light joining the spirit to it, her head and hands floppy like a rag doll.

"What?" she stammered. It was all she could manage to say.

He laughed, "I have transferred your consciousness from your physical body to your spirit, from Imaginari. You are now contained within this form, unable to return to that pathetic physical girl."

Ellie looked at her body, she was stunned and did not know what to do. Behind it, she could see her friends placing the necklace on the fifth and final stone.

"The best part," the Man mocked. "Is that you cannot return to your world in this form, and if you are separated from your body for too long, this spirit will die. Slowly of course, but it will happen. Now watch as your world burns," he threw Ellie, in her spirit form, across the realm where she fell in a heap on the floor.

As she looked up, he had moved over to the window and had flung her body through it, into the real world. He turned to face her.

"Farewell, Eleanor. Please feel free to watch," he cackled and moved through the window into the world where her friends were desperately trying to help her.

Ellie hurried over to the window, now floating rather than walking and tried to move through it. She could not. It was as though she was stuck on the wrong side of a huge sliding door that she could not open. She banged her fists on it and screamed out in frustration. As she watched, the Man descended on her friends, slamming them all to one side as he had before. Except this time, he picked up the necklace himself.

Annabelle scrambled to her feet first. She had not seen the Man arrive but knew they were in trouble. There was still one stone to go, and as she looked round, she saw him bending down and scooping the necklace into his hand.

"I have never seen an item like this before," he said, "Clever, very clever indeed."

"Where is Ellie?" Annabelle asked, defiantly. Taking a few

steps forward, she could see her friends getting to their feet and taking in the surroundings.

The Man turned to face her, "I'm very sorry Annabelle, but Eleanor will not be joining us. Well, her body will but her mind and spirit are, shall we say, lost."

He gave a gentle motion of his hand, as if directing Annabelle. Her eyes followed the direction he was gesturing, her heart sank. Lying on the floor, looking as white as a sheet, was Ellie. Annabelle hurried over, collapsed at her side putting Ellie's head on her lap.

"Ellie?" she cried out, "Come on, come back to me. I need you."

The boys hurried over, keeping a wide berth of the Man who was simply floating by the remaining stone, taking in the surroundings.

"What did you do to her?" Annabelle asked.

"I corrected her. She will be no trouble now."

"You corrected her?" Simon challenged, his hands clenched into fists.

"Yes," the Man replied. "I have corrected a wrong that is being repeated billions of times on this world. Physical form is not needed, or rather, it is needed for your survival, but not for the benefit of others. So, I removed Eleanor from her physical form."

"What does that mean?" Annabelle asked through clenched teeth.

"I have killed her," he stated calmly, as if requesting a glass of water.

"No," Simon shouted back, "I don't believe it."

He knelt beside Ellie and felt her forehead. It was cold. He checked her pulse, but there was not one. Every moment that passed felt like an eternity. Annabelle was sobbing floods of tears now, unable to speak. Simon was holding them back through anger and rage, trying to think of something. He rummaged in Ellie's pockets and took out the compass and telescope.

"There has to be something," he shouted. The compass pointed at him, and only him. He threw it to one side, "Hope," he exclaimed, feeling the burden of his friends' death setting in. In a final act of defiance, he picked up the telescope and peered through it. Nothing. Nothing but grey mist wherever he looked. As far as he could tell, his friend was lost. He took her cold lifeless hand in his and kissed it, holding it close to his cheek.

"I'm sorry, Ellie. We let you down," he sobbed into her hand, then he collapsed onto Annabelle's shoulder, where they sobbed and cried as one.

Dan, Leo, and Tyler also broke down in tears, the five friends felt that everything was lost, without Ellie, even if they could get the necklace back, they could not defeat him. The Man had won.

CHAPTER 16

Ellie collapsed to the floor, defeated, deflated, and broken. She was furious at herself for getting as cocky as she had so quickly. Who was she kidding, trying to take him on like that?

"I should have just played for time," she said aloud. "All I had to do was keep him away, I couldn't even do that."

In her new spirit form, she could not cry tears, she had the feeling of them in her throat, and the build up of pressure in her mind, but she could not physically do it. It took Ellie a few moments to realise this, and in that time, she began to understand the frustration of not having a physical form. Yes, it was fun and magical that she could create and move things, but not being able to touch, feel, or even experience physical pain was a strange sensation. She looked at her hands, her now glowing hands. They had a golden shade to them, translucent though as she could see the purple vapour of the floor through them. She tried to put her head in her hands, but it fell straight through.

"Damn it," she shouted, lifting herself to her feet.

Ellie looked through the window the Man had created, looking down on her world. It broke her heart to see Annabelle, Simon, and the others in mourning over her cold lifeless body. There was nothing she could do, she could not communicate with them nor pass through the portal to tell them she was ok, to keep fighting.

"What's the point?" she said, "Even if I could get there, we can't beat him." She had seen him pick up the necklace, "That was our only hope, and I blew it." Ellie turned away in shame, she could not watch her friends suffer like this, and if the

Man was true to his word, he would make them pay for her ignorance and failures. There was a realisation to this, the scene she had just turned away from matched her dream vision perfectly. Albeit a different angle, but it was the same. Her friends surrounding her body, the Man nearby gloating as he always did. It had come true after all. She moved away from the window, a vague attempt at blocking it from her mind and vision. What could she do now?

"Come on Ellie, think. You may not be able to beat him, but you don't have to give him the satisfaction of suffering either. What are your options?"

She looked around, in a room filled with nothing, surrounded by purple vapour, there were not many options to speak of.

"Can you get home? No," she stated to herself, as if doing a mental checklist. "Can you stay here? Yes, but do I want to? No," Ellie processed this as best she could, a methodical approach was soothing to her. "That leaves one then, Imaginari. Can I get there?" Ellie paused, the Man had stated that she could not get through the window into her world, but he had not mentioned her moving into Imaginari. Was it an oversight? Or had he not protected against that? "One way to find out," she stated and closed her eyes.

Whilst Ellie no longer had a physical form, she could still sense when her eyes were open or closed, and the darkness of them being closed was no different.

'I want to go to Imaginari,' she thought to herself.

She expected nothing to happen and to be at this for hours, trying over and over. But to her surprise, there was a gentle flowing sensation through her body. She imagined it would be the way water would feel as it flowed down a pipe, if water could feel that is. She opened her eyes, and never had she been so happy to see the grey landscape of Imaginari all around her. In her glowing form she felt like the brightest thing in the world. Ellie looked around and took in her surroundings, they were not unfamiliar to her. She was standing on what appeared to be a country road with high hedges on each side. The road was sloped slightly, and given there was nobody around, she decided to move up the incline. As before, Imaginari was silent and still, not a sound to be heard. Ellie was conscious that she would now be blending in more and with minimal effort and concentration she was able to turn her golden glow into a dull grey mist. From memory, this would make her match the other spirits that resided in Imaginari. Blending in was comforting to Ellie at the moment, being special and standing out had not got her far with the Man this time, maybe blending in was the way to go. Ellie carried on up the road until she reached a junction, the road she was on had met another giving her two options; left or right.

'Which way?' Ellie asked herself, the junction looked familiar to her, but she could not place why. Ellie turned to the left, and then to the right, neither way felt correct but neither felt wrong either, she was stumped and felt that she could not move until she knew of a certain route to take.

'Well this is a fine mess, isn't it Ellie?' she thought to herself, 'Can't even decide which way to go now can you? What hope did you have against him?'

She stopped herself, whatever happened next and going forward, Ellie realised that scolding herself at every opportunity was not going to help anyone. She shook her head in defiance of herself, then for no apparent reason, she repeated the last question in her mind.

'What hope did I have?'

Why did that stick in her mind so much?

'Hope. The compass, direction,' she thought excitedly and reached down to her pocket. Or rather, where her pocket was. Ellie's hand moved through her body like it was not there, because in physical terms, it was not.

'Damn it,' she thought to herself, 'I don't have it.' She turned on the spot, feeling more lost than ever as the desperation was beginning to set in. Then she stopped and thought calmly for a second, 'But, can I make it?'

The thought was a good one, she was in Imaginari after all, and she was now a spirit and they could allegedly create anything. 'Worth a try,' she decided.

Ellie put her palms together in front of her as if she was cupping water to drink from her hands. She closed her eyes once more and cleared her mind.

'Guidance, I need hope, and guidance. I need the compass that Alistair made.'

Her internal dialogue was strong now, she was used to just thinking to herself. Again, to her surprise, it took minimal effort. After a few moments Ellie opened her eyes and to her delight she was now holding the ghost like form of the compass in her hands. She could not feel it, but she could sense it, and whilst she knew that it was not physically real, to her mind it was there in her palms ready for her to use. She held it up to her face with one hand, every detail had been recreated; scratches on the casing, the size of the device, and its thin needle. Ellie smiled to herself, finally something positive. Next, was just to use it.

She held it out in front of her and thought, 'Guide me, give me hope.'

To her delight the needle spun once and then held firm in a position. She tested it by turning slowly on the spot, it kept pointing in the same direction. Grinning, she decided that the direction it had chosen was as good as any, she followed it. The needle was not pointing down one of the two routes specifically, but it was angled more to the left, so she went left.

The road carried on, the needle staying pretty much central to it once Ellie had rounded the first bend. What did surprise her is that she had not seen a single other spirit in her time there, were they avoiding her? Or just not around at the moment? It did not matter to Ellie, she was happy that she had some direction to follow, but where it was leading her she did not know. She also did not know how far away 'hope' was, would she be walking, floating, forever? Would she get there before her spirit form died as the Man had told her it would? These were just some of the questions that were pinging around in her mind. As Ellie moved along, the road levelled out and became less rural, buildings appeared, or at least the shape of them did, but there were still no spirits to talk to, greet her or even shout at her. The road straightened, and Ellie noticed that the needle had started to point to her right ever so slightly. She kept going, as she moved forwards the needle moved again as if it were actually pointing to something quite close that would soon be level with Ellie on her right-hand side. Shortly after, the needle was pointing directly to Ellie's right, she stopped and turned, making the needle point in front of her once more. She looked up. It was pointing at what would have been a gorgeous cottage. Even though it was made of grey mist, Ellie could make out intricate details all around it. The cottage had a small wooden effect door, a garden bursting with flowers and windows with an overhanging thatch roof. It was gorgeous, and Ellie concluded that if she had been asked to draw, or create, the picture postcard cottage; this was it.

'Why here?' Ellie asked, after allowing herself time to take in the view. She decided to investigate and moved forwards towards the gate. Instinctively, she went to open it with her hand, but it flowed straight through as did she. She smiled to herself, amused that she was making such silly errors. She reached the door and held her hand up to knock, then stopped.

'How do I knock?' she asked herself.

"You knock, by thinking of knocking," came a soft male voice in her head.

The sound made Ellie jump, after the silence and lack of contact this was truly a surprise.

'Do you live here?' she asked.

"I do, come in," the voice replied and instantly the door faded away, revealing an inside that was as quaint and picturesque as the outside.

Without hesitating, Ellie entered the building. She was greeted by a small staircase and short hallway with doors to the left and right.

"Come into the front room, the door on the right," the voice instructed.

Just as the front door had vanished, the door to Ellie's right did the same. She took one look behind her, the front door had appeared again, and then she decided to carry on. She moved into the room. Ellie was greeted with a modern looking space, basic furnishings and home comforts surrounded the walls with a small table in the middle. Ellie looked around and as she turned to her left, she saw what she assumed was the source of the voice in her head. A spirit was floating not far away, Ellie looked directly at it.

"Greetings, Eleanor." The voice said, "I am so glad we get to finally meet."

'Finally?' Ellie asked, confused.

"Our meeting was cut short last time, you needed to go soon after we said hello. I do not think that will happen this time."

'You're the spirit I met in the road, the last time I was here?' Ellie asked, putting the pieces together in her mind as she did so.

"Correct."

'You can help me then, can't you? They said that you could...'

"We will get to that," he interrupted, cutting Ellie short. "There is much to discuss, much to make sense of."

'Why are you here? Why do you make things look so, physical? How do you know me? Why are you watching me?'

"So many questions, all are valid, but we will deal with them and more, one at a time. Please sit."

This seemed strange to Ellie, why would they need to sit when they had no physical way of actually sitting. She decided not to argue and floated over to a chair and made the sitting motion. To her surprise, her spirit did just that and seemed quite at home, hovering above the seat in an apparent seating position. The other spirit did the same, and if anyone had looked in at that moment, they would have seen two grey ghost like forms apparently seated round a coffee table in a front room of a quaint little cottage.

"First, I think we should start with names, don't you?" he asked.

Ellie thought nothing, then decided to retort, 'You already know mine.'

"Indeed, I do, Eleanor Fields."

There was a pause, 'Do I get to know yours?'

"So direct, just as I knew you to be. Of course you do my name, is Christian Lloyd."

Ellie processed this, where had she heard that name before?

"I can sense you trying to place me, I fear you do know my

name and do know some of my story. Would you like me to bring you up to speed, with everything? Also, may I call you Ellie?"

'Yes, Ellie is fine. And that would be good, probably the first time anyone has done that in one go,' Ellie replied, relaxing a little.

"Very well. I believe there are two places you know my name from, there will be a third, but we can come to that later. The first is the notes from Alistair, the man who lived in your house before you. I am the one he was working with. Together we worked out that the Man had hidden part of his power in the stones, we created the compass and telescope."

Ellie shifted slightly, she had imagined putting the compass away when she walked into the house, she went to make it appear once more, but he stopped her.

"I know you used it to get here, child. Do not worry."

This only made Ellie a little uneasy, there was something familiar about this spirit, but she could not quite place it.

"The other place you will know me from is because of the excellent work that your friends did in researching the village of Mow Cop. They did find the articles of my disappearance did they not?"

This did hit home with Ellie, she remembered reviewing a list of names that had vanished without a trace from the hill.

'You were the first one that broke the pattern, and the last one to vanish I think?'

"Correct. I was the most recent and indeed the last one that the Man took from your world, our world."

'You mean, you were once human, like me?'

"Yes, I am not a true Imaginari spirit, I was made from my physical body and spirit when the Man took me. He imprisoned me here as punishment."

'Punishment?' Ellie was intrigued now, trying to piece it all together.

"For many things, I feel the need to tell you the full story, if you will allow me?"

Ellie nodded, 'If we have time? This sort of makes sense to what is going on with me right now. But my friends are in danger, and I think I am running out of time to stop him.'

"Thank you, I thought as much. I understand the current predicament, but remember time moves differently here. We have time."

There was a kindness to his voice, a gentle softness that seemed familiar and alien to Ellie at the same time. She sat and listened.

"This begins just under twenty years ago. The Man was trying to find a way to achieve his goal of absorbing all of the energy from our world, do you mind if I call it ours?"

Ellie shook her head.

"He wanted to destroy our world to use its energy to make this one physical, he had tried before as I'm sure you are aware. Millions of years ago, and then a couple of times in the last hundred years. Not to mention the time a few thousand years ago when he tricked Abijah into making the folly. All of this making sense to you?"

'Yes,' Ellie replied simply.

"Good, after the failure with Abijah he knew he needed a soul, he did not know it needed to be willing. He thought it needed to be a child willingly given. So, he was trying to find one. He was picking on unhappy people, angry people, lonely people. People that he thought he could manipulate into doing his bidding. Please know Ellie that I am not proud of why he chose me."

'Why did he choose you?' Ellie asked without thinking about it.

"Because I was unhappy. My new fiancé and I had just welcomed our baby boy into the world. We were tired, I was stressed with too much work and not enough pay. We were starting to struggle. She was not working you see as she was looking after our son. I was in a very dark place. It was not her fault and I am not proud of it, I never stopped loving either of them though. They were my world."

Ellie could only imagine what this felt like.

"It was a dark and rainy night, really bad storms had been hitting the area, I now know that was the Man all along," he continued. "Anyway, I was driving home from work. The night before we had argued, my fiancé and I, and I had gone to bed angry. That day at work I sat and stewed on the whole thing and went back and forth on what to do next. Eventually I realised that it was only words, I loved her, she loved me, and we were both simply exhausted. So, on the way home I picked up the ingredients for her favourite meal, pizza, and some lilies her favourite flower as a way of saying sorry and to start making amends."

'That's nice of you,' Ellie jumped in, 'Everyone gets angry and upset sometimes.'

"Thank you, child. Very wise of you. I'm sorry to say though that she never got the flowers or the meal. As I was driving up the hill to the village the Man stopped me. I did not know who or what he was at the time, damn near terrified me. I confronted him, he said that he insisted that I listen to him and took me, and my car, into the prison realm. The purple smoke place?" Seeing Ellie nod, he carried on, "He trapped me, tied me up and even took away my voice so all I could do was listen. He claimed there was a prophecy, and that the world he came from, this one, needed a sacrifice from someone in our world." He stopped, composing himself, "He wanted me to give up my son, he wanted me to sacrifice him at the folly."

Ellie clasped her hand to her mouth, the idea of asking someone to do that was low even for the Man.

"Remember," Christian continued, "he believed that he needed a child, he tried with Joanna and thought the reason it failed was because her mother was not as willing. He and we now know this not to be true and that he needs a willing soul from a specific bloodline. In exchange for this, he offered me the chance for my fiancé and I to have our lives the way they were. Before our son was born. Of course I refused. As punishment he banished me here, killing my physical body in the process and turning me into a spirit form stuck here in Imaginari. It did not take me long to realise I would never go home, so I made the most of it here. I learned how to create and enjoy this world as best as I could. I could watch my fiancé and my son grow up, using the power of my mind to see into our world. That was both a blessing and a curse, seeing them safe was wonderful, but seeing them mourn for me, or worse be angry at me, was horrendous. I'd give anything to be able to tell them the truth." He stopped, Ellie imagined he wanted to wipe away tears, but that was not possible. Not here.

'I'm sure deep down they know the truth, that you would never leave them,' she offered.

"For a time, this was true," he replied. "She searched for me, but eventually after being told many times that I must have left angry, abandoning her and our child, she started to believe it. She changed our sons name to hers and moved to a new house. She wanted to remove all connections to me. I do not blame her for that. Our son has grown up knowing nothing of me, except that I abandoned his mother."

Ellie looked around, 'Was this your house?' she asked, thinking she was a step ahead for once.

Christian nodded, "Yes, I made it look like this because to me this is home. This is the house that my family and I should have grown up in, together. I made it like this to try and ease my own pain."

Ellie did not know what to say to that, she just floated there in silence.

"I never saw the Man again, he left me to suffer the way he felt everyone does here."

'And they don't?'

"No, not at all. Everyone I have interacted with here is peaceful, balanced, and appreciates the world they have. All except him. He is hellbent on power and destruction. Which leads me onto Alistair."

'The man who lived in my house before me?'

"Yes, he, like you, could manipulate the energy, not to your level mind. He tried to get the council to listen, to stop worshipping the Man as a hero and try to stop him. Something you have since been able to achieve."

If Ellie could blush, she would have. She had never considered it an achievement before.

"Alistair made it here, and as the only other one to make it here and survive I sought him out and we agreed to work together. I believe you know the important parts of that relationship from his notes, yes?"

'I know about the compass, the telescope, and the stones,'

Ellie confirmed.

"Good, they are the key things to note, in the interest of time we will skip over the other parts of that relationship."

Ellie smiled, unsure of what else there could be that he was not telling her, 'How did you discover the secret of the stones?'

"By accident," Christian replied. "We noted that each time he passed into your world he would visit one of the five stones. Never all of them, and never the same one twice in a row. I focused hard and watched him, looking at what he did. Each time he visited one he would draw power from it. I came to realise that when left alone the stones were not only passing energy up to the folly as I know you have seen, but also storing some for him to use."

'Like batteries?' Ellie asked, wanting to offer something to the conversation.

"Sort of, yes. He was using them to store energy, so we realised that if they were no more, like any other spirit he would not be able to reform. From there it did not take us long to realise that to destroy them would need something similar to what created them."

'The last two Guardians helped me; we made my necklace powerful enough to do it.'

"I know, and I believe you and your friends managed to destroy four of the five stones?"

Ellie lowered her head in shame, 'Yes, before he beat me and banished me here, like you.'

"But that was not long ago, was it?"

'No,' Ellie could only manage simple replies now, she was feeling ashamed of how little she had achieved compared to Christian and Alistair.

"Ellie do not fear, for all is not lost. Not yet."

Ellie looked up at him once more.

"The next thing I need to tell you, is about you, your friends, and what we are going to do next."

Ellie was stunned at this, it felt like a real gear change and suddenly, there was hope once more. She said nothing, just floated in silence above her chair of mist.

"Listen, I have friends here, they feared me at first as they thought I was in league with the Man. Some still do fear it so even my friends do not speak of me publicly. You have met six of them, remember? When you were here before?"

Ellie nodded, recalling the group of spirits that at first had seemed to dislike her, but had then offered to help before then vanishing upon Christian's arrival.

'Did they mean you when they said, he? I thought they meant the Man?'

Christian nodded, "They did mean me, yes. I hope you do not mind but I have called for them, they will be here soon as we will need their help to do this, to beat him. The five will be here soon."

'Five?' Ellie asked, 'I thought I met six?'

"You did, all will become clear I assure you, please trust me Ellie."

'Ok, carry on. When will they get here?'

"Not long, but there is more that I wish to share with you before they arrive, then as a seven we will need to work together."

Ellie leaned forward, focused now, feeling thankful to have someone take charge and push her in what felt like the right direction, 'I'm listening.'

"First, I owe you an apology. The moment I realised you could use the energy better than Alistair I tried to contact you, I tried to help you reach this world."

Ellie's eyes widened, 'It was you? You made the purple strands appear on my hands in the field, you nearly dragged me in?'

"Yes, that was me, the Man sensed it though and tried to pull you into the prison realm instead. It was only the actions of Annabelle and Simon that broke the connection. They saved you, Ellie."

'How?'

"Because he attacked the connection, and because you were resisting it which I understand, your spirit would have been pulled apart in three ways. Them grabbing you and making you subconsciously aware that your physical body was in danger is what saved you, that broke the connection to Imaginari."

'I'll never hear the end of it if they find out they saved me, you know,' Ellie commented with a wry smile to herself.

"Indeed, they love you, they would do anything for you."

Ellie looked at him, a small amount of suspicion in her mind, 'That's a few times you have said something like that, how do you know so much about me and my friends?'

She sat back, waiting for the answer. She felt this was a key part to his story that he was not sharing.

He sighed, "Follow me," he said, getting up and floating out of the door that Ellie had entered through.

She did so, he led her out into the hall and up the stairs. Once up there he stopped outside of a door and waited for her. They faced each other, and he spoke once again.

"I have been watching you, and your friends for a long time. One of them for even longer. When you and your other friends arrived on the scene, I kept an eye on all of you."

Ellie moved back slightly, nervous again.

"Only because I cared, and I wanted to help," he defended.

"You remember I told you I had a son?"

Ellie nodded.

"And that his mother changed his name to her maiden name, the name she had when I was banished here?" He sighed once more, as if building up the strength to finish the thought.

"This is my son's bedroom, as it would have been."

He gestured, and the door dissolved, Ellie peered through, and then moved into the room.

It was a baby's room, a cot in the corner, bookshelves of baby books with a rocking chair, a typical baby boy's room. Toys on the floor, colourful fluffy teddies, all made of mist of course but Ellie could tell what they were, the attention to detail was astounding.

"The name of my son, the name she gave him, is Simon Lesley."

Ellie froze on the spot, the name sinking into her chest like an icicle. She turned slowly to face Christian, and immediately saw him in a new way. The jaw line, eyes and nose were identical to Simon. Yes, they were made of mist and vapour, but it was him none the less. She was annoyed she had not realised it before. She had been so focused on her own problems and challenges that she had not considered that Simon's dad may have been involved in all of this decades ago.

'You're. Simon's. Dad?' she managed to stutter out.

"Yes, I am," he replied. "Lloyd is the name he had, and that she would have taken if we were married. But we never got the chance."

'So, you were watching Simon, and then me and the others, because you're his dad?'

He nodded.

'I, I don't know what to say.'

"There is nothing you need to say, but I need to thank you."

'Thank me?'

Ellie did not know what for, as far as she could tell she had done nothing but endanger his son and end the world.

"You have made Simon the happiest I have ever seen him; you instantly became friends and I know you have his back as he does yours."

Ellie wanted to blush again, 'It doesn't do much good now though does it?' she added truthfully. 'I'm stuck here, the Man is destroying our world, they have no way to stop him or destroy the stones. What can I do?'

"You mean what can we do?" he replied, "And the answer is, anything," he turned and went back downstairs. "Come, the others are here."

Ellie stopped, taking a moment to look around the room that was a replica of where her friend first slept at home. She smiled to herself, amazed at what had unfolded in the last few moments. Here she was, in another world chatting clear as day with Simon's dad, when he did not even know his dads name. He had always been there, watching, looking out for his son. 'I'm coming Simon,' she said to herself and left the room.

Ellie headed downstairs and into the front room, there she was greeted by five new spirits, six including Christian. She looked around the room, they were all standing in a circle, Christian to her left then the others were all generic blank shapes in a circle back to Ellie's right, making a circle of seven in his front room.

"Ellie, these are my friends. We will do introductions in a second, but I think you will figure it out before we complete them, but I want to explain one more thing to you."

'Ok,' she said, still looking around the room at the spirits.

"As you know there are two types of spirit here in Imaginari. There are those that are created here..."

'And those that belong, or are linked to one of us, in our world,' Ellie interrupted, wanting to join in.

"Correct. The ones that are connected are controlled by us, and nearly everyone in our world will not know it. They will sense it now and then, when they dream, imagine anything, talk to themselves that sort of thing. All of those things are their spirit in Imaginari, making contact with them."

Ellie nodded.

"Before we introduce the others, have you ever wondered why your voice sounds so different on camera or video?"

Ellie looked at him, perplexed.

"You must have noticed that the voice you hear back on tape, is different to how you hear yourself when you speak normally?"

Ellie nodded, it did make sense to her.

"The reason, is because the voice you hear when you speak aloud, is actually your inner spirit voice. You are not hearing the sound through your ears you are hearing it echo through your head, through your spirit and into the mind. When you hear the recording, you hear the voice that is actually said aloud. Make sense?"

'Oddly, yes it does,' Ellie commented.

"Good, remember that and see if you can place these people, remember, you have met them all before."

Ellie went to think a response, begging for urgency.

"Do not worry, we have time, this will work," Christian comforted.

He turned to his left, and the spirit there spoke.

"Hi Ellie."

The voice instantly sounded familiar; the recognition was right on the tip of her tongue.

"How about some sweeties?" it added, as if giving a clue.

The realisation washed over her like a warm wave at the

beach. The moment she worked out it was Simon's spirit, it took his form, making a perfect grey glowing image of her friend.

Ellie beamed at him. She turned to the next one along, which spoke in turn.

"Hope your workouts are still going well."

Tyler appeared.

"I bet she never read all our notes and research, did she Dan?" Ellie chuckled as Leo came into view, followed quickly by Dan to his left.

"No, she never did or would," Dan added.

Finally, Ellie turned to the spirit on her left.

"I love you too," it said, and Annabelle, gorgeous Annabelle with her long flowing hair and glasses appeared.

They were all made of the same grey mist, but Ellie could see them all as clear as day. She looked at Annabelle, somehow, even though it was not possible, Ellie could see her deep brown eyes. She wanted nothing more than to stay in this moment forever, pretend that nothing else mattered and be here, with Annabelle, safe.

'I, I'm speechless,' Ellie said, projecting her thoughts to all of them.

"There's a first," Simon replied, to chuckles across the room.

It was a strange sensation, there was no sound, but Ellie felt at home instantly with her friends. She looked down, Annabelle's spirit was holding her hand, as she always did to comfort her. Ellie could not feel it in her hand, but she could in her soul, and that is where it mattered. They were here, together, and they were going to fight.

'Who was the other spirit?' Ellie asked, 'There was six wasn't there?'

They all looked at her, it did not take her long to realise that they all had the same look on their face. A look that said 'Really?'

"Ellie," Christian spoke, "Think. Who is missing from your group of friends?"

'Nobody,' she replied, 'we are all here.'

"Exactly," Leo commented.

"The sixth spirit you met that day, Ellie," Annabelle said,

"Was you."

Ellie could not process this, 'I met myself?'

"Yes, oddly it was you that told you it was time you left so that you wouldn't get stuck here," Simon replied with his usual chirpy tone.

"You are the six, and together, I think you can beat him," Christian stated.

Ellie felt a buzz of excitement, 'Ok, how?'

"First, we need to get you home, and this time with some help," Christian replied. "We have not got much time, so everyone do as I say," he moved into the middle of the group, "Ellie come here with me."

She did so.

"Annabelle, Simon close up together. Everyone else move round we need to form a circle around the two of us."

Her friends did so, they were now in a circle evenly spaced around Ellie and Christian in the centre.

"What we are about to do, has never been done, but in theory, it should work."

'Theory?' Ellie asked, nervously.

"It will be fine," Simon reassured.

Ellie smiled, not feeling confident.

Christian took Ellie's hands in his, as best a spirit could. "You others, join hands to make a circle, close your eyes and focus on your physical counterparts."

Looking around, Ellie saw her friends in grey mist form linking hands and closing their eyes. She wanted to burst out laughing but knew that she could not, this was serious.

"Ellie, here is what we are going to do," Christian said, looking straight at her. "We, you and I, are going to make a portal to your world, just big enough to let these spirits through. They will be drawn to your friends, their physical counterparts. Then, we will send you through to join them. Ok?"

'Ok, but then what?'

"Leo and Dan were right; you need to overload him with power. If this works, for a short time you will have more power than anyone in Imaginari or your world has ever had. You will have your own physical strength, the spirit power you have here and now, an extra spirit boost of power, and the left over from the portal. Use it. Get your friends to channel living energy into their spirits. Tie him down, it will overload him."

Ellie took all this in, 'What about the stones, he will never give up the necklace.'

"Use your body, keep your spirit form away from it, and get your body to be in contact with the stone. Will it to be so, and it will be powerful enough to destroy it."

'How?'

"You will be the perfect blend of the physical world and Imaginari, a unique blend for a short time."

'Right. Go back home, get my friends to team up with their spirits, use living world energy to tie him down and overload him whilst keeping my body touching the stone?'

Christian nodded.

'Easy,' Ellie smiled nervously.

Whilst they had been talking, a lot had changed in the room. It was no longer still, it was spinning round them, or they were spinning in it, Ellie could not tell. She focused on Christian.

'How do we do this?'

"Not we, I, let me focus."

Ellie did so, as she watched he closed his eyes.

Moments later, a black pin of nothing appeared above their heads, it grew slightly larger until it was the size of a football. Her friends were moving so fast around her that she could not tell who was who anymore, they were all a blur of grey. As Ellie watched, a golden strand of light reached down through the black hole like a rope being dangled from a hatch.

"Simon, you first," Christian called out, sounding exhausted from the effort.

Ellie saw a hand shoot up and grab the golden strand and instantly a grey blur was pulled through.

"Leo."

The same thing happened, with a silent pop another grey blur vanished.

"Dan, Tyler, get going."

Two in quick succession.

"Annabelle, you're the last one."

This left Ellie and Christian, standing under a black hole with a golden thread dangling down from it.

"Ellie, now for you, but before you go, you need something."

'What?' Ellie asked, wondering why he did not tell her this before.

"Me."

He thrust his hand into Ellie's chest, and she immediately felt a surge of energy, the same she had felt when testing her powers on the tree weeks before.

'What are you doing?' she asked.

"I'm giving you my spirit energy, you need the extra boost, and you will do more with it in the next few moments than I have ever done. I only ask one thing."

'What?' Ellie asked, unsure of what to say or do.

"Look after my son."

This broke Ellie's heart, but before she could say anything, there was a final surge of power in her chest. She did not know why but her hand instinctively reached up and grabbed the golden strand of light. The moment she touched it, Imaginari vanished, the grey mist, the cottage, all of it turned to black, and Ellie was flying through nothingness.

CHAPTER 17

Annabelle and Simon sobbed. Ellie's cold, lifeless body was lying on the ground with her head resting on Annabelle's lap. They had no idea how long they had been there for, but it felt like years. Leo, Dan, and Tyler had sat down, everyone was crying, and nobody knew what to say. The night seemed to have taken a cold turn, the wind had picked up and was cutting through their jackets as they sat on the hilltop. The only person who seemed unmoved by all this, was the Man. He was floating a few metres away, holding the necklace that had destroyed four of his five keys.

"This is genius," he spoke softly, "It is a shame that I had to kill them, and her, in order to achieve my goal. If they had only seen my way of thinking, they could have made great things when all this is over."

"Eleanor," Annabelle muttered.

"What?" the Man snapped, turning towards Annabelle.

"Her name," Annabelle snarled, "is Eleanor. Do not call her, her. And you do not get to call her Ellie. Ever."

He chuckled, "I am sorry, Annabelle, rest assured though I have no intentions of ever calling her Ellie." He glided over, "But I see no reason for the hostility, we can still achieve great things together."

"What?" she retorted, looking at him defiantly square in the face.

"I will need people to help me keep order in the new world, suffice to say that not everyone in Imaginari or here will be happy with my plans. You can help me, in exchange for your life."

"You think I would help you? After you killed Ellie in front of me?" Annabelle's tears had turned to anger now. "Never," she spat, turning away from the Man's gaze.

"That is disappointing I must say. Do any of you wish to help me?" he had turned to the boys now.

"Not a chance," Simon replied, "We will fight you to our last breath," he stood and positioned himself between the Man and his friends.

"Defiant I see, stupid boy. Do any of you see reason?"

They all stood, aligning themselves with Simon making a barrier between the Man and Ellie's body.

"We will never help you, Ellie died for that, we owe her to do the same," Annabelle stated.

"Very well," the Man said, before he began to rise up into the night sky. "You shall all witness the destruction of your world and the splendour of mine. I shall ensure that you are the last to die and that it is the slowest, most painful death, imaginable."

"I thought you needed a willing soul? From Ellie's family to open the gate?" Leo shouted up.

The Man looked at him, "Clever boy, yes that is true I did, but now I have assimilated the other Guardians, I am more powerful than any of them. I will be able to break that spirit rule and destroy the barrier between worlds, do not worry."

The five friends looked at each other, they all felt brave, and knew they were doing the right thing by challenging him, but they also knew it was hopeless and none of them could actually do anything.

"I think," the Man continued, "Yes, Annabelle, you shall suffer most for claiming to love Eleanor, I think it is fitting that you should suffer."

"I do love her," she shouted back, but it was the last thing she could say.

The Man reached down, and an invisible force grabbed Annabelle around the throat and lifted her into the air. She grabbed and thrashed with her hands, but there was nothing to grab onto. Her feet kicked but there was nothing there. She was floating up into the air, to her it felt like being lifted by the neck, but to the others, she was simply being lifted into the air by an invisible force.

"Annabelle," Simon called out, helpless.

The Man laughed, "Foolish mortals," he waved his other hand and a battering of air sent the boys sprawling to the floor in a scattered mess. "You cannot stop me," he turned to Annabelle once more, "And you, girl, will witness it all."

Annabelle was level with him now, he twisted his wrist turning Annabelle, so she was facing away from him out over the edge of the hill. With another swift movement he pulled her arms and legs out, so she was now a star shape, floating high above the hill, level with the Man and the top of the folly. "Now, the beginning, of the end," the Man said in a confident booming voice.

He spread his arms wide and floated a little higher above the top of the folly. As he did so the sky turned black, but not the colour black, it was as if all of the light in the sky had gone, swallowing up the stars in a cloud of nothing. Moments later, a bolt of light tore down from the sky, through the Man and into the centre of the folly tower. It lit up the sky and the top of the hill with a brilliant white light. The moment it made contact with the ground the earth shook and rumbled. The area of sky where it had come from opened, revealing a patch of grey in the middle of the black. As they watched, helpless, strands of golden light begin to move from the trees, bushes and ground into the sky. The smaller items soon turned to black, dead, as the energy was completely absorbed from them. The wind was battering the hilltop now, swirling round and round. The boys battled their way to the only remaining stone where Ellie's body was, around them the strands of light were merging to create thicker beams of light into the sky.

"Why is there nothing coming from us, or Ellie?" Simon asked, looking at his hands, having to shout above the noise of the wind.

"He wants us to watch," Leo shouted back, "So I guess we are immune?"

"And Ellie?" Simon asked.

"She is dead Simon, there is no life energy left for him to take."

This was hard to process, but Simon knew it to be true.

He looked up at Annabelle, hopelessly floating above all the destruction.

"We have to help her," he shouted, "We have to do something?"

"How?" Dan asked.

Simon did not have an answer. As the four looked at each other, there was another bolt of light that tore across the sky, the impact knocked them to their knees. Simon fell, and the telescope rolled into his leg, along with the compass. He threw the telescope to Leo.

"Can you see anything?" he shouted.

Simon picked up the compass and looked at it, shaking it to try and make it move.

"Show me hope, show me something," Simon pleaded with the device.

To his surprise it turned, and pointed to Ellie, lying lifeless in between them. He nudged Tyler.

"How can she help us? How is that hope?"

Tyler shook his head, "No idea, but I think everything has gone crazy now, surely?"

"Did you see anything?" Simon asked Leo.

Leo lowered the telescope and shook his head.

Simon dropped the compass and pulled Ellie into a hug, "What do I do, Ellie?" he sobbed into her shoulder. "Tell me how to fix it."

There he sat, holding her body as the hill shook and vibrated with destruction around him. Tyler, Leo, and Dan looked at each other. They all felt the same way, they were desperate to help, but the truth was none of them could think of anything that they could do. As they watched, the world around them was crumbling, anything living was turning to black, the life being drawn out of it and pulled into the black vortex above. Annabelle was out of reach and helpless, the last stone was secure, the Man had the only thing that could destroy it. What could they do?

The Man looked down at them, "Hope. Pathetic. I do not believe in hope, or luck. I believe in power," he leaned his head back, absorbing yet another bolt of light as he did so.

"He is too powerful now, it's over," Leo said to Simon, putting his arm around him.

Simon nodded, accepting defeat.

"Protect Ellie," Annabelle called down over the wind.

They looked up at her.

"Don't let her get destroyed by this, she deserves us to try and keep her body safe."

"I'm sorry Annabelle," Simon shouted back, "I can do that, but we can't get to you."

"Don't worry about me, just keep her as safe as you can."

The boys looked at Annabelle one last time. Then formed a circle around Ellie's body, putting their arms on each other's shoulders. Kneeling down to create a shield as best they could around their friend; their heads touching in the middle of the circle they had created.

Annabelle looked down on them, "Goodbye, I love you all."

She closed her eyes and lifted her head up. She would not beg; she would not crack and give him the satisfaction. If this was the end then so be it, she would not let him have that from her as well as victory. The boys kept a tight circle, shielding themselves as best they could from the destruction, with Ellie's body lying between them. Simon was the only one with his eyes open, the others had closed them to hold back the tears and fear. Simon watched his friend's body shake with the ground, feeling every bang and vibration himself. He was aware of more bolts of light overhead, more bangs and crashes as the world was falling apart around him. It was so tempting to turn and run, to run away and pray that he could escape. But he knew it would be no use to do that. He was about to close his eyes and wait for the inevitable end, when he noticed something new, that he had not seen before nor was he expecting. A golden spec of light had appeared on Ellie's chest, over where her heart would be. He blinked, clearing his vision to try and focus on it, not believing his eyes. It was definitely there though.

"What's that?" he asked his friends, calling over the noise of the wind and destruction.

They all opened their eyes, but Leo was the only one who spoke.

"No idea," he said.

As they watched the spec grew a little larger, to the size of a small coin. At the same time, it grew a little brighter, not beacon level bright but bright enough for the boys to need to squint a little. They relaxed their grip on each other and moved back, opening Ellie up to the elements around them a little. The moment they did so, strands of golden light stopped moving from the ground into the sky, but into Ellie's chest. They watched in amazement as the strands grew thicker, brighter, and stronger. Annabelle looked down and said nothing through fear of it not being real. Simon looked up, and shrugged his shoulders to Annabelle, as if saying he too had no idea what was going on. At this precise moment, the Man looked down as well.

"What is happening? What did you do?" he boomed.

They all said nothing, partly because they could sense his irritation, but mostly because they did not know what was going on anyway. The world was still in chaos, and the black hole was still drawing energy, but some of it was being diverted into Ellie, and nobody knew how or why. As they watched, golden lines of light began to flow from their hands into Ellie as well, merging with those from the ground. There was a moment of panic from Simon as he thought he would die too, but this was soon pushed from his mind. The golden light grew brighter, the strands now stretching up to Annabelle and linking all six friends, including Ellie, together in a web of gold, lighting up the hilltop with pure, clean, golden light. The Man moved down to investigate, but before he could get close, the situation changed completely. There was a silver flash from Ellie's chest, and a silver shape of light emerged from it and moved next to Simon. He retreated slightly, but the shape stayed with him, mirroring his every move. The light from this figure created a glow around him and the ground under his feet. He moved his arm; the figure moved the same one. He looked at the others in shock, unsure of what to say or do. He wanted to panic, but felt a level of reassurance from the figure, but he could not place why. Before anyone could say anything, there was another flash, the same thing happened but this time to Leo. He was left with a silver shadow copying his every move.

This was repeated for Dan, Tyler, and finally Annabelle, though Annabelle's simply floated up to be in front of her mirroring her forced star shape in the sky.

"What is the meaning of this?" the Man demanded.

Before anything else could be said or done, there was a blinding golden flash directly above Ellie's body. The force of the light sent the boys and their silver counterparts sprawling backwards to the floor. The Man was forced away a few metres and Annabelle felt the wind blast her face. A golden shape had appeared above Ellie, so bright they could not look directly at it as if a star had fallen from the sky. For a few moments, nothing happened, the wind and noise had stopped, as if stunned by the arrival of these ghost-like figures. As they watched, the golden light faded, and their eyes could make out its shape. The shape of a person, a girl, a girl they all knew and could not have been happier to see. Ellie. Ellie's spirit form was a perfect replica of her body, except glowing gold with power, she shone across the hilltop like a lighthouse, saturating everything with a golden, hopeful light. The wind and energy flow bellowed and moved once more, the chaos on the hill returned.

"Ellie," Simon stammered, "How?" he managed to finish.

"You look, different," Leo added.

"Strong," Tyler suggested.

Ellie turned and looked at Simon, "There is a long story to answer that, and it is worth telling. I promise I will explain it all, but for now, I need you all to listen and trust me."

Her voice boomed over the hill loud and clear. Her friends would always trust and follow her, but this felt different. This felt like orders rather than a request for help from a friend.

"You sound, powerful," Simon commented, a little scared by the volume of his friend's voice and her new appearance.

"You haven't seen anything yet," Ellie replied sharply, but with a gentle smile that amused him a little. It was the sort of wit he had come to expect from her.

She turned and moved away from her friends, so she was no longer over her own body. She looked up at the Man who had started to move back towards her and the others.

"This ends now," she shouted, lifting herself into the air slightly in his direction.

Ellie allowed herself to rise a little further keeping her eyes focused on the Man at all times. Then without warning she dived towards the hilltop, slamming her fist into the Earth and coming to rest on her knees. The moment she did so, a number of things happened. First, the flow of energy into the black hole stopped, the sky was still torn apart, but no more energy was flowing through. Second, Annabelle was released and began to fall, this did not last long though as the silver shape that had been with her seemingly caught her and lowered her gently to the ground near the others. Once there, the five friends moved forwards and gathered behind the spirit form of their friend, hope once more filling their hearts. Finally, Ellie stood floating just above the ground and pointed down towards the ground. She then moved both of her arms with purpose, moving them slowly out sideways. As she did so, the ground rumbled, shaking so much that Annabelle grabbed hold of Simon for support. Then, on the horizon a purple sphere began to appear out of the ground, as if it was being drawn by Ellie herself. She continued to lift her arms up, the purple sphere following their angle and speed. As she lifted them above her head her hands met. The moment they did the purple bubble's walls also met with a loud bang, sending one final vibration through the floor. The hill in Mow Cop was now encased in a giant snow globe of shimmering purple energy. Ellie faced the Man once more and began to lift her spirit off the ground. Never taking her eyes off him, her voice boomed over the hilltop.

"Ok, listen up."

Simon and the others knew she was talking to them.

Ellie continued, "He can't leave this bubble, he's trapped. We have one chance, one shot. These are your spirits from Imaginari, they are on our side and they are here to help. Everyone lead your spirit, spread out around the folly as evenly as you can. When you're in a good spot, find something that is still living. A tree, a bush, anything, grab it, and hold on, they will be with you to enhance that energy and allow me to use it. Simon, stay here with my body, keep it safe and in contact with that final stone. We are going to tie him down with power and overload him, just like you said, Leo."

They all looked at each other, and without question or another thought did as Ellie had told them and began to move away from the stone and spread out around the hill.

As she glided up in a spiral around the hilltop to be level with the Man, directly above the folly tower, she called out one last thing, "Let's finish this."

CHAPTER 18

Annabelle, Dan, Leo, and Tyler moved instinctively. The instruction from Ellie was clear and obvious, they needed to act fast. The four moved away from the final stone and Ellie's body in two groups, they were not quite sure how they had sorted out their directions without discussing it. On her own, Annabelle headed away from the stone with the folly on her right. She stayed low on the hill and scrambled over the many stones, bushes, and roots that were in her way. Her spirit glided behind her silently, never more than an arm's length away. After a few moments, she stopped and turned to take stock of where she was. Simon and the final stone were almost exactly south from where she was now facing, the direction she had just travelled in. She quickly pushed the thought of Ellie's body out of her mind. Looking to her left, she could see the folly. Annabelle knew this was where she was supposed to be but could not understand why. It was like an instinct or process that had made the decision for her without her realising it. She looked around, she needed something living as Ellie had told them to hold on to. She saw a small tree a few steps away, and without a moments hesitation she moved over to it and took hold of the thickest branch. Seconds later, her spirit reached out and took her other hand. The moment there was contact Annabelle felt a surge of energy and strength flow through her. It was so strong and powerful that it made her grip on the branch tighten, she did not want to let go but she was unsure she would be able to even if she tried. Looking up, she could see the golden spirit of her girlfriend, flying high circling around above the folly tower. All Annabelle had to do now was wait, and hope.

Dan, Leo, and Tyler all headed in the same direction at first. They climbed up the crest of the hill with the folly on their left. As they crossed the peak it did not take long for Leo to stop, allowing Tyler and Dan to carry on. Leo was now level with the wall of the folly, immediately making him aware that he was on the north south line. He could see Simon to his left, a little lower down starting to move Ellie's body. He looked away again, the sight of seeing one of his friends move the other was a little disconcerting. He looked at his spirit, like Annabelle's had never been too far away as he had ran the short distance to this spot. After a few seconds he glanced around and noticed a small bush behind him, close to the ground. He knelt and grabbed hold of some of the bristles and leaves. Instantly, the spirit took hold of his other hand and he too felt a surge of energy and power. It felt unbearable at first, but the sight of Ellie's glowing figure above the tower gave him hope. He closed his eyes, gritted his teeth, and waited.

Having left Leo with his spirit, Dan and Tyler crossed the top of the hill and down the steps by the side of the folly, the Man and Ellie glowing high above them. At the bottom of the stairs Tyler turned to the left and Dan to the right, again following instincts as they did so, their spirits in tow. Tyler rounded a corner, the folly high above him and slightly to his right, he stopped and looked around him and immediately to his right he saw Annabelle. One hand clenched around a tree branch, the other seemingly being held by her spirit companion. He looked around, the area he was in was one of gravel paths and there was not much in the way of foliage or life. He took a few steps to his left and peered round a rock, poking out of the other side of it was a small shrub.
"Will this do?" he asked himself out loud.
"This will do just fine," came a voice in his mind that sounded not too dissimilar to his own.
He looked at the spirit, "Was that you?" he asked, still trying to make sense of everything that was going on.

"It was, but we can discuss this later, please grab hold of the shrub."
Tyler frowned, but did not argue. He perched himself onto the rock and grabbed hold of as much of the tiny shrub as he could. He held out his hand for the spirit.
"Are you going to look after me?"
"I am going to look after us," came the reply.

Dan had the furthest to go. He moved down the steps with Tyler and then turned right, the folly towering over him as he worked his way around the hill. When he stopped, he could not see any of his friends except for Ellie's glowing golden spirit high above him. He faced the folly tower, he knew that Leo was to his left somewhere, beyond him was Simon and Tyler was to his right, back where he had come. Other than that, he was alone, except for his spirit of course. This area of the hill was reasonably lush and green, and it did not take him long to find something to hold on to, a tree, much bigger and stronger than that of Annabelle's. He moved towards the trunk. It had a low branch that he could lean against, taking the weight off of his feet as he did so. He rested his palm on the trunk and looked up at the crest of the hill. Ellie was level with the Man now, they were above the folly and facing each other. Dan closed his eyes and waited for whatever was going to happen.
"Come on, Ellie. You got this," he whispered to himself.

Simon did not have to move anywhere; he was initially thankful for this but soon felt less fortunate as he realised he needed to move Ellie's body to be touching the fifth and final keystone. The arrival of Ellie in spirit form had sent a wave of hope and positivity over them all, none more so than Simon who felt that he had failed her and did not want their friendship to end with the small argument about a necklace. It was also a strange experience for him to see his friend, and talk to her, hear her voice, but then have to touch and move her cold lifeless body. He moved himself so that he could lift her from behind under her arms, dragging her feet as he shuffled backwards towards the stone. She was heavy, her body unable to help in any way he needed to support her and move her safely and carefully as she had instructed. After a short while he lay her down, leaning her back against the stone and bending one of her hands round so it was touching it skin to rock to be absolutely sure. He went and sat on her other side, taking her other hand.

"Whatever you're up to, I believe in you," he said, lifting her hand and kissing the back of it.

With his other hand, he reached down and dug his fingers into the soft, wet, soil and mud. Clenching his hand around the living roots and blades of grass around him. He looked up, he had a clear view of the folly and could see Annabelle down the hillside as well, she was braced and prepared. None of his other friends were visible due to the shape of the hill and the location of them on it, he could only assume they were all where they needed to be. Simon glanced at his spirit, then up at his friend facing off against the Man in the sky.

"We can do this," he said.

Seconds later, his spirit glided down and placed its hand on top of Simon's. They were all set.

Whilst her friends had been preparing, Ellie had allowed her golden shining form to glide up to meet the Man. She had moved around the tower in a spiral, buying as much time as she could for her friends to do as she had asked them to. It was also giving her time to understand and explore this new form; she had used the energy before of course but had never felt power like this. Moments before she left Imaginari, when Christian had sacrificed himself to get her home, she felt a surge of power, and in that moment, she knew what she needed to do and how to do it. Imaginari was with her, it was with her friends, and if they did this right, they stood a chance. Ellie glided upwards and was now level with the Man, she knew he would not pay any attention to her friends, and she was right. He had stared at her golden form the entire time. Ellie was floating above the tower of the folly, the Man directly in front of her above the wall that ran along the north south line across the hilltop.

"Do you honestly think you can beat me?" he boomed,

confidently.

"I don't think," Ellie replied, "I know we will."

She glared at him, with her peripheral vision she could see Dan, Leo, and Simon all now seemingly in position with contact between their spirits and something living. Whilst she could not see clearly, she knew that Simon had also moved her body as she had asked. Ellie decided on faith that if those three were in position, Annabelle and Tyler must be too. She could not look as they were behind and below her and checking would mean taking her eyes off the Man for longer than she dared. She needed to trust them.

"You have not had practice or the time to use these powers, you do not deserve them. How you have been able to return, survive the splice and seal me here I do not know. But I know it will not be enough."

"You don't sound very sure though," Ellie replied politely, "Surely you would have tried to strike me down by now if you were that confident that you could beat me?"

It was a gamble. Ellie was in uncharted territory and knew that she would need to use her gut and instincts to win this particular battle. She had a plan, and it had to work.

"Foolish girl," he retorted, "Do you really think I am scared of you? And that your puny friends will save your pathetic world?" He raised his arms as he said this, gesturing to the world around him. "You cannot possibly hope to win."

This was where he made his mistake. In gloating and showing off he had momentarily taken his gaze away from Ellie, taking in his surroundings as a way of defiance. She noticed and decided to strike. In the second that his focus was shifted, she shot forward. A golden streak behind her as she flew through the air above the folly. He of course noticed this and turned back towards her, reaching out to grab her just as he had in the prison realm not so long ago. Ellie was ready for that. She kept her aim true and headed straight for him, the folly wall guiding her as she flew at him. Just before she reached his outstretched grasp, she dived down towards the ground. This sudden and strange manoeuvre took the Man by surprise, his hands reached out and clasped nothing but air. He looked down, Ellie had shot underneath him and was heading towards the ground. He grinned.

"You cannot even fly straight yet," he muttered to himself.

If only he had looked closer, instead of trying to gloat over Ellie he would have seen the truth of the situation. Yes, Ellie had missed him, she had dived down below his feet and carried on towards the ground at a steady speed. This was however intentional, she was now aiming straight for Leo, who still had his eyes closed, and his spirit. As she reached them she handed to the spirit a golden strand of light so fine it was almost invisible. The spirit grabbed hold and the moment he did it glowed with power. Leo felt a surge of energy at this and opened his eyes just in time to see Ellie soar over his head and circle back around. To his amazement his spirit, whilst still holding his hand, was also now holding a glowing golden rope in the other. He followed the rope with his eyes, at the other end of the rope with the appearance of a kite was the Man. Leo smiled to himself, Ellie had a plan. The Man also realised this at the same time and immediately let out a howl of rage and fury that tore across the sky like a thunderbolt. He reached down to try and free his ankle that was now tethered to the ground by the golden strand of light. The moment his fingers touched it, was the moment that the surge of energy from Leo and his spirit reached the Man. The jolt of power made him lurch back and scream out in pain once again. Ellie did not have time to look and see what was going on, she needed to stick to her plan and see it through, she could not afford to make the same mistakes that the Man had made and lose focus. After she had handed over the strand to Leo's spirit, she banked right and keeping her speed up shot over to where Simon was waiting with his. She swooped across and gave the end of a new strand of light to his spirit, not stopping to look at him or her own body leaning on the stone. She turned right again and headed up to where the Man was still reeling from the first surge of energy. The Man faced her, steadying himself to try and defend himself once more but Ellie was ready, she swerved to the side and attached Simon's thread to his other ankle, lashing it tight as she did so. Just as before there was a surge of energy up the thread that hit the Man as strong as the first. As he cried out Ellie circled around him, making sure the strands were holding strong. They were; the Man struggled and wriggled but could not get himself free. Ellie smiled to herself, pleased that her plan was not only apparently working but also that he was angry about it. She lingered too long though and very nearly got caught out. The Man surged forward towards her, the lines going slack as he was moving in the direction they were tethered and reached out his hand. Ellie reacted quickly and just in time, she dodged to the side and wrapped a new thread around the Man's outstretched wrist. She dived, soaring towards Dan this time who looked reasonably relaxed perched against his tree. As before, she handed over the thread to the spirit and it glowed with power. Soaring around once more Ellie rounded the tree and began to head back towards the Man.

Three out of five, she thought to herself, proudly as she moved towards the flailing, flapping Man who could now only move one arm freely. It was all he needed though. As Ellie approached, he lashed out, sending a wave of static power surging towards her. She could not react in time, it hit her square in the chest and sent her slamming into her own purple barrier. It pinned her there, unable to escape its pulsating grip.

"You cannot stop me," the Man yelled.

He was right, she could not. The power was too great, and she could not get free from its hold. The Man however, had not counted on Ellie's friends. Specifically, the three that he was currently tethered to. Simon looked up and could see Ellie pinned unable to move. He closed his eyes and willed another surge of energy from the ground into the golden rope of light. It worked, and it seemed to him that Leo and Dan had the same idea. Together they sent another shockwave up each of their threads that met the Man's ankles and wrist simultaneously. The result was a blinding flash, a deafening bang, and the Man being thrown back once again, his focus lost. Instantly Ellie was free, and she moved to get back on top of the confrontation. She could not waste time thanking her friends for their help and she headed straight for his only free arm. He was still recovering from the attack and it was easier this time for her to grab his wrist, attach another new thread of light and head straight for Annabelle. Ellie had never been so happy to see Annabelle. She greeted Ellie with a grin, knowing that this would be a fleeting visit it was all she could manage. Ellie swooped over handing the thread down to a spirit for the fourth time, again sending a new surge of energy up to the Man. Ellie turned to her right and surveyed the scene that was unfolding above the hill. The Man was now tethered by both arms and legs spreadeagled over the crest of the hill. His feet were tied to Simon and Leo, his hands to Annabelle and Dan. The strands were holding firm though were not pulling tight, he could move but not a great deal in any particular direction. As Ellie looked, he lifted his body upright to face her once more, the golden strands of light hanging from his limbs like strings from a puppet.

"What now, girl?" he called out to her.

Ellie smiled to herself, and in one commanding powerful breath called out, "Pull."

The four spirits attached to the Man reacted immediately, they did not need to pull in the physical sense, all they needed to do was absorb as much of the golden strands of light as they could. The effect however was the same. As they did this, the Man was pulled tight and twisted onto his back as the strands stretched his arms and legs. This meant he was now facing up, being pulled down towards the folly as the strands tightened.

After a few seconds, Ellie called out, "Stop."

They did so. The Man was now being held tight and fast across the top of the folly tower unable to move, his arms and legs being held fast by the bonds that Ellie and her friends had trapped him with.

"Everyone stay strong, this is not over yet," she called out once more, moving up towards the tower as she did so.

When she got there, she moved herself so she was by the Man's side, facing up towards his head.

"You think you have beaten me, girl?" he asked, defiant as ever. "Do you think that your friends can keep me here forever?"

She said nothing.

"They will tire and then the power holding me here will weaken and I shall be free."

"I know," Ellie said, calmly.

"Then what is the meaning of this futile effort to imprison me?"

Ellie moved round so that she was now by his head, looking down at him as if he were hanging upside down. The stones of the folly were crumbling a little under the pressure from the strands of light, and she knew she did not have long before it fell apart. She also meant it when she said he was right, he was. Her friends could not sustain this level of exertion for long, this would end soon, one way or the other.

"I am going to give you a choice," Ellie said.

"What choice?" the Man said, "I know I will be free soon, so why should I make a bargain with you?" he snarled.

"Because," Ellie retorted, still calm and collected, "The choice is freedom with conditions. Or death."

The Man stared at her, "What do you mean, conditions?"

"I am here representing Imaginari and my world. We need each other to survive. You want to destroy my world which will eventually destroy yours as well. So, the choice is simple. Agree to stop this nonsense of destruction and power, and live. Or resist. And die."

She waited for a response, expecting it to be one of wit and repulsion.

"You will not kill me, you do not have the power or courage to do so."

"You could be right, but you are judging me based on the past, and not what I am here and now," Ellie replied. "When you left my spirit form in the prison realm, you stopped me from coming here but you didn't stop me getting into Imaginari. When I was there I found my friends, I found Christian."

The Man shifted at his name, clearly remembering him.

"Together we joined our spirit forms and he sacrificed himself to send me here to beat you. You see, you're not fighting me right now, you are fighting all of us as one. That is why I have been able to overpower you. When people work together amazing things can happen, when we trust each other and believe in each other, we can do anything."

Ellie paused, she could see the way this was going, he was playing for time and she would only destroy him as a last resort. She decided to take a stand, she reached out both her hands and held them above his chest as he lay there.

"This will hurt, but you have until I return to make up your mind."

He shifted, pulling against his restraints but they did not yield. Her friends and their spirits were holding him exactly where he was. She clicked her fingers and in an instant a strand of golden light appeared between her hands. She lowered her hands, aligning the strand with his throat as she did so. When it made contact, there was a hissing sound as the power clashed with that of the Man. She lowered herself, allowing the thread to get longer as she did so. Turning, she headed down the tower, so she was now facing Tyler, perched over his rock, the only one not currently joined to the Man. Ellie glided down slowly, taking her time to ensure this was done right. As she got to Tyler and his spirit, she paused and tied the two ends of light together, making one thicker strand. She handed it to the spirit and she saw the surge of power from the ground flow through Tyler, into the spirit and up the golden thread. She turned and allowed her eyes to follow the thread back up to the top of the tower, where it was tightening around the Man's throat. Once more, Ellie glided back up to the top of the tower, where the Man was completely immobile now, his throat, wrists, and ankles beginning to crack under the power of the golden light.

"Last chance," she said softly, looking down on him.

The Man said nothing.

"Very well, then this is the end," Ellie stated. She knew what she needed to do, "It is time to end the Man." She called out to her friends and their spirits, "I have tried to reason with him, and he has chosen to die. Stay strong, this will be over soon."

With one last pity filled look at the Man, she glided away towards Tyler.

"What happens now?" Tyler spluttered, struggling under the energy pressure.

"We kill him," Ellie said coldly, "Stay strong."

He smiled at her and closed his eyes to concentrate once

again.

Ellie gave the spirit another golden strand of light and sped away towards Dan and his tree. She was there in seconds and allowed the spirit there to grab hold but rather than let go herself, she swooped up the hillside continuing the same thread. She reached Leo and did the same thing and moments later was with Simon. There she allowed the spirit to take hold before moving on to Annabelle, who smiled her beaming smile before Ellie moved back to Tyler. She let go, giving his spirit the other end. She had made a golden circle of light all around the hilltop joining her friends together with a continuous strand of gold. Once released she soared up above the folly, the Man still held fast at the top of the tower, struggling against his bonds as her friends' power pulsated all around. There was still one more thing to do, before she could finish him off. Ellie flew back to Simon, more specifically to her body. It was odd for her to see herself like this, a true out of body experience. She reached down and placed the end of a new piece of golden light in her own hand, the one that was touching the stone.

"Ellie, hurry," Simon murmured.

She looked at him, he had gone white and she realised she was running out of time as her friends' strength would not last much longer. She moved quickly, gliding towards Annabelle once again with the new thread, she handed it to the spirit and glided away once more but this time back over the hill to Leo. She wasted no time there and immediately sped back up past the tower to Tyler and then finally to Dan. Each time handing the thread to the spirit to hold whilst she sped away. When she was with Dan, she let go, giving his spirit the end.

She looked at his spirit, "Pull that last one tight."

The spirit did so, and instantly the threads she had just laid out were pulled tight back and forth across the hilltop between her friends.

"Hang in there Dan, nearly done," she comforted.

Ellie shot into the air high above the tower and looked all around her. The purple bubble was still holding strong, rippling with power. As she looked, the Man was hardly moving now, clearly accepting his fate. The golden circle of light was rippling slightly in a perfect ring around the hill. The last few strands she had laid down made a different shape though, from where she was high above the folly looking down on it from the south side, she could see the perfect, pulsating golden shape of the letter M, encased in the golden circle just like the necklace. She looked down at Simon and her body. She could see the stone, the fifth and final key beginning to vibrate with power. It was going to work. Ellie moved towards the tower and positioned herself by the Man's head once again. She said nothing but looked down at him.

"Pathetic girl," he snarled.

Ellie frowned, and placed her hands on his temples, instantly feeling the energy flowing through him and his restraints. It was like a static charge that fizzed and sparked between her hands and his head. She closed her eyes and began to squeeze his head. She focused hard, picturing the energy flowing up from the ground, through her friends up the strands of light and into the Man and finally into her. She felt every pulse, wave, and ripple, and with each moment the feeling got stronger. Through her eyelids she could see the light of the Man growing in intensity, it was blinding her even though she had her eyes closed. He began to howl in pain and scream like she had never heard before. She focused harder, ignoring his screeching and pushing harder to keep the energy in him from the ground; that was the only way, to keep the energy bottled in him.

"You want power," she snarled without thinking about it, "Have. It. All."

The Man let out a final ear shattering yell of pain and Ellie pushed her hands together. In a moment the Man vanished, exploding in a ball of brilliant white light that filled the sky and blasted outwards. It expanded as a sphere, passing through Ellie as it did so. When it reached the ground, it scorched the earth to black. It reached her friends and knocked them all over, forcing them to release their spirits and the living things they had clutched so tightly. Like Ellie, the spirits were unmoved by the force. It expanded all the way until it reached the barrier Ellie had created where it stopped and instead of growing in size it grew in intensity and power. The white sphere absorbed all the energy on the hill, taking with it the golden strands that had imprisoned the Man and destroying them the same as they had him. The fifth keystone was blasted to dust and Ellie's lifeless body rolled down the hill a short distance, Simon unable to hold it still and safe.

Moments later, the light faded and shrunk almost as fast as it had grown, it condensed itself to the size of a football, hovering above the tower in front of Ellie's still glowing golden spirit. She reached out to touch it, curious as to what would happen. Before she could it shot towards her chest and sent her flying backwards. She looked around, it had not come out again, but yet she felt no pain.

"Where did it go?" she asked aloud.

Before she could think on it, she was arched back her arms dangling by her sides and five beams of white light shot out of her chest. They pierced the darkness in the same way the sphere had, but they were much smaller and more concentrated. Ellie could not see exactly where they went, but she was fairly sure they were aiming for her friends across the hill. She could not move, fixed in place by the beams of light. After a few seconds, with a loud bang, they vanished, releasing Ellie to straighten up and move freely once again. She looked around, there was a circle of black scorched earth around the folly and over the hilltop. The folly itself was still standing but looked a little blackened around the edges.

"Everyone ok?" Ellie called out, "Meet me where the stones used to be."

She glided over the tower and surveyed the scene, to her delight, she could make out five figures moving over the hill to where the keystones once were; her friends were alive.

CHAPTER 19

Ellie arrived silently at Simon's side, he had managed to get to his feet and climb back up the hill and was looking down at Ellie's body. It had fallen onto its back and rolled off slightly, rather unceremoniously in fact, as the stone that was supporting it had now vanished to dust.

"Did we do it?" he asked, not looking up as if in fear of getting an answer he did not like.

"I think we did," Ellie replied with a smile.

"Will you be ok?" he asked, a lump forming in his throat.

"I think so, time will tell," Ellie had not considered what would happen next, her focus had been on beating the Man, outwitting him and destroying him properly. She believed they had done that.

Shortly after, the others arrived, Annabelle and Leo first, followed by Tyler and Dan. They all looked exhausted and worse for ware, the amount of energy they had used and that had flowed through them was truly extraordinary. After hugs and mutterings of surprise and congratulations, the five friends formed a circle with their spirit counterparts and Ellie's spirit in there as well.

"Thank you," Ellie said simply, after the general chattering had died down. "We did it, together, I couldn't have done it without you and the world was saved because of your actions and bravery."

Her friends looked at her blankly, unsure they were worthy of her praise and thanks.

"All we did was hold on," Annabelle commented with a smirk.

"You trusted me," Ellie replied. "You trusted each other, and you delivered the decisive push that was needed. You were the energy and the driving force."

"Is this the part where you tell us what just happened? How you are here and there?" Leo asked, gesturing towards Ellie's body on the floor. "Will you be able to go back?"

"I think I owe you all an explanation," Ellie stated, "I shall share with you everything that happened after we got to the hill."

Ellie did so, she explained everything that happened in the prison realm, starting with how he split her spirit out again. They gasped when she said she could see them and was desperate to help when she could not. Their interest was piqued however when she got to Christian in Imaginari.

"You mean the compass led you to him?" Annabelle asked.

"Yes, it leads to hope, and he was my hope. It led me through the village I'm not sure where, but it was definitely the village. Or rather here but recreated there. He was the one that had been working with your spirits, your counterparts."

"And that's how you found them?" Dan commented.

"I had met them before but didn't know it, I had also technically met myself."

"What?"

"My spirit, this form," she gestured to her golden self. "We have two, one that keeps our bodies alive, and one that exists in Imaginari. When I went there before I met this golden one, when he spliced my spirit out of me it draws out the one from Imaginari it seems. That is why mine is golden and yours are silver"

"This is true," Leo's spirit confirmed. "If we were to merge with you now, we would turn golden when we emerged, and your bodies would collapse. Like Ellie's has."

"Christian summoned your spirits to him, after we had discussed what my predicament was, and then they channelled enough energy to push through to here, our world," Ellie added.

"Is that when they all came through and mirrored us and stuff?" Tyler asked, keen to join in.

"Yes, they needed you to trust them instantly, and fortunately, you did," Ellie responded.

"How did you get back then?" Annabelle asked Ellie.

"Sacrifice. Christian forced his remaining spirit energy into my golden form, as such I became instantly aware of his feelings, thoughts, memories, and expressions, and I knew the plan he had formed. Yes, I carried it out here with your help, but it was all down to him, his ideas." Ellie resisted the urge to look at Simon at this point, she needed to tell him but wanted the moment to be right, "When he did that, I was also able to draw in more power from Imaginari, that is what gave me the strength to create the bonds to hold the Man down. We literally had the power of that world on our side tonight."

"So, he is gone? You beat him?" Annabelle queried.

"We did, yes, together."

"Explain how that works to me?" Simon asked.

"What do you mean?"

"How did we help? How did we know where to go and what exactly did we just do?"

"You knew what to do because we told you," Simon's spirit replied. "We also were aware of Christian's plan and the Man's mistakes, when we arrived you allowed us to join you. Though you did not know it, we shared a connection, meaning we could transfer the smallest amount of knowledge and energy to you."

"That's why we knew where to run," Tyler joined in, excited to understand something that was being discussed.

"Exactly. The positioning was crucial," Ellie stated.

"The letter M," Annabelle's spirit finished off. "The web would be strong enough to hold him, but the power he put in that symbol over the centuries meant that it would be his undoing. Starting from the final keystone, we created the shape needed for Ellie to make the golden 'M' symbol over the hilltop. This is what contained the energy in him, causing him to dissolve and vaporise."

"What other mistakes did he make?" Simon asked.

Tyler's spirit responded first, "Many. In his constant pursuit of power, he killed many mortals and dissolved many spirits. He assumed that individual strength could be greater than strength in numbers. That led to his failure tonight."

"He also helped Ellie," Simon's spirit added. "When he spliced her soul apart to make Emilia he inadvertently prepared her for the battle tonight. If he had not done that, she would not have been able to stay away from her body as long as she did to fight him. She would have died quite quickly."

"Emilia helped?" Annabelle asked, softly, looking at Ellie's lifeless body as she did so.

"She did, in her own way," Ellie replied, herself holding back a lump in her throat.

"She taught you to be brave, to fight and to resist him," Simon's Spirit reassured.

"Is he dead?" Dan asked quietly, as if not wanting to hear the answer.

"His form is gone, yes. His energy dispersed and absorbed," his own spirit confirmed.

"But that which is borrowed must be returned," Ellie concluded, solemnly.

"What does that mean?" Simon asked nervously.

"It means there is still more to do," Tyler's spirit added. "Ellie, you must return to your body. We can continue this conversation once part of the balance has been restored. Then, you know what we must do."

Ellie nodded, "Will this hurt?"

"No, it will be like waking up from a dream," the spirit comforted.

Ellie smiled softly and glided over to her own body, still lying on the floor where it had fallen. She turned to face her friends who watched in wonder and awe of her.

She winked at Annabelle, "See you in a minute."

Ellie closed her eyes and gently allowed herself to lie back onto the ground over her body. As she made contact, her golden form vanished inside it, the way a dolphin vanishes beneath the waves. After a few seconds the golden light had vanished completely, and the circle of friends was now stood in grey darkness, looking at Ellie who was still lifeless on the floor. There was a shudder and a rumble from the ground. Around them the purple sphere had started to fade and shrink back the way it had arrived, opening up like a flower in spring to reveal the clear black sky. After it had vanished beneath the horizon and the rumbling had subsided, Ellie opened her eyes. She took a gasp of air as if breathing for the first time, gulping down oxygen as much as she could. Her friends, led by Annabelle let out small cheers of celebration and delight as Ellie, back in her physical body, climbed to her feet. Annabelle rushed over and wrapped her in the tightest of hugs.

"I love you," she whispered.

"I know, I love you too," Ellie replied.

After hugs and congratulations had been shared, they once again ended up standing in a circle, alternating between human, their spirit companion, and then the next human. Ellie was facing the folly with Annabelle to her left and her, now silver spirit, to the right.

"Wow that was fun," she beamed, causing everyone to chuckle a nervous, but comforting laugh.

"Is that it now then?" Dan asked, wanting to conclude everything as fast as possible.

"There is still the matter of the borrowed power," Ellie's spirt replied, taking Ellie by surprise.

"I thought we just did that, with Ellie and everything," Dan responded, confused.

"We rebalanced mine, but we need to agree a way to keep the rest of it in check," Ellie added. "It all makes sense now though. I saw my own death. I saw my body exactly like that on the floor, there in a dream weeks ago. It was true, it needed to happen."

They looked at her, in shock.

"I'm sorry I didn't tell any of you that. I was scared."

Annabelle took her hand, "We understand."

Ellie smiled, "Thank you. But we still need to ensure he stays gone for good. When we destroyed him, his power was transferred to you five," she stopped, allowing that to sink in.

"Us?" Simon asked, fear seeping into his voice.

"Don't panic," his spirit comforted, "There is a plan and there will be balance. His spirit was split five ways because there were five Guardians. When he rebuilt himself this year he destroyed his own spirit form to do it, which is why there is five and not six."

"Those five pieces," Tyler's spirit continued, "Were shared

out across the hill to all of you."

"You mean he is in all of us? Except Ellie?" Simon asked, trying to make sense of it all.

"Correct. He has been split into five parts, and provided they never merge, and stay as five parts, then he is gone forever."

"How do we keep them apart?" Dan asked.

"Quite simple actually," Ellie responded. "We need to keep you away from your own spirits, and the ability to use the energy. Your five spirits will return to Imaginari, never to come back here. Without them it would not be possible for his energy in you to surface, keeping it locked and hidden away," she paused, waiting for any kind of response.

"Ellie is right," Dan's spirit spoke first, "Doing this will stop him from returning, and will keep the balance and flow of power even. Christian worked this out, I trust him."

Everyone nodded in agreement and understanding.

"Will it affect us in any way?" Leo asked curiously.

"No," his spirit offered. "You will live a normal life, your dreams and imagination will feed Imaginari, and me, so be nice, all it means is that we shall never return. And you shall never see us again."

"Seems fair," Leo agreed.

Ellie smiled to herself, a smirk almost as she looked at her friends.

"What is it?" Annabelle asked, a puzzled look on her face.

"I just realised who you all are."

"Well that's a nice thing to say to your girlfriend isn't it," Annabelle teased.

"I know who you are, who you all are," Ellie replied, looking round the circle at her friends. "You are the most important group of people I have ever met, I would not be who I am now without you and the world would be lost if we had not worked together."

They all shifted on the spot, looking at their feet or the sky in embarrassment.

"Don't you see?" Ellie pleaded, "You are the new Guardians of Imaginari. You five, standing here with me right here and now are the ones that will keep both worlds safe. You will keep the Man at bay, whilst your spirits ensure the security and use of the energy flow in Imaginari."

They all stared at her, perplexed and amazed at what she had just said.

"But you did most of the work," Leo commented.

"That doesn't mean anything, you did the honourable thing. Don't argue with me, your spirits know I am right. My friends, Imaginari's Guardians."

She could sense the reluctant pride that was spreading through the group, she knew she was right and moments later this was confirmed.

"We are the spirits of the Guardians," The five spirits spoke at once. "We shall uphold the oath, protect the realm, and ensure the continued existence of our world."

Ellie beamed, her friends looked shocked and amazed. As they watched, silver strands of light joined the five spirits together in a web, meeting in the middle of the circle. It was not blindingly bright, but it was bright enough to illuminate the hilltop.

"What about you?" Simon asked Ellie from across the circle. "Where do you fit in all this?"

"We are the gatekeepers," Ellie's spirit replied, "I shall ensure that the portal between worlds and the prison realm remains closed to humans and spirits alike forevermore."

Ellie's spirit moved forward to the point where the silver strands met. The moment she made contact the five strands became one and shot up into the sky and down into the ground like a huge shining pole. The beam of light seemed to stretch for infinity as they watched in awe. Ellie's spirit turned to face her once again.

"Goodbye Ellie, dream well and strong. Keep your word to Christian," it said.

Ellie swallowed, glancing at Simon who fortunately was looking up at the sky so did not notice.

She looked at her spirit straight in the face, "I will. I promise."

The other spirits spoke as one to the group, "Farewell Guardians."

There was a blinding flash, and they had gone, taking the silver light with them, leaving Ellie and her five friends in the moonlight on the hilltop, the breeze gently rustling through the trees on the winter's night.

CHAPTER 20

The six friends stood in silence for a minute or two, enjoying the peace and tranquility that now surrounded them. They were still in the circle they were in before, but now the gaps between them were larger now the spirits had left them. Ellie looked at her friends, happy in the knowledge that it was over, the Man was gone. She could finally enjoy her life and do what she wanted to do, when she wanted to do it.

"There is still one thing I don't understand," Simon stated, breaking the silence.

They all looked at him.

"Who was this Christian that you kept mentioning? How did he help and fit into all this?"

Ellie swallowed, she knew in this moment she had a choice. She could tell him and face up to whatever his reaction was, or forever keep it a secret. If her exploits had taught her anything since moving to Mow Cop, it was that being brave and telling the truth was always the best option.

"He was someone that the Man tried to use," Ellie started. "The Man tried many times over the centuries to win, yeah? We all remember that?"

They nodded.

"Well, he was one of the spirits that the Man tried to manipulate to his will. The most recent in fact, he was on the list that Leo and Dan pulled together." She looked at them, they smiled, pleased that they had helped and been right after all. She continued, "The Man was trying anything, he was picking people that he thought he could bend to his will all over the place. They all resisted, failed, or died I suppose but Christian stood up to him, so the Man punished him in the most severe way."

"How?" Annabelle asked.

"He spliced his soul apart, like he did with me, but he forced his spirit into Imaginari and I assume destroyed his body somehow. That is what would have happened to me tonight, as the spirits said, if he hadn't prepared me by making Emilia."

"Sounds like a brave man," Leo commented, to nods of agreement from the circle.

"He was, to the end he was planning and scheming to keep both worlds safe," Ellie added, taking a deep breath as she did so.

"What is it?" Annabelle asked, sensing something was wrong with Ellie.

Ellie looked at her, then at Simon.

"Simon," she said, "Do you know why the compass pointed at you when I made it change to point for hope and guidance?"

"No," he shook his head. "I just thought it was broken or only worked in Imaginari or something."

Ellie looked at him, his soft eyes big and wide with wonder. "It pointed to you because you were my hope. It pointed to Christian because he was our hope. The compass was pointing not to you, or him, but to your bloodline." She paused, took a breath then continued, "It pointed to you both, because he was your dad."

Silence, nobody dared breathe. They all knew the stories that Simon had shared, how his dad had disappeared when he was still a baby, but this? This was something new.

"What?" Simon mumbled.

Ellie took a step towards him, "He was your dad, Simon. He didn't run away from you or abandon you. He was taken by the Man. Your mum raised you and kept you safe, but he never stopped loving you. Protecting you. Watching you."

"The Man chose him?" he asked.

Ellie nodded.

"Because he was weak. You said so yourself," Simon snapped, a flicker of rage entering his eyes. "The Man was picking people he thought were weak and pathetic."

"Yes, the Man chose him because he thought he was weak,"

Ellie agreed, taking another cautious step forward. "But he failed because your dad resisted him, he refused his offer of power and relief. The Man wanted you, his son, to be given up the way Joanna was. Your dad refused, to protect you. He sacrificed himself then and again tonight to keep you, us, safe. He was a brave man, Simon."

Ellie was aware that everyone was welling up and nobody knew what to say, she was imploring Simon to listen to her and take it all in. Simon said nothing, just stared at her, through her even, as if she was still a spirit.

"Simon, say something. I had to tell you, but it's true. He saved us."

Simon wiped his eyes, holding back the tears, sniffed and turned on his heel, storming up the crest towards the folly. Ellie and the others watched in silence, not knowing what to say or do to comfort their friend. Ellie felt the wind behind her, pushing her a little. Thinking this felt like the energy telling her what to do, she announced, "Stay here. I'll go talk to him."

And she did, Ellie headed up the hill to her friend who had fallen to his knees, tears streaming down his face. She put her hand on his shoulder, he did not flinch or move it away.

"I had to tell you," she whispered.

"I know, thank you," he sniffed. "I'm not upset about that; I would have wanted you to tell me."

"What is it then?"

"I have lived my life so angry at him, so deeply angry and resentful towards him for leaving us. I'm now angry at myself for not even thinking that it was possible he left for a good, decent reason."

Ellie smiled to herself slightly, squeezing her friend's shoulder as she did so.

"Did he say anything about me?"

"He made his house the same there as the one you were living in. He had your room exactly as it was. He loved you, you were his world. He watched over you, it was him that was trying to pull me into Imaginari in the field, remember the strands of light on my hands?"

Simon nodded.

"That was him trying to get me there, so he could help. He sacrificed himself, twice, to save us."

"You already said that," Simon said with a chuckle, his humour returning a little.

"I know but think about it. When he resisted the Man himself, he saved you at the time yeah? Well, if he hadn't resisted, he wouldn't have been in Imaginari now to help me. He saved us, for real, you twice, and the world once. Be proud of him Simon, he was proud of you."

It was all she could manage, she did not know what else to say, fortunately, Simon did not need to hear anything.

He stood and wrapped his friend in a hug, "Thank you Ellie."

"I'm always here," she replied, hugging her friend for as long as he needed it.

"I can't tell my mum though, it will break her heart."

"I know, whatever you think is best I will be there to help."

"Thank you."

"You can stop thanking me now," she replied, chuckling.

He sniggered too, humour and cheekiness were the foundations of their friendship after all.

Seeing what was happening, the others headed up the hill, soft smiles and gentle words of support and encouragement were offered which Simon graciously accepted.

"I have two final questions," Leo asked the group once calm had been restored. "One, does this mean we have to meet like a council? Wear silly hats and badges and chant to the moon and stuff?"

They laughed.

"No, you are Guardians, not council members, I think keeping it quiet and secret from the world is the best thing to do, don't you?" Ellie replied kindly.

They all agreed.

"That said, I do think we should keep a tradition," Ellie added.

They looked at her.

"I think that at the first full moon of each winter, we should come to this folly. Every year. Not to celebrate or sacrifice anything, but just to remember what we did here. Our secret, but our tradition."

They smiled.

"Every year," Simon agreed.
Ellie beamed at her friends, "Good, that means we will always see each other at least once a year. No excuses, that includes you, Tyler. No more holidays during critical moments," she had never forgotten that he had not actually met Emilia.
"And the second?" Simon asked Leo.
"Can we get off this hill now? It's freezing."

The rest of that weekend was spent recovering and telling stories from each person's point of view, everyone seemed to enjoy telling Ellie how much they loved watching her swoop and soar around the hilltop. Ellie would miss being able to do that, but she was far happier to be able to put it all behind them. As agreed by the folly they were keeping that evening's events to themselves, allowing people to make up more stories of what had happened. The purple bubble it seemed had shielded everything from view, but it had not prevented the earth from being scorched and the top of the tower being broken slightly. Local news and gossips alike again blamed youths lighting fires, attributing the tower damage to the latest storms to batter the hill and surrounding areas. The simple fact was that only they knew what had happened, and they found it endlessly amusing to hear other people's suggestions and ideas. As the days and weeks rolled on, life returned to normal for Ellie and her friends. Normal daily activities soon took over and that weekend became a distant memory.

A few months later after Christmas, Ellie and Annabelle were walking over the hilltop, a fresh dusting of snow had turned the hill and everything around it white, giving it a pure clean look. They climbed the steps as they had done many times over and looked across the hillside at their surroundings. Everything was white, the only bits that were not were the grey roads where the cars had washed the snow aside. Annabelle leant on Ellie's shoulder and sighed.
"Simple life is good, isn't it?" she commented softly.
"Yes, but I don't think you will ever let it be simple, will you?" Ellie replied with a grin.

Annabelle tapped her, "Don't be horrid. I just meant that everything seems so clean and new now, a fresh start."

Ellie nodded, she too felt the same way. "Yes, you're right. All just normal and simple now, I like it. Adventures can be fun but exhausting," Ellie kissed Annabelle on the top of her head, "But as long as I have you, and we are together, I'm always happy."

"Softie," Annabelle teased, lifting her head up.

They turned and looked at the folly, standing proud with its own dusting of white snow.

"Do you think it is closed for good? The portal I mean," Annabelle asked.

"I think so, everyone is happy now, balance and power restored and all that."

"Can you still feel it, the energy around you?" Annabelle asked curiously.

"Not really, I used to be able to sense it, but now I can't even if I try. That's ok though, means I don't need to use it I suppose."

They turned and headed down the hill to where the five keystones had been, there was nothing there now except a circle of raised land.

"It was so hard seeing your body here you know," Annabelle stated.

"Even harder seeing your own body, I can tell you."

Annabelle chuckled, "Ok, you win. Do you think we will be here every year, like we said?"

"I will be. It's the right thing to do, and you should be here too, Guardian," Ellie nudged her.

They hugged and kissed, even though this hill and specific spot held unpleasant memories for them, it was also the moment and place they told each other they loved each other for the first time. That is a moment they would never forget.

"Come on, lets head back. I want a hot chocolate, it's your turn to cook tonight and we are going to finally decide which is the best dunking biscuit," Ellie stated, turning and moving away as she did so. After a few steps, she felt something hard and cold hit the back of her head, turning she saw Annabelle's beaming face, her hand covered in a dusting of snow from where the snowball had been.

"You are so dead," Ellie stated, and ran towards Annabelle who turned and fled down the hillside screaming and howling with laughter.

That is how Ellie, Annabelle, and the others spent their time, having fun and enjoying each other's company, as any young group of friends should.

They kept their word, all of them. Every year at the first full moon of winter come rain or shine they were all there. The five Guardians and the Gatekeeper. Protecting our world, Imaginari, and everywhere else in between. As they grew older, the group grew larger too. Ellie and Annabelle stayed together, Simon and Sophie parted but remained great friends. Leo, Dan, and Tyler all had long lasting relationships, each built with one statement and request. That every year, at the first full moon, these six people and anyone that wished to join them went to the folly in Mow Cop. They stood and admired the tower above them, standing in a specific spot just to the left. A small circular area that was unusually flat for the hill. They would not say why they did this, that was between the original six. But anyone that joined them knew that the reason was an important one and respected the tradition all the same. They were also keen to impart the knowledge that dreams and imagination, can be a very powerful thing indeed.

The end of The Book Of Imaginari.

ABOUT THE AUTHOR

Richard Hayden

At the time of writing The Book Of Imaginari (it began in 2019), Richard lived in the village of Mow Cop where it is set. He would often visit the folly and look out over the surrounding areas – it is this that led him to the inspiration for Imaginari.

Each part took around four months from concept to first draft, all three parts are available now.

The book was written for pleasure, creating it would fill his spare time and this opportunity was increased massively during the pandemic of 2020 – the goal being to create something that at least one person would find and enjoy reading it.

Let him know what you think of Imaginari, he can be contacted on Twitter and Instagram (@R_C_Hayden) and on Facebook (Richard Hayden Author, @rchaydenauthor), he would love to hear what you think of the story.

Printed in Great Britain
by Amazon